PASSPORT
TO
TERROR
Passport Time Travel Series | Book One

Christy Cooper-Burnett

Black Rose Writing | Texas

ISBN: 978-1-68513-028-2
PUBLISHED BY BLACK ROSE WRITING
www.blackrosewriting.com

Printed in the United States of America
Suggested Retail Price (SRP) $19.95

Passport to Terror is printed in Garamond Premier Pro

*As a planet-friendly publisher, Black Rose Writing does its best to eliminate unnecessary waste to reduce paper usage and energy costs, while never compromising the reading experience. As a result, the final word count vs. page count may not meet common expectations.

OTHER TITLES BY
CHRISTY COOPER-BURNETT

The Christine Stewart Time Travel Series

No Way Home

Finding Home

Escaping Home

For my son Mychael, who is my everything.
And to my dad, Philip C. Cooper, Detective (Retired),
Ontario, California PD

PASSPORT
TO
TERROR

PROLOGUE
MADISON

1888, London, England

The rain kept rhythm with my racing heart as droplets of icy water mixed with my tears and spilled down my cheeks. I stood frozen in place. All I managed to do was to blink rapidly to clear my vision. My eyes remained fixed on the lifeless woman splayed out in the alley before me as my mind slowly registered the image. My hand flew to my mouth, and I stumbled backward.

I didn't want to see her. I didn't want to believe it.

This was all wrong.

But I couldn't pull my gaze away, and it forced me to accept the truth. Alysha Beck lay murdered in a Whitechapel alley in 1888.

How did this happen? No. How could I let this happen?

The woman behind me continued to scream. "Ripper! It's the Ripper!" she shrieked.

Her cries echoed loudly in the narrow passageway, making the entire scene reminiscent of some horror movie playing out in a seedy, dim theater.

Which was ironic because the slain woman was a film star. And not just your run-of-the-mill average actress. She was one of the world's most popular leading ladies.

Admired everywhere. Box office gold. And now, very dead.

The man next to me leaned over to be sick. His name was Derek Porter, and he knew Alysha much better than I did. I'd met her just three days ago and only witnessed her entitled, rude side. Guilt surged through me almost instantly. I was sure she had likable traits. Maybe I just hadn't known her long enough to find any.

A trickle of dread started at my spine and worked its way up as I realized with absolute certainty her murder would affect every facet of my life from that moment forward. I just had no idea how profoundly. Things were about to get much, much worse in ways I never imagined, as this began a seemingly endless stream of events that would change everything. Forever.

They always say, "Be careful what you wish for."

I wish I had been careful. But it was too late for that.

ONE
MADISON

2022, Los Angeles, California

The day my father discovered time travel started like any other Sunday. I was twenty years old and living on my own for the first time. I made the drive from my run-down apartment in Glendale to my parents' home in Burbank every week when my mother insisted I come over for Sunday dinner. She always made too much food and sent me home with a care package. It was her not-so-subtle way of making sure I had food in my refrigerator. Not that I minded. I was perpetually broke, even though I worked forty-plus hours a week lining someone else's pockets with money. I was living the American dream. A very broke American dream.

Like most people my age, I was nothing more than a flea on a big dog. Which wasn't where I wanted to be. Because let's face it—no one likes fleas. And like *all* people my age, I was coasting along, waiting for something to happen to shake up my life and make it more interesting.

That something happened, all right. And I never saw it coming.

My father, who worked as a mid-level scientist for a large biotech company, made history. And by default, so did I.

My father was a self-proclaimed inventor. He was constantly working and tinkering with something in his workspace. My mother always grumbled that he devoted more time to his work and hobbies than his family. And she was right. Don't get me wrong—he loved us. He just loved his workshop and projects as much as he did the two of us.

I will never forget the day my father changed all our lives forever. That Sunday afternoon mom and I stood at the kitchen counter cleaning vegetables for the stew we were preparing for dinner. Also known as my Sunday night handout. My dad came bounding up the stairs from his workshop, skidding across the tile floor and almost hurling himself through the French doors to the backyard.

"I did it, Brenda! I really did it!"

"Did what, Jim?" my mother asked, shaking the water from her hands.

She picked up a knife and reached for another potato without bothering to turn around to face him.

"Time travel. I can time travel! My machine really works. I can hardly believe it myself, but I swear, it works."

I watched my mother lay the knife down and twist to glance at him. I turned my attention back to the potatoes and rolled my eyes so hard they nearly settled in the back of my head.

"You've said that before, Jim," she said, wiping her hands on a dish towel.

"Yeah, I know. Well, this time, I'm sure. Come on."

He grabbed her hand and tugged her toward the basement door. She turned toward me and offered a half smile. I shot her a look of pity before I resumed cleaning potatoes. We had both heard this before. One too many times to fake any enthusiasm about hearing the same thing yet again. I loved my dad, but he was a dreamer. Unlike him I was firmly planted in the real world.

Nothing could have prepared me for when my mother came back upstairs and confirmed my father was right. I really didn't see that coming. He had unlocked the key to time travel.

He always talked about how incredible it would be to see history firsthand. He wanted to stand in the crowd at Lincoln's Gettysburg address or Martin Luther King's famous "I Have a Dream" speech. And now he could.

We spent the rest of that night discussing what to do about his discovery. He was adamant that we didn't share the news with anyone until he decided on the best course of action. My parents weren't staunch anti-government types, but they had a certain wariness of the people in power in our nation.

After two days of deliberation, my dad decided he needed a patent on his technology. I figured he would waltz into the patent office, fill out some forms and just like that he would own the rights. That wasn't even close to what happened. Dad hired a patent attorney who set things in motion. A very slow motion. My parents were nervous about keeping their secret, but I think they were most worried that I would let something slip to one of my friends. One of them might tell someone else and before we knew it the news would be out. Who knew what some nutjob might do to get their hands on the technology?

The six months before the patent office granted my dad protection on his invention turned out to be the longest of my life. I had to carry on like everything was normal when it was anything but. When the attorney finally told my dad the decision had been made and the patent was his, we were beyond relieved. It didn't take long for word to leak out though. It was only later, when the news made its way to the government, that all hell broke loose. That's when things hit warp speed.

Reality hit, and it transformed our family in ways we never could have imagined. My dad's picture was all over the internet and the news. They called it the biggest discovery of our time. News crews parked outside my parents' house twenty-four hours a day. After a while, the novelty of living next door to someone famous wore off, and their neighbors complained. Things went rapidly downhill from there. None of us could go anywhere without being tracked by the press. My already lacking social life circled the drain and died a slow death. None of my friends could stand the invasiveness after a month, and my boyfriend cut and ran after only a couple of weeks. It was all the excuse I needed to stay home and turn into a near recluse.

Once the Feds learned of Dad's technology, they were on him day and night. Of course, they wanted the device for themselves. They said it would go to good use. It would save millions of lives. But he refused to sell his patent to anyone, least of all the government. They pleaded, they threatened, they tried to intimidate him. They tried to guilt him into selling it by telling him they could use it for everything from disease research to geopolitics. And they promised him more cash than my parents could ever spend in a lifetime. Still, my father never wavered. He told mom and I that integrity was priceless, and he didn't believe for one moment that the government wouldn't exploit the technology if they got their hands on it.

Then one day he sat me down for a serious talk. If I didn't know better, I'd think he had a premonition of what was coming.

"Maddie, after I'm gone, my patent will be yours. Don't listen to anything the government tells you, that patent is rock solid. I made sure of that. It goes to you if anything happens to your mom or me. I had lawyers make sure you would inherit it, so don't let the Feds tell you they can take it. As long as you renew the patent at every expiration term, it's yours. Always use a patent attorney for that so there is no room for error."

"Dad, nothing is going to happen to you and Mom. I'm really sick of your invention, to be honest. Ever since the world found out about it, our lives have been on a rollercoaster. I can't even hang out with any of my friends. I wish you'd never discovered the stupid thing."

"Maddie, don't say that. This is my legacy. It's all I have to leave you besides this house and my retirement account. And one day you may feel differently about it."

"I doubt that," I said, shaking my head.

"I just need you to promise me one thing."

I didn't respond. I already guessed what he was going to say. I remained silent, trying to wait him out. But one thing my dad excelled at was perseverance. I did not.

"Fine. What?" I asked, sighing heavily.

"Just don't sell it to the government. No good will come of it if you do. They'll only exploit it. Probably use it to go back and change the outcome of wars to their benefit. And who knows what else? That's not what I want. Promise me, Maddie."

He looked so worried in that moment that I couldn't help but soften my attitude.

"Okay. I promise, Dad."

Six months later, both of my parents were dead. It was officially ruled an accident. They took a curve too fast in the rain and went off the side of a hill. But I've always had my doubts. How could I not?

After their deaths my entire world plunged into a tailspin when I became the sole beneficiary of my father's will. For the first time in my life, I was completely and utterly alone.

I owned the blueprint to the world's only working time travel technology. And not one clue what to do with it.

TWO
MADISON

2032, Los Angeles, California

I touched the glass top of my desk, awakening my computer. My company logo danced across the screen.

The Taylor Travel Group. Bringing History to Life.

It still gave me a surge of pride to see that. I founded my company just over eight years ago, and since then it had become wildly successful.

I got the idea for The Taylor Travel Group after thinking about my dad's vision for his technology. Why couldn't I share his dream with the world? There were no *time police*. There was no one to stop me from taking people back in time if they wanted to go. Of course, there were so many things to consider. The safety of the travelers and the integrity of the timeline, for starters. I used all my savings and my cash inheritance from Mom and Dad to hire a think tank, so I made sure I didn't miss any safety issues. Next were insanely expensive lawyers to draft an equally insanely long disclaimer. It took them one hundred pages of lawyer-speak to say guests vacationed at their own risk. If they were injured or killed during travel, they could not hold me culpable. Legally, anyway. But I knew if anything ever happened to a guest, they would be certain to blame me for everything socially and morally.

So now my travel group escorted wealthy tourists back in time to historical events every week, and we had tours scheduled out for at least six months. The average person couldn't afford my fees, so most of our clients were in the top echelon of the nation's income bracket.

I frequently accompanied tours if the event was something that intrigued me or if a VIP was in the group. I'd met a ton of prominent people and experienced just as many one-of-a-kind historical moments. I loved what I did. And I made an excellent living doing it. I spent many hours at my office, taking care of every aspect of the tours. I have always been very detail oriented. Admittedly, it might be more accurate to say I was a control freak. An anal-retentive train wreck. My Director of Client Services, Tori, was constantly telling me to relax. "Let go", she would say. I tried. I honestly did. But it wasn't very likely to happen. At the very least it would require a lot of wine on my part.

I swiveled my chair around to gaze out the ceiling-to-floor window behind me. The morning was already in full swing, and Los Angeles was alive and bustling. Pedestrians lined the sidewalks and crosswalks. A few taxis still made the rounds, but practically everyone took the new super-fast subway if they didn't have their own car. Some locals still complained about the crowds and the noise, but I embraced the sounds of the city. It was music to my ears. In fact, I loved everything about Los Angeles. All of it. The dirt, the grit, the crowds. It was the greatest place on earth. It was home and I would never leave.

Tori interrupted my thoughts as she burst through my office door. "Boss, you will never believe who booked a rush tour with us." She rested her hands on her hips, eyebrows raised, prompting me to guess.

"Good morning to you too, Tori. Who booked a vacation?"

"Don't you even want to try to guess?"

"Not really, no."

"You know, you're not much fun, Maddie."

Tori was the only person I allowed to call me Maddie. We had been friends since we were teenagers. So I let her get away with it, although I didn't like it.

"I never claimed to be fun. Fun is overrated."

"Whatever," she said, waving her hand in a dismissive motion. "Okay, get ready. Derek Porter."

She nodded once and smiled, waiting for my reaction. I stared at her blankly. I presumed she expected me to be impressed with whoever Derek Porter was. But I'd never heard of the man.

"Seriously, Madison?"

Uh-oh. She used my given name. Apparently, she was serious about this being a big deal.

"He discovered Alysha Beck. He's Hollywood's premier producer and director!"

I nodded, unimpressed, and I still didn't recognize the name. When I didn't respond she sank into the chair across from me in frustration.

"Oh, come on. *Tarnished Souls?* Have you really not seen it? It's only the biggest hit movie of the year. Everyone has seen it. You need to get out more, Maddie."

My eyes flickered down to my lap to concentrate on an imaginary piece of lint there.

"You really haven't seen it? Stream a movie once in a while, Maddie. Have you even heard of it?"

Of course I had heard of it. That ridiculous film was on every billboard, every accessible space in the city. You couldn't move ten feet in any direction without having a visual of it smack you in the face.

Her love. His destiny. Their future.

What a load of crap. I despised those sugary romance movies that sold unrealistic plots to women. I wasn't a romantic. I was a realist. And that wasn't real life. What about the girl who settled for someone she met on the subway or in a club? Or at work? Or how about the number one way people met—online? That was the real world. Not on a vacation to find yourself in Italy. No one went on a European trip and came back with a husband. Or if they did, he was probably looking for a green card. The idea was ridiculous, and I was baffled as to why everyone was so freaked out about this film. It was only a movie. And judging from the teasers I'd seen, it appeared to be an awful one, at that.

I glanced up at Tori, who was waiting for my answer. I could tell she was about thirty seconds away from giving me a lecture on my social life. Which

I looked forward to about as much as I would a root canal with no anesthesia.

"Of course I'm familiar with the movie. But when do I have time for movies? Between work and Fred, that leaves me about an hour of free time a day."

"Maddie, Fred is a cat. And a jerk who barely registers your existence even when you're home. If he could open his own can of cat food, he would ignore you completely and probably already be long gone. It's so wrong to blame a pet on your lack of social skills. I ask you to go out all the time. If it wasn't for work, I'd never see you."

"All the more reason for me to spend some quality time with Fred. His behavior is a clear cry for attention."

"Fred's behavior is an unmistakable plea for freedom. And don't change the subject."

There was the lecture I knew was coming. I sighed and leaned further back in my chair, bracing for the rest of it.

"Are you going to tell me about the tour or scold me because I haven't watched some stupid movie?"

"Fine. They want to go to nineteenth-century London."

"To see what, exactly?"

"That's the thing. They don't want to see anything. Well, I mean nothing specific, anyway. They prefer to *immerse themselves* in nineteenth-century London for a few days. They're doing research for an upcoming movie. Derek Porter, the set designer, the costume designer, and some assistant. But the best part is that Alysha Beck and Jake Martin are coming too."

She practically squealed at the last part. Although, I had to admit, I could get on board with Jake Martin coming along. He was easy to look at.

"Okay, so when did they schedule for?"

"This weekend. I used the VIP slot for them."

We always reserved VIP space for last-minute tours that would pay a premium for a rush tour. I wasn't stupid. If you wanted special service, then you paid a special price.

"And are they willing to pay the rush fee?"

"Not only that, but the motion picture studio paid a ten percent bonus above that to secure the last-minute booking and to ensure our confidentiality because of the stars' participation."

"Wow. I won't complain about that."

At that moment, one of my tour guides, Tyler, barged into my office. Well, as much as a gay man who appeared to be in a minor state of panic could barge. It was closer to an over-acted theatrical entrance.

"Is it true?" He grabbed Tori's shoulder to turn her toward him. "Did Jake Martin and Alysha Beck book a tour with us to do some kind of method-actor immersion thing?"

"Yep. This weekend," she said. They both shrieked, jumping up and down, holding hands like children.

"Stop it, you two. They're only people," I said, shaking my head at how absurd they were acting.

"*Excuse me*? Jake Martin is a God. Not that he would ever notice a lowly peasant like *moi*. But stranger things have happened, yes? Maybe he's gay, and the studio is pressuring him to hide it. Or he doesn't realize he's gay yet. What if once he meets me, he realizes I'm all he'll ever need?" Tyler mused.

"Sure, Tyler. The biggest star in the world is going to take one look in your direction and fall head over heels in gay love with you. Even though he's not gay," said Tori.

"Not that we *know* of," said Tyler, smiling.

"What about your husband, Julio? Forgotten about the Spanish hunk already?" asked Tori, rolling her eyes.

"Like I said, stranger things have happened. Don't count me out just yet. It would shock you, the power I have over men. Besides, Julio would understand. It's Jake-friggin-Martin!"

He turned his attention to me next. "Madison, please, please. I am begging you with all I have, with all things holy, to assign me to this tour. Cassidy can take my tour tomorrow to see the Titanic off. It'll be a piece of cake for her. I'll even waive my commission on this one. Whatever it takes, Boss."

He stepped closer, leaning on his elbows over my desk.

"Oh, for God's sake, get off my desk, Tyler," I said, waving my arms to shoo him off my furniture.

"Well, am I on the tour?" he asked, hands clasped together, his face pleading. There was a good chance he would burst into tears if I said no.

"Of course you are. You're my best tour guide. Plus, I don't think I could bear to be around you with you pouting over this for the next year."

"Thank you, Madison! I won't let you down."

He high-fived Tori and they glided out of my office arm in arm. I could practically hear an imaginary director yell, "Cut! That's a wrap."

I couldn't help but smile to myself as I looked around my office. This tour was a big deal for me and my company. If we could pull this off without a hitch, it would be an enormous boon for business.

Looking back, I remember being pretty pleased with myself at that moment. Of course, back then I didn't know what was coming. I didn't realize my world was about to crumble and I would need every ounce of the determination and strength I'd always prided myself on. Or that my very life would depend on it as I tumbled down a rabbit hole that would challenge everything I knew about myself. I might come out of it smarter and stronger. I might come out of it unemployed. Or maybe even dead.

THREE
DEREK

2032, Los Angeles, California

So I guess this was really happening. How I let the studio heads rope me into this I will never know. Did I want to put my life in the hands of some thirty-year-old glorified travel agent who inherited her father's time travel technology? Of course not. I had socks older than her. I'd have to be insane to want to. Nevertheless, I was doing just that. Normally, I wouldn't touch something like this with a stick. But when Len Palmer, the CEO of Majestic Motion Pictures, asked you to do him a favor, you did it. I knew exactly where I ranked on the food chain. Plus, I needed his big Hollywood budget for my next movie.

"Shit!" I shouted as I launched my water bottle across the room. I was under tremendous pressure with this next film. *Tarnished Souls* had been a blessing and a curse. It was a colossal hit and put me on the map in the movie industry. Especially after I discovered Alysha Beck, the newest up-and-coming starlet to storm Hollywood. But now everything I did after that had to meet or exceed that level or everyone would regard my next movie as a flop. That was the only reason I agreed to go on this trip to 1888 London. This movie needed to be just as good, if not better than the last one. It had to feel authentic. Not like some cheap copycat of every other period piece done before it.

If I was honest, I had never been so frightened about anything in my life. I was scared shitless. Was this time travel thing even safe? I researched Madison Taylor and her company, or rather, I hired the best people money could buy to research her. She seemed like a solid CEO, if not a little naïve.

She should have dumped her time travel machine with the government and skated on easy street for the rest of her life. But then I wouldn't be able to research this movie, so I suppose I was glad she hadn't. But still. Flung back almost one hundred fifty years to the Victorian era was never going to be on my bucket list.

A soft *ping* sounded from my desktop. I tapped my finger on the glass at the phone icon and saw my secretary, Harper's, face light up on the desk. Oh, pardon me. My *Executive Engineer,* as she insisted on being titled. These generation alphas were getting more absurd every year.

"Yes, Harper?"

"Alysha Beck on line one, Mr. Porter."

Sonofabitch. "Great. Perfect. The last person I want to talk to right now," I mumbled.

"Should I tell her you're unavailable?"

"No. I'll take it." *Like I had a choice.*

I inhaled a deep breath and plastered a fake smile on my face. I read somewhere if you smile when you talk, it will come across in your inflection. I figured it was a bunch of bullshit, but I could use all the help I could get not to sound as irritated as I really felt.

"Alysha, what a delightful surprise. How's my rising star today, sweetheart?"

"Cut the crap, Derek. Did you find out if I can bring my protein shakes on this stupid *vacation* you're dragging me on?"

I collapsed into my chair, wishing a tumbler of scotch would magically appear in front of me.

"Not yet, no. I have a call out to our coordinator at Taylor Travel. But honestly, I think we should prepare for the alternative at this point. I don't imagine they're going to allow us to take special protein shakes in your luggage. Not where we're going."

"We're only going to London, Derek. Not another planet."

I closed my eyes and pinched the bridge of my nose while I tried to keep my temper in check. This girl was as dumb as a box of rocks sometimes. How she ever managed to memorize lines was a mystery to me.

"Yes, I understand *where* we will be. But I think the issue is *when* we will be. I'm fairly certain 1888 London didn't have protein shakes. Remember, we agreed to their rules that nothing modern-day go with us."

Just saying it out loud made my stomach do another flip.

"Well, maybe they aren't aware that I am vegan, gluten intolerant and on a very strict calorie intake."

Of course she was. Protein shakes, my ass. I was surprised she wasn't allergic to air.

"Yes, I'm sure they will consider all those *extremely* important points, Alysha," I said, struggling to keep the frustration out of my voice.

"Just make it happen, Derek."

With that, the line went dead.

"Bitch," I murmured to myself, as my battered patience with Alysha came to an abrupt end.

I paced the room, running my hands through my new hair plugs. Is this seriously how far I had fallen? Catering to the demands of a spoiled actress who was a nobody until I plucked her from obscurity out of a restaurant in West Hills? Apparently, it was. But I was filthy rich for doing it. And people respected me too. I was a somebody in this town. And I resolved to stay that way. So if I had to kiss a little starlet ass to remain on top of my game, then so be it. Lots of people in this city did much worse than that to maintain their status.

I stuck my head out my office door. "Harper!"

She appeared almost instantly. I was never clear how she did that. It was as if she lurked close by, no matter where I was. It creeped me out.

"Yes, Mr. Porter?"

"Book me a massage and one of those hot rock treatment things I like for tonight."

"Yes, Mr. Porter."

"And I'll have a scotch, neat. A very large one."

She disappeared around the corner, and I sat at my desk to make the call I dreaded.

They answered on the first ring. "Taylor Travel Group, Aaron speaking. How may I assist you?"

"I need to speak to Tori, please."

"Certainly, sir. May I ask who's calling, please?"

"Derek Porter."

"Oh, Mr. Porter, certainly, sir. Right away. Just hold on one moment, please."

I won't lie. I reveled in the way my name tripped people up, the way it put them on edge. That didn't mean I didn't work for it. I paid my dues just like anyone else in this shitty town. Maybe even more so. And now I was one of Hollywood's best-known producers and directors. Aaron the receptionist had presumably never spoken to anyone as famous as me. He would go home and tell his roommates about how he got to talk to Derek Porter today. He'd probably embellish our chat to suggest we exchanged pleasantries. Whatever. He could have his moment. I hated being on hold and was about to hang up when Tori picked up the line.

"Hello, Mr. Porter, this is Tori. What can I help you with today?"

"I seem to have a dilemma on my hands, Tori. Alysha Beck has very strict dietary requirements and needs to bring the appropriate nutritional drinks on our vacation. Now, I realize that normally you don't allow this sort of thing, but surely we can make an exception for Ms. Beck, can't we, Tori?"

"I'm very sorry, Mr. Porter, but no. We can't. Nothing from our timeline but our costumes and luggage are allowed on our vacations. I wish I could accommodate your request. I really do. But unfortunately, it's a hard no."

Tori was decidedly less impressed with me than Aaron. I sighed and closed my eyes while I reined in my annoyance. Time to bring out the big guns.

"Listen, Tori. I didn't want to do this, but you will leave me no choice but to bring this to the owner's attention if you won't help me."

That ought to do it. No employee wanted me to complain about their level of service to their boss. That would be career suicide coming from someone like me. I knew the studio was paying top dollar for this stupid trip, and Madison Taylor wouldn't want to jeopardize that if she had half a brain cell functioning.

"I'm happy to see if Ms. Taylor is available to speak with you."

Before I could say another word, she put me on hold again. That didn't go how I assumed it would. Tori probably loathed her job and wanted to get fired. I couldn't say I blamed her. But after a full two minutes on hold, I was fuming. Evidently, they were not on their A game when it came to customer service. That did nothing to ease my already frayed nerves regarding this organization and my upcoming trip.

"This is Madison Taylor. Good afternoon, Mr. Porter."

She sounded older than her years. With a level of confidence that only developed with experience or necessity. I shook my head and focused on the issue at hand. I needed Alysha off my back about her ridiculous shakes.

"Ms. Taylor, your employee, our travel coordinator, Tori, is being very uncooperative with a sensitive matter I am trying to resolve. I'm afraid I am going to require that you step in and iron this out for me."

"Really? Ms. Beck's protein shakes are a sensitive matter? You will be in 1888 for three days, Mr. Porter. I'm confident we can find Ms. Beck an alternative source of nutrition while there. We are well aware of her special dietary needs. She was very precise on her questionnaire. Your tour guide, Tyler, will take excellent care of Ms. Beck. Now, is that all I can help you with today?"

This was not going at all the way I expected. These women were trying to break my balls at every turn. I genuinely didn't need this nonsense. Between Alysha and my nerves over the trip, this was the last thing I wanted to deal with.

"And what if Tyler can't do that? Then what, Ms. Taylor? Are you really prepared to jeopardize the trip over this?"

I was certain I heard her sigh in exasperation.

Who did she think she was talking to? She wasn't even trying to be apologetic.

"Mr. Porter, one of two things can take place here. Either you can cancel your vacation, or simply take Alysha off the travel roster. Or she can travel with us to 1888, and if she becomes ill or cannot tolerate the food there, I can always send her home on emergency transport. I will be on this tour myself, so you have my word that we will do all we can to accommodate her dietary requirements. If that isn't acceptable, then I can cancel the tour and refund the studio's money, minus the deposit. But nothing from our timeline other than our wardrobe is traveling back to London with us. I hope I've made myself clear, Mr. Porter. The answer is no. I understand you're probably not used to hearing that word a lot. But I cannot make an exception to this rule."

I was furious. If my phone wasn't built into the glass of my desktop, I would have thrown it across the room. I missed the good old days when you could slam a phone down in someone's ears. God, was I really *that* old to remember desktop phones? Instead, I punched the disconnect icon and hoped it would somehow have the same affect.

So much for getting Alysha off my ass. Well, I tried. But it wasn't a hill I was willing to die on, that was for sure. Even so, she was going to make this already miserable trip a living hell. I was positively screwed.

FOUR
MADISON

2032, Los Angeles, California

I waved my hand over the lock outside my apartment and slung my purse farther up my arm. The place was pitch black and smelled of cat. Lovely of Fred to leave me a present after the day I'd had. I was convinced he refused to use his very expensive self-cleaning cat litter box to punish me for leaving him alone all day. The automatic light switched on, highlighting Fred sprawled across the back of the couch, dozing. He opened one eye and got up to stretch.

"Hi, furball. Mom's home. And I have a treat."

He turned his back to me and lay down again, completely indifferent to my arrival home.

"Tori's right. You really are a jerk, Fred."

He ignored me as I tossed my coat and purse on the dining room table. Two could play this game. I poured myself a glass of wine as my frozen meal heated. At the last minute, I opened Fred's dinner. Finally, something that got his attention. He hopped up on the counter, and we dug in together. His purring relaxed me, and the alcohol didn't hurt either. By the time I finished eating, I almost felt okay about my day. Although Derek Porter had really put a dent in my mood. That man was seriously too much. Why he thought I would allow Alysha Beck to bring protein shakes, of all things, on our trip to 1888 was beyond me. Usually, guests want to bring a camera or cell phone. How they thought their phones would work was a mystery. We were just all so addicted to them. I guess we couldn't imagine being without that safety net.

As if on cue, my phone chime sounded. I walked to the table to dig through my purse as Fred stretched his hind leg out. I saw what was coming and tried to lung for my drink, but I was too slow. His paw connected with my wineglass, sending it crashing to the floor.

"Oh, Fred! No! What is wrong with you, cat?"

He never even looked back at me, just sauntered off to the bedroom without a care in the world. To sleep and shed on my comforter, no doubt.

"Terrorist fleabag," I mumbled after him.

After I cleaned up the broken glass, I went in search of another bottle of wine. A little spill wasn't enough to dissuade me from my nightcap. I collapsed on the sofa and my gaze fell to the picture of my parents on the bookshelf. I missed them more than ever, and I couldn't help but wonder if they would be proud of me. I knew in my heart it would thrill my dad to know I founded The Taylor Travel Group. I was living his dream.

Taking a gulp of my wine, I opened my tablet. There was a lot to get finished by tomorrow if I was going to pull off this trip to 1888 London at such short notice. My mind wandered to Derek Porter and his group once again. If the rest of the group behaved anything like Derek, we would have our hands full. At least Tyler wasn't booked and could take the lead as their guide. Most people underestimated Tyler. He came across as everyone's friend. But there was a tough side to him that only Tori, I, and his husband ever got to witness. He was professional but firm with our clients and everyone loved him. His good-natured personality sometimes seemed at odds with his background as a linguistics expert who spoke six languages. He also had a degree in world history. And most recently earned a black belt in karate. Don't judge a book by its cover was never truer than in Tyler's case.

By the time I had checked wardrobe, run a system check, and confirmed all the guests' disclaimers were on file it was almost midnight. There were employees to do all those tasks, of course. I had a dedicated wardrobe department, archival and historical research, and IT staff. But this was my company, and my obsession to ensure things were perfect wouldn't allow me to leave all the details to them. I worked for another hour until my yawning reminded me I needed to sleep. Tomorrow was a big day, and I had to be sharp.

Fred protested as I climbed into bed, not happy about losing his spot on my pillow. I fluffed it and turned it over, too exhausted to get up and grab a fresh pillowcase. What could a bit of cat fur hurt among friends, right? Grabbing my phone from the bedside table, I made myself a note to fill Fred's self-feeder before I left. He would not be happy to have only dry nuggets for the next three days, but sacrifices had to be made. I slipped into sleep as thoughts about tomorrow bounced around my head.

My alarm woke me at six o'clock. I slapped my hand around the nightstand randomly until it found the alarm icon to stop the obnoxious buzzing sound. I was tired after staying up late last night, but I was also excited. Butterflies fluttered in my stomach. Today was the day. The movie staff would arrive at ten o'clock.

Stepping into the shower, I let the warm water soothe my nerves. I used extra conditioner on my hair to look as put together as possible. I wanted to appear professional, but not like I was trying too hard to impress them. Which was clearly the case. In the end, I chose a navy blue pencil skirt and a white silk blouse. I added plain silver hoop earrings and a silver bracelet. Classic. Understated. I pulled my hair into a sleek ponytail and finished with a bit of mascara and a swipe of lip gloss.

I studied myself in the mirror while Fred glared at me from the bed. My look was all business, but not too uptight. Perfect. Just what I was going for.

As I suspected, Fred was none too happy about having dry food for breakfast. I leaned down and stroked his head, which earned me a hiss and a nip on the hand.

As I stepped out of my apartment into the hallway, Mrs. Fitzgerald peeked one eye out her door. Maybe if I pretended not to notice her, she would just close the door and go back inside.

"Hello, dear," came the raspy voice from the apartment directly across from mine.

Perfect. The building's number one gossiper. "Hi, Mrs. Fitzgerald." My voice sounded whiny, and I cleared my throat.

"Going on another trip or just a day at the office?"

"Taking a trip for a few days."

"A few days? Oh my. Don't you ever worry that your *patrons* will disrupt the timeline? It could happen, you know. The butterfly effect and all that. I've seen that movie. With that pretty actress. What's her name? I can picture her face. Oh, never mind. The point is no one should dabble in history like you do, young lady. It's not right, if you ask me."

I didn't ask you, but when has that ever stopped you?

She pushed the door open further, wagging her finger at me. "My Marty always used to say that we should leave the past where it was. He was right. Did I ever tell you he was a rocket scientist? Smartest man I ever knew, my Marty."

"You may have mentioned that before," I said. *Only about five hundred times.*

"I'm sorry. I'm running behind today, so I have to go. See you at the end of the week, Mrs. Fitzgerald." *Or never, you old busybody.* I didn't care that I was probably going to hell for those thoughts.

She didn't even try to hide her disdain, shaking her head as she closed the door.

If I'd known the turn my life was about to take that morning, I would have almost certainly done things differently. I might have even listened to old Mrs. Fitzgerald for once. But I was still blissfully unaware of the nightmare my life would become only a few days later.

I was traveling to nineteenth-century London with a couple of Hollywood's biggest stars for some method-actor immersion. Piece of cake. Or so I thought. Everyone knows what they say about hindsight. So I went on with my day without a clue the universe was conspiring against me.

I caught the subway downtown and walked the three blocks to my office. The morning was balmy, but then again, most every day in Los Angeles was mild-weathered. I glanced up at the electronic billboard across the street just in time for the poster of *Tarnished Souls* to flash across it. An eight-foot-high likeness of Alysha Beck and Jake Martin glittered in the sunlight. I squinted up at it, wondering what it would be like to have your face plastered all over the city. No privacy, ever. You could never throw on sweats and a baseball hat and run into the grocery store anonymously. I had to think that kind of life would grow weary after a while.

I pulled my gaze away and continued down Sunset Boulevard toward my office. As I rounded the intersection onto Vine Street and then took a quick left onto Leland Way, the sign on my building drew my eyes upward.

The Taylor Travel Group

The vivid blue letters stood out against the muted gray stone of the building. The double glass doors opened, and I watched Tyler sprint across the pavement to the sandwich shop. There was little traffic on the road. The building was tucked away on a short street that ran between Vine and North El Centro Avenue. Just around the corner from all the action on Sunset, but once you turned onto Leland Way, that all seemed a million miles away. Trees lined the sidewalk, shading the entire block. A small sandwich shop doubled as a coffee house in the early morning, and all the employees in the businesses on our block frequented it.

I stepped into my office building to an empty lobby, except for my receptionist, Aaron. Normally, we had a few potential customers waiting for appointments with the sales staff, but the movie studio had requested that we block the time so it would be vacant when Alysha and Jake arrived. I guess they thought sighting a star would be too much for the average person to handle. Or maybe they were just über-paranoid that word would leak out they were taking a tour. I was uncertain why it was such a secret, but it was their money, and they paid handsomely for a discreet trip.

"Hey, Madison! Are you ready for today? I can hardly stand it, I'm so excited," said Aaron.

"Yep. It's a big day. I'm going to head upstairs. Will you tell Tyler to find me when he gets back from the coffee shop?"

"Sure thing, Boss."

I headed up the spiral staircase rather than riding the elevator to the second floor, hoping the exercise would take some of the edge off my nerves.

They are only people, Madison. Calm down.

I repeated that over and over to myself as I settled in for the morning. After I reviewed the final details with Tyler, somehow, I was even more tense. At fifteen minutes to ten, I stepped into the bathroom to give myself a once over before heading downstairs to wait for our guests. I wanted to make a good impression and felt I should be there when they arrived.

I inhaled a deep breath and pushed my shoulders back, hoping my posture would convey confidence. I walked out of my office and the first thing I heard was the sound of a crowd. If I didn't know better, I would think there was a party in full swing somewhere in the office. My shoulders slumped, and I wrung my hands anxiously before making my way to the stairs. Whatever was happening down there, I had to fix it quickly, before the movie group arrived. There was no way I was going to let some over-enthusiastic employees blow this opportunity for me.

FIVE
MADISON

2032, Los Angeles, California

I hurried toward the stairs and got as far as the third step before I froze. The lobby was swarming with paparazzi, cameras clicking away furiously. Tyler and Tori were trying in vain to push them out the front door. And in the midst of it all were Alysha Beck and Jake Martin. Alysha played to the cameras, throwing her head back each time she laughed at something one of them said.

I'd never seen anyone exude such confidence, and her perfect posture and relaxed smile looked completely natural on her. She was all curves and cleavage and glossy red lips, and her dress left little to the imagination. And she worked it to her advantage expertly. She probably did yoga in her sleep and considered an olive and a stalk of celery a meal. Or whatever diet drink she was passing off as protein shakes. No one could look like that and actually *eat*. I was convinced she hadn't seen an ounce of fat or a carb since she was a teenager. Which was presumably only a couple of years ago.

I glanced down at my simple navy skirt and white blouse and never felt dowdier in my life. Why hadn't I at least worn some kick-ass heels or trendier jewelry? Well, it was too late now. I had to work with what I had. I wasn't unattractive but compared to Alysha Beck I felt like a frump.

Alysha had every photographer in the room eating right out of her hand. Jake smiled as he leaned over to whisper something in her ear, his arm around her waist. She shot him a smile, but she looked bothered and immediately turned her attention back to the photographers.

I felt a pang of jealousy with how at ease she was with herself. At least that's what I told myself. But that was a big fat lie. I was envious of the way she looked. I was already irritated, and I hadn't even met her yet. I told myself to stop being so petty. I was the CEO of a very successful business. But that did little to boost my waning confidence.

I stood up straighter and started down the stairs again. My movement caught Jake's attention, and his gaze shifted up to me. I stopped mid-step and gawked at him like a complete idiot.

Walk, Madison. You must look like a twit.

I knew this wasn't headed in the right direction. But I couldn't help myself. I was mesmerized. I'd never seen such a handsome man before. His hair was perfectly messy. He had just enough stubble to be masculine without looking unkempt. And those eyes. They were the color of jade. Could that color even be real? He must wear contacts. When he smiled at me, his dimples appeared, and I almost passed out. Instead, I lost my footing and tripped, grabbing onto the handrail as I narrowly missed tumbling down the staircase into an epic faceplant.

I would have preferred fainting.

Every eye in the place was on me at once as I untangled my heel from the edge of the stair riser. Smoothing my skirt down I straightened up, acting as though nothing happened and tried to redeem myself. Thankfully, a photographer distracted Jake and the room lost interest in me quickly. All but Tyler and Tori who ran up to help me.

"Oh my God, are you okay?" asked Tyler, taking my arm like I was an invalid.

I shook loose from his grip. "I'm fine. What are all these, these, whoever they are, doing here?" I said, sweeping my arm in a full circle.

"We don't know how they found out," said Tori. "They showed up a few minutes ago, right after Alysha and Jake got here."

"You have to admit, it's pretty cool, right? Maybe one of our pictures will make it into a gossip magazine. Or on the news or something," said Tyler.

"No, I do not think it's cool, Tyler. We should have prevented this from happening. And clearly, we have failed miserably," I said.

At that moment, the door opened, and a middle-aged man walked in. He looked at the swarm of photographers and shook his head. A few cameramen turned his way to get pictures. He smiled warmly, even shaking the hands of some.

"Uh-oh. Derek Porter," said Tyler.

"Shit. Time for damage control," I said under my breath.

Before I could move around Tori and Tyler, Derek headed up the stairs two at a time straight for us. He made a good first impression. His jeans and button-down shirt were impeccably pressed, and I recognized the designer logo on his leather shoes. He stopped in front of me, frowning slightly. My gaze was drawn upward to his forehead, to what looked like recently healed hair plugs.

Really? Hair plugs?

His voice snapped me back to attention, where I tried my best to focus on his eyes.

"Madison Taylor, I presume?" he said, offering his hand.

"Mr. Porter, it's nice to meet you. I'm very sorry about all this," I said, my gaze sweeping across the scene below us. "I don't know how it leaked out that Jake and Alysha were going to be here. I can assure you we are completely confidential with our client's privacy."

He looked down at the pack of paparazzi and waved his hand dismissively. "Are you kidding me? Alysha probably sent out engraved invitations to every gossip rag in town a week ago."

My gaze traveled to Alysha again. Jake had moved away from her, leaving her alone in the circle of paparazzi. She was in her element, that was undeniable. She preened and posed while the press continued to snap pictures and hurl questions at her.

What a circus. And she was eating it up. I wouldn't put it past her to have arranged this, just like Derek said.

Derek moved up a step and clapped his hands to get the crowd's attention, reeling me back from my thoughts.

"Listen up, people. Thank you all for coming to see us off. But I really must get my two stars ready to travel to 1888 London. We'll hold a press conference when we return. Until then, the world is going to have to survive without Hollywood's hottest leading lady and man."

"Which way are we heading?" he asked, leaning over to speak to me in a hushed tone.

"Right this way to the elevators," I said, making my way down the stairs.

Tori and Tyler both hurried ahead to lead Jake, Alysha, and the rest of the movie staff to the elevators.

Derek followed me and I was overcome with pressure to fill the uncomfortable silence with conversation. A bad habit I couldn't seem to break.

"Welcome to Taylor Travel, Mr. Porter. I'm certain you'll find your vacation to be an adventure like no other."

He weaved around me and twisted to face me when he reached the lobby floor. "Vacation, yeah. Whatever. Just get us home safely and that'll be great." With that, he jogged across the marble floor to the elevators where he found Jake, slapping his back in greeting.

I could tell these people would be a challenge. One I was not looking forward to. Tyler was herding the group onto the elevators, and I picked up the pace to catch up to them. A few of the press were still taking pictures as the lift doors clicked shut.

How many pictures can they possibly need of these two?

Once we were in the elevator and away from the press, I breathed a sigh of relief. Alysha and Jake stood directly in front of me.

"The press is gone. Get your hands off me," said Alysha, twisting away from Jake.

"Don't get your panties in a ruffle, princess. The last thing I want to do is touch you," said Jake, moving to the opposite side of the elevator.

Derek sighed and let his chin drop to his chest, while his assistant fidgeted nervously. The movie set designer and wardrobe manager ignored the feuding couple. Tyler and Tori exchanged a glance, while I cringed inwardly. This was shaping up to be worse than I imagined. The two stars could barely stand to be in the same elevator together. To their credit they were talented actors, because when they were playing to the press, I was convinced they were happily in love.

The lift stopped at the fourth floor and Tori directed everyone toward the wardrobe department.

"If I can have everyone's attention, please," she said. "I'm Tori, your Travel Coordinator. I will be on vacation with you, so if you find you need anything before we leave or while we are in the past, please see me. This is our wardrobe department. We have clothing prepared for each of you. Our research department spends many hours to get this just right. So please, do not adjust the costumes in any way. They are authentic to the time, and it is imperative that we blend into this timeline accurately. You will each receive two additional sets of clothing, one for each day we spend in 1888. Our hairstylists will also attend to you here to make sure we style you correctly for the timeline. No makeup is allowed, ladies. Tattoos are covered with a special waterproof makeup. This makeup will last for the duration of the trip, and we will remove it when we arrive back here in a few days. You each have an assigned locker where you can store your purses, wallets, cell phones, and anything else modern day. Remember, nothing from this era can go with us. Jewelry, including wedding rings, must be left in the secure lockers. If you have piercings, they must come out, no matter where they are on your body."

Tyler stepped up next. "Hi all. My name is Tyler," he said, giving the group a wave. "I'm your tour guide for your journey to London. I am an expert in linguistics and speech. I will do all the talking when we are in 1888. I can speak in a nearly perfect scouser or posh British accent. Chances are, you will not be as good as I am. Language is the foremost thing to give us away if we are not discreet. Think of yourselves as mutes while we are there. Do not engage in conversation with anyone outside your fellow travelers. Our goal is to integrate seamlessly and not bring any undue attention to ourselves. When you talk amongst yourselves, you are to do so only when we are alone. In other words, don't have a conversation with your fellow vacationers when nineteenth-century people are within earshot. Because we will be in the past for three days, this is extremely important. Also, no one is to go out alone. Ever. All our time in the city will be spent on group tours. Someone from The Taylor Travel Group must accompany a vacationer at all times. No exceptions. This is for everyone's safety. I'll turn things over to Madison now."

I stepped up to face the group. My palms were sweaty, and I knew I must look as uneasy as I felt.

"Good morning. My name is Madison Taylor, and I am the CEO and founder of The Taylor Travel Group. My objective is to give each of you a once-in-a-lifetime experience. I know you are all here to do research for an upcoming movie. We hope that spending time in 1888 London will provide you an excellent reference for that research. I do, however, need to be certain all of you understand the importance of following the rules we set forth for your vacation. If anyone violates any of those rules, I will have no choice but to send you home on emergency transport. And you may also incur a hefty monetary penalty. There are absolutely no exceptions to that policy. With that being said, I welcome you all and look forward to giving you the vacation of your dreams. If you will follow Tori and Tyler into wardrobe, we can get started on your preparations."

The group followed their guides without hesitation. All but Alysha, who rolled her eyes and went back to texting on her phone. I watched Tyler lead her out of the hallway and made a mental note to myself to watch her carefully. If I were a betting woman, my money would be on her to be the one I had to send home early. She didn't strike me as someone who felt the rules applied to her. I realized she had probably gotten by on her looks her entire life. And now she was a spoiled celebrity, the public adoration she received only reinforcing her inflated opinion of herself. Perfect.

I forced myself to smile as I followed them into wardrobe, bracing for what was certain to be the vacation from hell.

SIX
MADISON

2032, Los Angeles, California

Two hours later I stepped out of wardrobe in a tiered skirt and ruffled, fitted blouse with huge top sleeves that tapered down to narrow, lace-trimmed cuffs. The boning of the decorative corset I wore over the blouse was crushing my ribcage. I couldn't decide which was worse—the spring sided boots or the itchy ribbed stockings. But the thing that bothered me most was the hat. It sat precariously perched on top of my updo, all feathers and flowers. Wardrobe assured me it was period appropriate. All I knew was that it was a pain in my neck—literally. I plucked a stray piece of feather fluff off my bottom lip and wondered how I would get through the trip in Victorian clothing. The lace ruffle from my blouse tickled my chin, and I batted it away in frustration. It was a wonder to me how women in the nineteenth century wore this every day. I wanted to rip it all off and put on jeans and a tee shirt, but instead I inhaled a deep breath and reminded myself it would only be for three days.

Tori and Tyler walked out next. Tori appeared as miserable as me in her get-up. Tyler, on the other hand, appeared completely comfortable in his clothing. He wore a close-fitting shirt with cuffed sleeves and an English square necktie. His double-breasted waistcoat had notched lapels, small pockets, and a pocket watch. His trousers were high-waistband, and spats covered his spring-sided boots. A morning coat, inverness cape, and leather gloves completed his ensemble.

He spun once, holding his arms out to show off his outfit.

"Aren't you hot in all those layers?" asked Tori.

"Girl, yeeeesss! It's way too much clothing for LA. But we *are* going to London in November. I'll be glad I have it when we get there."

I was struggling to sit comfortably in my skirt, but finally settled into a chair, albeit it perched awkwardly on the edge. My petticoats took up so much room they almost needed their own seat.

"Well, you look quite smart, Tyler," I said.

"I do, don't I? Here. Take a picture of me so I can send it to Julio. He will love this," he said, tossing his cell to Tori.

Tori took several pictures as Tyler modeled over-the-top poses, while we laughed at his antics.

In the middle of Tyler's runway performance, the door opened, and Alysha strolled into the room like she was born to wear the clothing. The stays accentuated her small waist, and somehow on her, the ruffles and ruched skirt looked high fashion. Even Tyler stood with his mouth agape. And he was gay.

I realized I resented her just a little bit because she was perfectly at ease in her clothing, whereas I felt like ten pounds of potatoes stuffed into a five-pound sack.

I had little time to feel sorry for myself though before Jake joined us, along with Derek, his assistant, the wardrobe manager, and the set designer. Jake's hair looked great slicked back under his hat, showing off his features even more than usual. The heat spread across my cheeks when he caught me staring at him. Derek seemed less comfortable and pulled and tugged on his waistcoat, adjusting his suspenders. Maybe Jake and Alysha were just accustomed to wearing costumes for their movie roles, so they were naturally more at ease than the rest of us. Whatever the reason, they were right at home in their new clothes.

Tori stepped up to address the group. "Everyone relax for a moment while IT does their final systems check for our trip. When we arrive in 1888, we will transport in outside the city to a predetermined landing zone. We will have just under a mile to walk to reach our hotel. Tyler was there two days ago to make hotel arrangements and do some recon for us."

I wiggled my toes inside my boots, not looking forward to a one-mile hike in them. Just walking around the office had been dicey. Paula in wardrobe was not my favorite person.

Tyler made the rounds to do a last-minute wardrobe check. He reached Alysha and smiled.

"Simply stunning, really. But I am going to need you to use this to remove your makeup, please," he said, handing her a makeup wipe. "Better take two," he said, holding out another one.

She stared at the wipes in his hand but made no move to take them. "What are those for?"

"Kudos to you for trying. I can't say I blame a gal for that. But you cannot wear any makeup on the trip. It's in our contract. You need to lose the false eyelashes, eye shadow and lipstick. And it looks like a little blush may have made its way onto your face too," he said, stretching his hand closer to her.

Alysha faced Derek, who looked as if he wanted to be anywhere else but at the receiving end of the starlet's scorn.

"Derek, how am I expected to go without eyelashes? This is insane. I have an image to think about," she whined.

Derek opened his mouth to speak, but before he could respond, Tyler jumped in to smooth things over.

"I get it, honey. I really do. I can't wear any either. My eyes are downright tragic without them. But the good news is, there are no paparazzi there. So that means no pictures. This will be our little secret. And trust me, I'm a vault, sweetheart," he said, winking at her.

Jake chuckled, turning to look at Alysha. "You're the only one who cares about your eyelashes, Alysha. I don't know why women bother with that, anyway. Seriously, it's not even in my top five hundred things I notice about a woman."

"Oh, shut up, Jake. Everyone's heard that joke before. And no one cares what you find appealing in a date. The press is gone, so you can stop acting now," she said, glaring at him.

"Derek?" Alysha looked at the director again.

"Take the damn makeup off, Alysha. It's in the contract," Derek snapped back.

Alysha snatched the wipes from Tyler, turning her back to us to remove her makeup. I steeled myself for an outburst, but against all odds, she didn't spiral into a stage-five meltdown.

Tyler stepped back and stood next to me.

"Listen to Jake and Alysha bickering like an old married couple. Can a scandalous sex tape be far off?" he whispered to me.

"Stop, Tyler."

"You know I'm right. There's a video somewhere just waiting to be found. I'd bet my next two paychecks on it."

Tyler was about as subtle as a sledgehammer. I couldn't say I disagreed with him, but I still shot him a look to make sure he knew I had heard enough.

Alysha spun to face us, and if looks could kill, well, I was just glad they couldn't. She held the used wipes out to Tyler, who glanced at the trash can in the room's corner. Alysha's eyes followed. She raised her eyebrows impatiently and waved the tissues at him. She was a piece of work. She honestly thought she was too entitled to throw her own trash away.

I said a little prayer to whatever patron saint might be responsible for keeping my temper in check and stepped forward to hold out my hand. Even without makeup she was unfairly gorgeous. I bristled when she smiled and dropped the dirty tissues into my palm, then walked away without so much as a thank you. By the time she crossed the room to Derek's side to unleash her latest tirade on him, I was seething. I could only guess what she was unhappy about now. I felt bad for Derek, even though I didn't like him much more than I did Alysha.

Tori interrupted my thoughts when she received a communication from IT.

"We're cleared to leave, Boss."

"Okay. Tyler, can you round them up and save Mr. Porter from Alysha's wrath?" I whispered.

"Okay, everyone. Operations has confirmed we are ready to travel. Can you please follow me?" Tyler said, waving them over.

He led us into the transportation room. It was empty except for the plastic arch that resembled an airport-security metal detector.

Tori stepped over to the transport portal and cleared her throat to get everyone's attention.

"This is the transport portal. When it is turned on you will see the energy field around it. It will distort the atmosphere and look much like a heat wave coming off a fire. The gravitational field immediately underneath the arch will be altered. It is important that you follow our instructions to the letter. We will walk through one person at a time. The person before you must be completely through the portal and no longer visible before you step into it. Tyler and I will go first, then Madison will direct you through one at a time. She will go through last. We will arrive approximately fifteen minutes apart, even though we walk through the arch within sixty seconds of each other. Does anyone have any questions?"

"Yeah. Is this safe? Are there any health risks? And how do we know where we come out the other side is safe? What if there are other people around from that timeline? We just suddenly appear and expect them to carry on like nothing happened?" asked Mark, the set designer.

I stepped forward, knowing I should be the one to answer this.

"It is perfectly safe, Mark. There are no known health risks. During our testing procedures we continually monitored everyone who transported. We compared before and after tests and no one experienced any physical changes. World-renowned health experts reviewed the results and signed off on the portal's safety. Five years on, we have had no issues whatsoever. I personally have transported hundreds of times over the past five years with not one problem. As far as the other side, the system chooses our landing spot based on our date and time of travel. Once IT powers up the portal, the system also does a final check to confirm it is safe and no one is there. That's why we come in so far from our hotel and at the time we do. The time zone doesn't affect our travel. We program for an early morning arrival in London, and it will take us to the date and time we select."

Mark nodded, seemingly satisfied with my explanation.

I glanced at the others, who all seemed relaxed. Everyone except Derek.

I saw beads of perspiration on his forehead, and his hands were balled into fists at his sides. I tried to catch his eye to reassure him. But as the built-in speakers began our countdown to transport, he squeezed his eyes shut tightly and mouthed something only he heard as Tyler stepped through and disappeared.

Was he praying?

A twinge of guilt surged through me for not reassuring him before now. I knew he was nervous, and as the owner of the company, I should have taken the opportunity to make him more comfortable when I had the chance. We hadn't even transported yet, and I was already jeopardizing the most important trip of my career. Then again, I still had no clue just how much worse things would get over the next few days.

Some people get a sense of dread when something bad is about to happen. The hair on the back of their neck stands on end. Their stomach does a flip. Something feels *off.*

Not me.

If I had, I would have refunded the movie studio's money and bolted. But I didn't have one inkling the trip ahead was about to go so wrong. And I went into it head-on with no hesitation other than the dislike of my clients.

I continued to stare at Derek. That's when a moment of foreboding would have been helpful. Even a hint of uneasiness. While there was still time to call it off. But it never came. Or if it did, I ignored it. And so, I carried on. I followed the others through the portal without a clue anything bad was coming.

Fate is a funny thing. It can guide your life in the right direction or slap you in the face when you least expect it. Little did I know I was on a collision course with fate, and it was about to deliver me a kick in the chops I wouldn't soon forget.

SEVEN
MADISON

1888, London, England

When I got to 1888, the others were already recovered from the transport. Mark stretched and twisted from side to side to crack his back, while Lacy, the wardrobe designer, and Harper, Derek's assistant, relaxed on a bench. I shook my head and blinked rapidly, clearing my mind. I was a little light-headed, but other than that, I felt fine. Tyler and Tori moved around the group checking on our guests, who all seemed in good shape.

All but Derek. Again.

I was convinced it was his age. Most travelers who had any short-term adverse reaction to time traveling were advanced-age clients. I glanced over at him again just in time to watch him lean over and be sick. He rested his hands on his knees as he took in long drags of air. I couldn't help but feel bad for him. It was obvious it wasn't his choice to be on this trip. The studio probably insisted he come, and he was struggling to keep up with his much younger staff.

I laid my hand on his back gently. "Some people have this reaction. It's perfectly normal and nothing to worry about. The nausea only lasts a few minutes before your body adjusts," I said softly.

He didn't respond but waved a hand above his head in a sort of acknowledgment. I was uncertain if I should stay with him or leave him to recover alone. He decided for me when he turned his face upward and grimaced.

"Some privacy please, Ms. Taylor," he said between gulps of air.

I nodded and walked toward the rest of the group.

"That was some trick. One minute I was in that room, and the next, bam! Here I am. I don't remember a thing," said Jake.

Alysha busied herself primping while Mark, the set designer and Lacy, the wardrobe manager, were busy taking in their surroundings. We stood in what looked to be a park. A large grassy area stretched before us, and iron benches dotted the landscape at the tree line. The fog prevented me from seeing very far, but I got the sensation we were on a hill judging how the landscape sloped. It was much colder than Los Angeles, with a constant drizzle. Not full-on rain—just enough to make everything feel damp and soggy. Including me.

After a moment, Derek joined us, looking only slightly better than he did a few minutes ago.

"As soon as everyone is up to it, we can make our way to the hotel," said Tyler, glancing at Derek. "Your luggage, with a change of clothing, arrived at the hotel staging area ahead of us. The hotel staff expect us to check in this morning. We still have some time until then, so once we reach the heart of the city, we can sightsee a bit before we check in if you'd all like to do that?"

Nods came from all around. Except for Alysha, who was still fussing with her hair, even though not a strand was out of place. She fascinated me, but for all the wrong reasons. I wasn't starstruck—I had just never met anyone as smug and self-indulgent as her. Derek's assistant, Harper, helped her tuck imaginary stray hairs under her hat and fluff her skirt. Alysha waved her off, and poor Harper literally gave her a little bow as she backed away. If this is how people treated Alysha, it was no wonder she acted so entitled.

It's only three days, Madison. Then you'll never have to see her again.

Tyler took an old compass from his jacket pocket and twisted it from side to side until he located the direction he wanted.

"All right, let's get this tour on the road, shall we?" he said, smiling.

He led the way down the hill, which was steeper than I'd originally anticipated. The heels of my boots sunk into the wet grass with each step, slowing me down, and I saw Tori having the same problem. I looked over at Alysha, who was right behind Tyler with no trouble keeping up.

Of course.

Tyler took pity on Tori and I and slowed to let us catch up so he could begin his tour.

"We are staying at the Langham Hotel in the district of Marylebone. This parish was likely in place since at least the twelfth century. The hotel was built between and 1863 and 1865 so is still relatively new by this timeline's standards. It is the largest and most modern hotel in the city, and the first to have hydraulic lifts. Of special significance to all of you, the hotel has been featured in many films in our timeline, starting with the James Bond classic *GoldenEye* in 1995.

"The hotel is a just over four miles from Whitechapel, which I understand particularly interests this group. We can take a carriage to Whitechapel, but I'm afraid I must set limits on how far into the area we can go. The Whitechapel and Spitalfields areas are the slums of East London in this timeline, and they are rife with crime, disease, and prostitution. It would be risky for us to venture too deep into that section of the city."

"That is unacceptable. Derek, tell him. That's the very part of London we need to visit the most. I need to observe firsthand the way these women lived," said Alysha as she hurried to catch up to Derek.

"As much as I hate to agree with anything Alysha says, she's right. We need to experience this for ourselves if we are going to play our roles with any authenticity at all," said Jake. "I hoped to spend one of our nights there. There must be a hotel or a room we can rent. Me and Alysha can stay together. It's nothing we haven't done before," he said, grinning.

I expected a shouting match, but Alysha just glared at him.

Tori guffawed. "That is entirely out of the question. Our research shows that to be the most dangerous part of London. People live in absolute squalid, overcrowded conditions, in badly maintained properties. The so-called doss houses are communal rooms and the only thing people there can afford. There are no safe hotels, Jake."

Jake and Alysha both turned to Derek.

Derek shrugged. "What? I can't force them to take us. And honestly, it doesn't sound like anywhere we should be," he said.

"Derek is right. The Whitechapel police patrol in numbers around Flower, Dean and Dorset Streets for their own safety. That should tell you all you need to know about all those infamous streets that branch off Commercial Street. The locals nicknamed Dorset Street *Dosset Street* because there are so many doss houses there. Besides, our clothing is much too posh. We would stand out like sore thumbs and be huge targets," said Tyler.

"What exactly is a doss house?" asked Harper.

"Common lodge houses with communal rooms and kitchens. Entire extended families share one room, and often complete strangers move in and share beds. It's a nasty situation, for sure. They rent for about four pence. That's why it's thought the prostitutes in the east end charge that amount. To make rent," said Tyler.

"That sounds horrible," said Lacy. "But I actually need to see what they wear for myself. I know how they are supposed to look, but I want to model most of the wardrobe for this film after real people."

"Yeah, I'd like to design the set after actual streets I have seen with my own eyes. Nothing will ever be as convincing and authentic as that," said Mark.

"Well, as I said, we'll travel to Whitechapel, but we just cannot go to Dorset, Flower or Dean Streets. Those are where the worst doss houses are. That area is well known for housing the most unstable class of people," said Tyler. "And of course, we all know the story of Jack the Ripper. Most thought him to reside in Whitechapel. That's where his victims were found, anyway. I don't know what your movie is about, but we seriously have no business messing about in that part of Whitechapel. I don't know if any of you realize it or not, but we are here smack in the middle of the Ripper murder spree."

I bit the inside of my cheek as I studied Tyler. I became more nervous with each word he added. That's why Whitechapel sounded so familiar to me. It was the setting behind the Jack the Ripper legend. I shuddered as I realized he was alive, seemingly well, and occupying the same timeline we were. It was time I took control of this conversation.

"Listen, everyone. I realize it's necessary for you to experience vintage Whitechapel. And like Tyler said, we can get close. I'm confident you will find plenty to inspire you while we are here. But your safety is of the utmost concern to me. So I give you my word, we will see as much as possible while keeping you safe. Fair enough?" I said, glancing around the group.

They all mumbled their agreement. What choice did they have? I had no intention of leading this group of snowflake Hollywood types into Jack the Ripper territory, completely unprepared and vulnerable.

Nope. Not a chance in hell. Not on my watch.

My contract was to take them sightseeing to 1888 London on a historical research vacation. Nowhere in that contract did it say we had to traipse through the most treacherous part of the city like a bunch of idiot tourists looking for trouble. And trouble is precisely what we would find. I had no doubt about that.

It was only then that the slightest fragment of apprehension crept into my mind. But I was too busy listening to my little voice to notice it. The same voice that told me everything would be fine, and I had the situation under control.

What a fool I was. That little voice was not to be trusted.

EIGHT
MADISON

1888, London, England

We wandered through the foggy city, reaching our hotel in thirty minutes. I stood on Langham Place in awe of the building in front of me. It was a traditional grand hotel built to resemble a Florentine palace. The Langham Place Hotel was an architectural beauty, even by our timeline's standards.

It was still very early, so there wasn't much sightseeing we could do yet. We sat on benches and marveled at our temporary home for the next few days. As always, Tyler was more than prepared to fill us in on a bit of history.

"This is much nicer than I thought it would be," said Harper.

"It sure is. Does anyone know anything about its history?" asked Lacy.

Tyler stood to face the group. "I was trying to avoid going all *boring tour guide* on you so soon, but since you asked, I'm happy to tell you about it. It was named after Sir James Langham, who had a mansion on this site. In 1867, they appointed James Sanderson as the general manager. He was, or is, a former American Union Army officer. He was known for developing a large American clientele. Mark Twain and financier Hetty Green were among the famous guests here. Not to mention Napoleon III, Oscar Wilde, Dvorak, Toscanini and Sibelius. So keep your eyes open. We might see someone famous as a rare perk. When the hotel opened, the Prince of Wales was here and many members of Victorian high society. We chose this hotel for your stay because it's the closest we come to any modern-day amenities. It has electric lights, hydraulic lifts, climate control, and hot and cold running water. These are uncommon indulgences for this era."

"Well, thank God for that. I'm glad you found somewhere with at least a few conveniences. I don't think I would stay without them," said Alysha.

"What are you talking about? Look at that place," said Jake, pointing to the hotel. "It's fantastic. It rivals any hotel in our contemporary world. I swear, Alysha, sometimes you are so spoiled and so rude. It's as if nothing is ever good enough for you. Like you assume you deserve the finest of everything life has to offer," he said. "Forget it, you'll never change."

Jake walked away from the group to lean against the lamppost on the corner.

"Someone needs a drink. Am I right, ladies?" said Alysha, turning to Harper and Lacy.

Harper frowned at her, and Lacy shook her head.

"This from the same woman who insists she needs to explore the slums of East London. My money says you'll be the first one to complain when we get there," mumbled Lacy, before she stood to go join Jake.

"Go on, Lacy. Run to your crush over there and make sure his feelings aren't bruised," Alysha called after her.

"I think we could all use a strong drink, sweetie. But seriously, you should have two. This is supposed to be fun. You're going to have a miserable time if you continue to fight with everyone," said Tyler, looking at Alysha.

He angled toward me and mouthed *biatch*. Tyler might have been momentarily dazzled by the glitterati, but he was obviously over it now.

"Who the hell do you think you are? You can't speak to me like that. I want him fired. Immediately!" she twisted toward me when she said it, her eyes blazing.

I chuckled. "That's not happening."

"Derek," she turned to Derek next for back-up.

The long-suffering Derek, I thought as I watched his face crumple. I could tell he was at the end of his Alysha rope, and it was only day one. He strode over to her, arms gesturing excitedly.

"Oh, for God's sake Alysha, can it, will you? Let's just get through the next three days and then you and Jake can resume killing each other or screwing. Whatever it is you two do together in your free time. Honestly, I really don't care anymore."

"Really? Let's see how you feel when my attorney gets me out of my contract for this movie. We'll see how much you care then. Have fun replacing me," said Alysha.

Derek stood glaring at Alysha, but didn't respond.

Jake and Lacy walked a wide berth around Derek and Alysha on their way back to the group and wisely ignored them.

When Alysha stomped past Derek, bumping his elbow in a huff, he collapsed onto the bench and closed his eyes in exasperation.

Mark sighed heavily before looking at Derek. "I'll go after her. I think it's my turn, anyway."

"Yep," was all Derek said, as Mark jogged after Alysha.

Mark and Harper hadn't even looked at Alysha during her outburst. It bothered me that everyone seemed to be accustomed to her tirades, and even more worrisome, they tolerated them.

"Well, that escalated quickly," said Tori.

"I apologize for her. She's. . . temperamental," said Derek.

"Is that the new word for bitchy?" asked Tyler.

"That's enough, Tyler. Mr. Porter is right. Let's do our best to make it through the next few days and get along," I said.

Lacy laughed as she sat next to Derek. "Good luck with that. We all get along fine. It's *her* you have to worry about," she said, glancing over at Alysha.

"That's the truth. You haven't seen anything yet. It gets worse," said Harper.

Derek looked at Harper sharply. "Sorry, Mr. Porter. But you know it's true. Someone has to warn them. And it just isn't right, the way she treats people. Especially you, after everything you've done for her," said Harper.

Derek waved his hand dismissively. "That's why I get the big bucks."

"You should get a damn gold mine to deal with that one," said Jake, nodding toward Alysha and Mark.

"So moving on, were any of you aware that Arthur Conan Doyle set the Sherlock Holmes stories *A Scandal in Bohemia* and *The Sign of Four* partly at this hotel? I'll bet you didn't know that," said Tyler, trying to distract them.

I turned to Alysha and Mark. He held her hands, then lifted her chin. They seemed very familiar with each other.

Was there anyone this woman hadn't slept with?

I know that sounded unfair of me to assume, but I had eyes. I could look at them and tell they were more than coworkers.

I liked Alysha less with every passing minute and made a mental note to stay as far away from her as possible. I couldn't afford to have a fight with a famous actress and blow any potential future tours with this movie company. I forced myself to tune back to Tyler, who had a never-ending stream of history about our hotel.

"Diana, Princess of Wales, Winston Churchill and Charles de Gaulle all considered the Langham one of their favorite spots."

"I can't wait to see it. I'll bet the interior is insane," said Lacy.

"We can go in anytime. Mr. Porter, if you want to go round up Cruella de Vil and Mark, we'll get checked in," said Tyler.

Derek chuckled and left to get Alysha and Mark. Once the group was together, we started across the street. The city was coming awake now, and we got our first look at the Londoners who lived in this timeline.

No one paid us any attention as we strolled toward the Langham Hotel. We all longed to get settled into our rooms and then explore the city. But first we had to get through check-in, and Alysha was still sulking as we stepped into the hotel. But even she gasped at the opulent lobby with its chandeliers and marble. It was positively breathtaking.

Tyler approached the reception desk and we got checked in without a snag. As he gathered the room keys, the concierge asked if there was anything he could do to make our stay more memorable. Alysha stepped forward, about to say something, but Tyler spoke up first.

"I'll be certain to inquire, thank you. Sadly, my fellow travelers do not speak English. They are visiting your lovely city from Hungary. I am their guide while here and will translate for them. So unless someone speaks Hungarian, I fear that will leave the task to me."

Tyler patted Alysha's arm and smiled at her, leaning over to say something in a low tone. It sounded Hungarian, although I wouldn't know the difference between Hungarian and Swahili. It must have convinced the concierge though, as he turned his attention back to Tyler.

"I see. Well, do ask if something arises. The Langham takes tremendous pride in providing the absolute highest level of comfort and service to our lodgers," he said. "The bell captain will bring your luggage up to your rooms straight away, sir."

Tyler bowed his head in response, and we followed him to the elevators. We had a lift to ourselves, and unsurprisingly, the moment the doors were closed, Alysha turned to Tyler.

"Hungary? Really? Why can't we be Americans, like we *are*? This is unbelievable," she said.

Tyler faced her with hands on his hips. "Honey, you need to learn how to follow directions before we have to send your little actress ass home. We just got here, and you've already tried to break the number one rule—no conversation with people in this timeline. We already went over this. Language and accent are the things most likely to cast suspicion on us faster than anything else. You are accustomed to our current day words and idioms. We are one-hundred-forty-four years in the past. Our language in the United States and the United Kingdom vary enough in our own timeline. Here it would be a disaster waiting to happen."

"It's not that big of a deal. Don't be such a drama queen," Alysha said, glaring at Tyler.

"Oh, you haven't met my drama queen yet, sweetheart. But you're about to, if you keep flapping your gums."

"Both of you stop it," I said.

Jake chuckled and Lacy sighed loudly while Derek closed his eyes and rubbed his temples. This tour was not off to a great start. And it wasn't lost on me that Alysha was the common denominator in every skirmish so far.

"Alysha, please refrain from speaking to any locals while here. That rule is in place for all of our safety. It's very easy to slip up and say the wrong thing. We are only trying to avoid a situation like that. Now, let's all get settled and meet in the lobby in an hour, okay? We can grab a bite to eat and go see the city," I said as cheerfully as I could manage.

We reached the fourth floor, and everyone scattered for their rooms. But not before I pulled Tyler and Tori aside.

"We have got to get this group back on track. Tyler, I have never seen you so annoyed with a guest. What is going on with you?" I asked.

"I know. I'm sorry, Madison. But she really gets under my skin. She is so spoiled and bitchy. I was really looking forward to this trip with them, but she seems hellbent on making everyone as miserable as she is."

"She *is* pretty horrible," said Tori.

"I agree. She is . . . unpleasant. But she is still our client, and this trip could open an entire new branch of my business if we convince the motion picture industry we're useful to them. So please, you are both my best guides. Do it for me. Suck it up for the rest of the trip and avoid speaking to her whenever possible. No one can maintain this degree of insufferable bitchiness forever. Not even Alysha. She'll have to mellow out eventually."

"I hope so. And I will give it my all. Not for her, but for you. I'll come and get you both in an hour," said Tyler, checking his pocket watch.

My room was only two doors down. On impulse, I stopped right before I put the key in and turned back to them.

"Hey," I called out.

When they both turned, I smiled. "First one of you who wins her over and gets her in line has a bonus coming. I know you can do it. She may be an actress, but you're both better. You take people on time travel tours where you have to blend in. That's real life, not a script."

They both grinned and nodded, high-fiving as they continued to their rooms. I wasn't sure if I believed my own words or if my determination to tame Alysha was just more to spite her. But either way, I was committed to the promise of a bonus now.

The problem was, I didn't realize what a worthy opponent Alysha would turn out to be.

NINE
MADISON

1888, London, England

Time flew by and before I knew it, Tyler and Tori knocked at my door. We picked up the others on our way to the dining area for a light lunch.

Lunch went well, and I was glad to see my bonus tactic worked. We were having fun, although it was clear to me Alysha was forcing herself to be decent. Our fun didn't include a new man, so I'm sure she was unhappy.

I reminded myself to stop thinking like that. I didn't know her at all and had no business passing judgment about her personal life. Besides, it was very unprofessional of me. Even if I kept my opinion to myself. All I knew was she was behaving herself. And for that, I remained grateful.

Tyler pulled out a chair for Alysha and both he and Tori fawned over her at lunch. She eyed them suspiciously but played along.

Derek appeared considerably more relaxed now that Alysha's tantrums had subsided. He sat with his arms extended across the back of his chair, and even joined the others in an afternoon libation. Before long, I eased up and enjoyed myself, too.

We agreed to take a walking tour of the west end of London through the Marylebone area of the city and venture closer to Whitechapel tomorrow.

We walked just over two miles to Buckingham Palace and by the time we arrived, no one wanted to walk back. Our period footwear didn't come close to modern-day walking shoes, and we were feeling the difference. My abused feet were screaming for a pair of Skechers. But my Skechers weren't approved Victorian footwear and Paula in wardrobe would hyperventilate if I suggested bringing them.

It took two carriages to carry the group, and even so, Harper still had to sit on Mark's lap for all of us to fit. But she was so petite, he didn't mind.

Tyler suggested we visit the Museum of Natural History next. It had only been open for seven years at that point and was a popular tourist destination. After that we had the carriages drop us a few blocks from our hotel where we window shopped and took in the sights and sounds of the city.

We couldn't buy anything, although everyone saw something they wanted. But taking something home from this timeline was prohibited. The Fair Trade Law had expanded to include my time travel trips. The government didn't want any of my guests to profit by bringing back antiquities or artifacts they could sell later. Or to have an unfair advantage in acquiring them, even if they planned to keep them for private ownership. Besides that, Tyler and Tori held all the period money we brought for convenience and safety's sake. I normally didn't worry about poaching much, but with Alysha along, who knows what she would dream up if she had the money to do so.

Our sightseeing made for a long day, and once we arrived at the hotel, we planned to freshen up and change clothes before dinner in the formal dining room that evening.

I was looking forward to getting upstairs to be alone. My feet hurt, my stay was as uncomfortable as anything I'd ever worn, and I was tired. Babysitting Alysha was exhausting. I'd never been more thankful to be back in my suite, alone with my thoughts. I drew a hot bath and poured myself a half glass of gin, then dipped my toe into the tub to test the water. It was heavenly. Settling in, I let the warmth wrap around me and soothe my aching feet. I rested my head against the edge of the tub and sipped my drink as I closed my eyes and sank further into the water. After soaking for thirty minutes and another shot of gin, I was ready to face my clients again.

My dinner dress proved easier to get into than my day wear. Although it still had plenty of layers of lace, it was a beautiful dress. It was sleeveless with the most over-the-top bow embellishments on the shoulders. That part wasn't great. They resembled wings and I felt like the first strong breeze could send me soaring. But the built-in stay wasn't as tight as the dress I wore earlier. Which was a good thing, because I wasn't sure how I would eat anything with that other corset squeezing my ribs together. I pinned my curls up and decided not to wear the small hat made to go with the dress. Paula in wardrobe would be so disappointed if she knew I left the hat off. But I could only take so much of this clothing. I had been a good sport so far, but being the boss had its advantages. I made an executive decision and tossed the hat back in my suitcase. I fastened a choker around my neck and slipped on the matching earrings, then pulled on the gloves that reached my elbows to complete the look. I stood in front of the mirror, admiring myself. I had to give Paula credit. The dress fit perfectly. Once I got the shoulder bows to settle down, I didn't look half bad. I grabbed my evening bag, tossing my room key into it, and headed for Tori's room. I helped her pin her long hair up and secure her hat, and we finished just before Tyler knocked on the door.

He gave us an exaggerated bow and held an arm out for each of us.

"Shall we retire to tea, ladies?"

I smiled and looped my arm through his. We stood in the hallway, where the others joined us one by one. Of course, Alysha kept us all waiting in the hall for another ten minutes.

The moment we stepped into the room, all the diner's eyes turned to us. I realized they were looking at Alysha. And so did she. She was stunning, as always. Even with no makeup. What was the deal with her complexion anyway? Did she live at the spa? Skin like that must cost her a fortune in products. I hated that I was so envious of Alysha's looks, but it was hard not to be.

She glanced around the space, a small smile playing at the corners of her mouth. She worked the room like a pro, I'd give her that. We found a table large enough to accommodate us in the corner, and I was glad we were seated away from the other diners so they wouldn't hear our conversation.

Mark turned his menu over, then leaned closer to peer at Lacy's. The paper menus offered soup, joint of meat and peas for the dinner selection.

"So not a choice, then? Just joint of meat. That sounds kind of vague. I wonder what that is?" he said.

"Chicken leg? I have no idea," said Jake.

"It might be a couple of things. Beef, pork, or even a leg of lamb," said Tyler.

"Great. Mystery dinner," said Alysha, letting her menu flutter to the table.

"It'll be a surprise. All part of the adventure, right?" said Tyler, grinning at her.

Before she responded, the staff appeared with soup tureens. We ate in silence, hungry after our long day. Soon after, they replaced the soup with a platter of assorted meats and fish, still considered our first course. The second course was mostly meat, including game birds, beef and pork with peas, asparagus, and a variety of sauces. They served burgundy wine, and while I would have preferred water, I knew the water here might not be safe for us to consume. We each had hydration pouches hidden in the secret compartment in our luggage to drink in our rooms.

I was already stuffed when they served the dessert or "after's" course, which was a huge assortment of pastries, creams, jellies, fruits, and nuts. After dessert, ratafia for the women and port for the men arrived, as after-dinner drinks.

We laughed and chatted for an hour, making plans to go to the outskirts of Whitechapel the next day. I finally felt this trip was on track. Alysha had settled down, and the others were enjoying themselves.

Tyler got both Lacy and Mark pencils and paper from the concierge, and they sketched details about their surroundings every chance they had. I watched Derek observe the people around him and could almost see his wheels turning. Alysha and Jake both studied people in the timeline closely, no doubt to mimic their mannerisms later in the movie. It was a productive vacation for them so far. And tomorrow would only lend more authenticity to it.

I went to my room that night feeling good about our time there. The studio was getting their money's worth. The guests were having fun and getting what they came for. And I'd sleep knowing my business would likely increase because of a successful tour.

I had no idea the following day was one of the last times I would wake up unafraid for what would seem like a very long time.

TEN
MADISON

1888, London, England

Excitement filled the air the following morning as we ate a quick breakfast and prepared for our day on the outskirts of Whitechapel. The truth was my nerves were getting the best of me. With everything Tori and Tyler had told us about the east end, it contradicted all my instincts to go there. But this is what the movie studio paid for. So I went along and did my best to seem enthusiastic.

Breakfast included eggs, sliced ham, toast and coffee, but I had a hard time getting much down. I took my chances drinking the coffee brewed with the local water. I figured the caffeine was worth the risk.

The weather proved exactly what I expected from London. Drizzly with patches of fog. And it was cold. I pulled my wrap tighter as we climbed into the hooded carriages. Gusts of wind blew through the buggy occasionally as I stared out the side opening, listening to the horse's hooves on the cobblestone street. I rode with Derek, Lacy, and Mark, while Tyler and Tori rode with Alysha, Jake, and Harper in a larger carriage. I was getting very good at avoiding Alysha. We pointed out interesting landmarks along the way and made small talk, but mostly we rode in silence. By the time the driver stopped to let us out on Commercial Street, I was totally lost. I had no idea where I was.

The moment I stepped out of the buggy, I could sense the difference. The entire atmosphere was in direct contrast to West London. The smell was horrendous. Like nothing I had experienced before, even in the worst parts of LA. Garbage and waste wafted through the air. Shouts and laughter carried on the breeze through the streets. Everything appeared to have a layer of grit on it. The buildings were filthy. The roads were pitted and in need of repair. People dressed in mismatched clothing that had undoubtedly been cobbled together for no other purpose than to stave off the bitter cold.

We stood there and glanced around at our surroundings. No one spoke as we took it all in. It was obvious poverty was a way of life there. Very different that the west end we had just come from.

Whitechapel was a maze of dingy alleyways and dark courtyards. Even the daylight couldn't hide the gloomy, shadowy corners. They were nearly as dark as night. Plenty of places for criminals to hide. Pubs dotted every corner, and they all had their fair share of customers, despite the early hour.

I looked at Tyler, whose face reflected his disappointment. No matter how much you read about Whitechapel or Spitalfields, it was entirely different to experience it in person. He recovered quickly though and smiled as he gathered everyone around.

"Okay. So, Buckingham Palace, it is not. But this is what you came to see, right? So let's go see it, people. No one wanders off, understood? We stick together."

We all nodded, but I didn't think any of us intended to go anywhere alone there.

"Let's start right where we are, shall we? Right across the street there is the Ten Bells. This is the most famous pub in Whitechapel. Annie Chapman was allegedly seen drinking here an hour before she was found murdered by Jack the Ripper. Elizabeth Stride, another Ripper victim, was thrown out on more than one occasion. And Mary Jane Kelly was a regular, most notably on her last night alive before becoming the Ripper's last victim."

"That's so gory," said Harper.

"I know, sorry. You know what, let's go to 4 Princelet Street. In our timeline the decaying building is used as a popular film location, as I'm sure you're all aware. But we'll have the opportunity to see it in its original design. That won't be so gruesome. We can walk through one of the many street markets on the way back if you'd like. And if you're brave enough, we can pass by 13 Millers Court. That's where Mary Jane Kelly lived. Um, I mean lives," said Tyler.

"Wait. Let's stay in this area for a while," said Derek. "Jake, Alysha, let's get a feel for some shots with you two in them. Against that building over there and near that alley between the houses," he said, pointing down a side street.

"Mark, can you sketch that area with them there? And Lacy, get that woman over there. Her clothing is perfect for the scene when Thomas finds Mary after searching so many years for her."

He glanced at Harper. "Are you getting all this down?" he asked.

"Yes sir," she nodded, scribbling notes furiously on a piece of paper.

"Why we couldn't bring the location manager is beyond me," he said.

Lacy and Mark both sketched on their pads while Jake and Alysha posed in front of the areas Derek selected.

"Harper, make certain all this gets to script breakdown when we get back. I want Mark and the production coordinator on the same page with set design. And it needs to get to pre-production ahead of schedule. No compromises on this."

Harper nodded and continued to scribble notes as fast as Derek barked them at her. It fascinated me to watch them. I never realized how much work it took to make a movie. We spent most of the afternoon walking the peripheries of Whitechapel while Derek dictated notes to Harper, and Mark and Lacy sketched anything of importance.

The novelty wore off quickly, and I became bored after a couple of hours. I didn't complain, but I could tell Tyler and Tori were ready to move on too. Many times, the tours we are on don't interest us. But this wasn't our vacation. So we smiled and remained in the background while they did their work. More than once, Alysha tried to talk us into going further into Whitechapel, but I wouldn't allow it. We only walked a few hundred feet down any side street and going even that far made me jumpy. I couldn't believe this was part of London. The west and east ends were worlds apart. Not to mention I couldn't stop thinking maybe Jack the Ripper walked the same routes. I looked at every man we passed, wondering if it was him. I was relieved when Derek said they had everything they needed and we were on the way back to our hotel.

Mark and Lacy chatted excitedly on the ride to the hotel. I got in the buggy with them and Tori, so I could spare myself from Alysha's complaining that we didn't get far enough into the city.

"Thank you for doing what you do, Madison. It makes all the difference for us," said Lacy.

Her words surprised me. In all the time I had my company, no guest ever expressed appreciation like that before. Sure, sometimes they mumbled an insincere thanks as they left the building. More as an afterthought or simply out of habit. But Lacy sounded genuinely grateful.

"I, er, you're welcome, Lacy," I stammered.

"Ditto. Without this, what we do is guesswork and history books. To be here, to experience it for ourselves, well, it's inspiring. This set will be like no other I've built because I have the small details now. Details I wouldn't have had before coming here," said Mark.

I smiled, feeling pretty good about myself. We would leave for home early the coming morning, and it looked like we made it through without a major speed bump. I will admit, I had my doubts at first. I sighed and peered out the window as the sun faded. I looked forward to dinner and a hot bath.

Two hours later, we were in the dining room waiting for the first course of dinner. Tyler sat next to Alysha, and she seemed to have forgotten they ever had words. She laughed at his jokes and leaned over to touch his arm when she spoke to him. He looked at me and winked as Tori glared at him. He was the obvious winner of the promised bonus.

Much to my surprise, I was completely relaxed and enjoying the company. It was our last night in London, the studio would get what they wanted out of the trip, and Alysha was behaving. I thought we had actually pulled it off.

Spoiler alert. I was mistaken.

I underestimated how far Alysha was willing to go to get what she wanted. That woman hadn't even gotten started yet.

ELEVEN
ALYSHA

1888, London, England

My God, these people were insufferable. I knew I would snap if I had to listen to one more of Tyler's stupid jokes. I was ready to scream. Not a puny little squeal, either. I mean a scream worthy of a blockbuster horror-movie. I wanted to strangle him with my bare hands at that point.

And Derek. He made me want to throw my wine glass at him. A has-been after making one good movie. And honestly, the reason it was so profitable was because Jake and I starred in it. Derek had his day in the spotlight, and now it was time for him to step aside and let a younger and more energetic director take over. Someone with a fresh perspective. He'll probably screw this film up, anyway. Let's be honest. His last hit was a fluke. He will never duplicate that success a second time. Jake and I obviously add to the box office demand, and because of that, sales will be decent for this movie. But he won't hit the same heights he did with *Tarnished Souls*. Everyone knows that. I wasn't even sure why the studio was taking a risk like that with him. Probably because if there was even a miniscule chance they could make some money, they would try. They were riding the wave while they still could.

And that mousy assistant of his, Harper, didn't make him more likable either. She can't even look anyone in the eye, least of all me. I know I intimidate most women, but the girl acts like she's about to faint when she's around me. And I don't mean that in a semi-endearing-mega-fan sort of way.

I glanced across the table at Mark, who met my gaze and held it longer than he should. He looked so pitiful. It depressed me to be around him. Sure, we slept together a few times. So what? It was only sex. It wasn't like I wanted to marry him. But of course, he became too attached and ruined everything. I had no other option but to move on. Now his sad puppy dog eyes merely looked pathetic and did nothing more than inspire me to tell him to grow a pair.

Jake laughed loudly and drew my attention. I stifled a yawn, which summed up our entire relationship. Don't even get me started on him. There was a point when I thought—hoped—he was *the one*. But that was a long time ago. Like all the other men before him, eventually things got stale. *He* got stale.

Madison sat next to Jake and my gaze traveled to her next. She was a tough one to figure out. She spoke up when she had to, but other than that, I hadn't heard her talk much on this trip. Honestly, I'm sure I'd missed most of what she said. I hadn't exactly hung on her every word. I didn't imagine she had anything to say that might be of actual interest to me. Of course, I'd heard about her before I came on this so-called vacation. You'd have to live on another planet not to recognize her name. She owned the only time travel technology in existence. I had never seen a picture of her though. She did an admirable job of keeping her face out of the limelight. But I expected her to be more ... I don't know . . . interesting.

Tyler asked me a question, snapping me back to my current hell.

"Don't you agree, Alysha?" he said, beaming at me like a kid trying to impress his teacher.

Shit. I had no clue what he was talking about. I couldn't be expected to pay attention to everything these people said to me. That was absurd.

Oh well. It didn't actually matter. I was a world-renowned actress. I'd bluff my way through it. I threw my head back and laughed.

"You know I do, Tyler," I said, smiling at him.

He looked pleased with himself and patted my hand that rested on his arm. Thankfully, his attention span rivaled a three-year-old's, and he turned to Tori almost immediately. I suppressed another yawn, wishing the night was over.

Wait a minute. Who was that?

I watched a man make his way across the dining room from the entrance behind our table. I swear I felt my breath leave my lungs with a *whoosh*. This was no ordinary nineteenth-century man. Every other woman in the place watched him too. That might intimidate some women, but not me. I knew what I brought to the table. But this man, he might be the first one to give my confidence a run for its money. He was gorgeous. Impeccably dressed, and he carried himself with an air of refinement. Just my type.

My night suddenly became a lot more interesting.

I snuck a glance at him every few minutes. I caught him looking back more than once, and that told me everything. If I wanted him, I could have him. And the more I considered it, the better it sounded. Why not? I was leaving tomorrow. I'd never see him again. What harm could going horizontal with him possibly do? Not a thing. I decided right then that was exactly what I would do. I hatched a plan, all the while sneaking glances at him. My timing had to be perfect for this to work. As long as I got that right, the rest was a forgone conclusion. Men didn't turn me down. Ever.

But this wasn't all about me sleeping with him. That was just a perk. I needed his help to get to Whitechapel. I had to see it at night. When the city would show me what it truly felt like to live in fear of the Ripper. If I wanted to play my part in this film like a pro, *like Meryl*, I had to draw from that same fear later. I wanted to experience what it meant to roam the streets when Jack the Ripper might be out. I wasn't senseless enough to go there alone, and none of my colleagues would have the guts to go with me. I knew that much. I had come up with the ideal solution. A gentleman to escort me. And it was my last chance. We were leaving for home in the morning, so it was now or never. I was certain once I had this guy in my clutches, I could talk him into virtually anything. And I intended to do just that.

I grabbed my drink and excused myself for some fresh air as the man put his napkin on his plate and rose.

He paused outside the entrance to the dining room, and I saw my opening. I inhaled deeply and switched to actress mode. As I moved to step around him, I feigned tripping, falling against his chest where my drink splashed over his white shirt.

Strong arms caught me as I leaned in closer. I stared up at him, fluttering my eyelashes. The corners of his mouth lifted slightly in a smile.

Got him.

"Oh, my. I'm so sorry." I said, sounding as flustered as possible.

"Are you all right, miss?" he asked.

"Oh, I'm fine. It's just . . . look at your shirt. Oh, dear," I said, covering my mouth with a gloved hand.

"I fear we shall not save it, but you are safe, and that is all that matters," he replied, smiling.

"I insist you come up to my suite so I can try to remove the stain. I must have some club soda in there."

He raised his eyebrows and gazed at me peculiarly.

"I realize it must seem highly improper for me to suggest that. I'm sure you have deduced I am American, judging by my accent. We do things differently there. I promise I don't bite."

Well, not always, anyway.

He laughed then, and I smiled at him. I looked down at his arm, then back up at him, hoping he would get my hint. He did and held his arm out for me. I looped my arm through his and accompanied him to the lifts.

When we reached my room, the gloves came off, literally and figuratively. I removed my hat and unpinned my hair, letting it fall loosely down my back. Taking the bottle of club soda and a towel, I stood close enough to him that I felt his breath on my cheek.

"It might work better if you take this off so I can rinse it," I said, my eyes flitting upward to meet his.

His eyes widened as I slipped my hands under his coat to slide it off. He didn't speak as I unbuttoned his vest and he shrugged it off. He stood still as I unfastened his shirt and it fell to the floor. I stood on my tiptoes and moved to kiss him. He hesitated at first, but after a few seconds he gave in, powerless to resist any longer. I took the lead from there as I pulled him toward the bed.

I planned to enjoy myself, even though I had no idea how this would turn out. I wasn't too worried. I was Alysha Beck, after all. Things always went my way. No matter what.

TWELVE
ALYSHA

1888, London, England

I turned toward . . . wait . . . I didn't know his name. Well, it wasn't the first time I'd found myself in that dilemma, and it might not be the last.

He lay with his hands behind his head, eyes closed. But he wasn't asleep. He must have sensed me staring at him, because he opened his eyes and angled his head toward me.

"I'm Alysha," I said.

He didn't answer, just offered me a small smile.

"And you are?" I asked, somewhat annoyed that he hadn't responded with his name.

"Does that really matter?"

The way he said it made it seem disrespectful, somehow. Not that I really cared one way or another what his name was. He was a means to an end for me. And a bit of fun in the process. But there was something very calculated about him. I couldn't put my finger on it. And I didn't like his attitude very much.

"So, *Mister no-name*, what do you do here in London?"

"A little of this, a little of that."

Again with the noncommittal answers? He was beginning to irritate me. I was only making small talk before I got to the real reason I brought him to my room. But it was like pulling teeth to get anything out of him. And the funny part was, I really did not give two shits what he did for work. Maybe I was conditioned to the men from my timeline, who were all too eager to tell me all about themselves.

Every. Boring. Detail.

Maybe it wasn't a bad thing that he didn't want to tell me his name or anything about his job. It would spare me having to pretend I was interested. Plus, it added to the mystery.

I reached over for the bottle of gin on the night table. Sitting up, I took a long pull straight from the bottle. No point in losing my buzz now. I was well on the road to being drunk, so I had another swallow. And then another. When I lay back down, I felt the effect of the alcohol.

He stared at the ceiling while I studied his face. He was unquestionably good-looking. Even more handsome than Jake.

"I'm here for inspiration on a film I'm starring in."

"A film?"

"Yes. About Jack the Ripper. Well, actually, it's a love story. I play Mary Jane Kelly, the Ripper's last victim. It focuses on her life leading up to her murder. It's fiction, of course. Who really knows what her life was like before her murder? She was fairly anonymous, I imagine. But it certainly wasn't the romantic nonsense we are making it out to be. But the audience will love it. And they'll pay me millions of dollars to do it. So, whatever."

"What did you say about Mary Jane Kelly?" he asked, sitting up.

"You know, she was Jack the Ripper's last victim."

"The most recent murders attributed to him are Catherine Eddowes and Elizabeth Stride. All the papers reported it."

"I've done my research, believe me. Mary Ann Nichols found August 31, Annie Chapman, found September 8, Elizabeth Stride and Catherine Eddowes both found September 30, and Mary Jane Kelly found November 9."

"But today's date is 8 November. How could you possibly know Mary Jane Kelly is to be the Ripper's last victim tomorrow?"

He sat on the corner of the bed now. He looked at me suspiciously, and a moment of panic overtook me. That was a stupid mistake.

Dammit.

I took a drink to stall, while I tried to figure out how to cover up my mistake. What could I possibly say? That I had confused the dates? No. That wouldn't work.

I said Mary Jane Kelly's name. And when they discovered her body tomorrow, he would realize I had told the truth. What did it matter if I told him everything? If I revealed the truth? Maybe he would help me after hearing that. I would be gone tomorrow, anyway. I took yet another drink and lay back down, patting the bed beside me.

"Lie down. I'm about to tell you something unbelievable. But I swear it's the truth. Just hear me out."

He lay down on his side to face me.

"I am from America, but just not when you think I am. I live in the year 2032. The Jack the Ripper murders are the most legendary unsolved crimes in history. It will make a fascinating movie. Of course, many movies have been done about him before, but this one will be different. It's the first big screen production with a love story twist. Anyway, I wanted to go to the east end so I can get an understanding for where Mary Jane Kelly lived. *How* she lived. But my travel companions wouldn't go into the heart of the slums. I need to go there tonight. I have to go to the Ten Bells pub, where she was a regular. And to where her body is discovered tomorrow. 13 Miller's Court in Spitalfields. Will you take me?" I asked, propping up on one elbow to look at him.

He sat up, his mouth agape. "Do you take me for a complete simpleton?"

He sprang from the bed, his face red, the anger practically radiating off him in waves.

"Wait! I am telling you the truth. We leave for our timeline tomorrow morning. This is my only chance to get this right."

I knew I sounded frantic, and he probably thought I was crazy. But I had to convince him to take me to Whitechapel. He continued to gather his clothing as I rushed around the bed to stand in front of him.

"I smuggled some things into this timeline with me. I wasn't supposed to, but I did. They will prove I am not lying. Just look at them," I said, already reaching for the dress I wore my first day here.

I turned the dress inside out and took the safety pin out that held the layers together like a pocket. I pulled out the coin and papers I smuggled in and handed them to him.

"My father's lucky silver dollar. See the date on it? 2021. It's a commemorative minting of the Morgan silver dollar. I am never without it, that's why I snuck it in. He gave it to me before he died, and it never leaves me. And check this out. Here is a printout on all the Jack the Ripper facts. It's from a tour company in my timeline. They take people on tours of Whitechapel and Spitalfields for fun. The mystery surrounding him is still alive and well," I said, handing him the tour brochure.

He reached for the leaflet and coin and returned to the edge of the bed to study them. I could tell what he saw shocked him. He turned the coin over several times, looking at it from all angles, and read the printout at least three times. Each time he studied the brochure he scoffed or huffed at something on it. I didn't speak, allowing him the time to come to grips with what I had just told him.

"I don't understand," was all he said.

"I get it. It's a shock, I'm sure. I didn't mean to tell you. It just slipped out. Here," I said, passing him the gin bottle.

He held the bottle, staring at it blankly for a moment before taking a long drink.

"Time travel is possible where I come from. We go on vacations to the past to see historical events. Or to sightsee, or do research, like we are."

"But how?"

"Don't ask me to explain how it works. I don't have a clue. I just know it does. And I don't want to waste my entire trip here without seeing what I came here to see. So, will you help me?"

Before he answered, a knock on the door interrupted us.

"Alysha, you in there, girlfriend?" Tyler called from the hall.

"Hang on, Tyler," I called out.

I twisted to the man on the bed. "Listen, I'm going to offer you more proof."

I wrapped a sheet around me and headed for the door, where I opened it a sliver.

"Hey, where did you go? I was worried about you. You left the table and never came back."

"I'm sorry, Tyler. I'm just tired, and the drinks gave me a headache. What time do we leave in the morning?"

"Five o'clock, sharp."

"Okay. So we go through the time portal in the same place we arrived, right? In that park on the hill west of the hotel, right?"

"Look at you with all your directions right. Of course that's where we're transporting from. Are you all right?"

"Yeah, I'm just tired, like I said."

"Well, don't worry girlfriend, I've got you. I'll carry you up that hill myself if I have to," he said, laughing.

"Deal. I can't wait to go back to 2032. I've had enough of 1888."

"Me too. The first thing I'm doing is getting one of those huge carnitas burritos from Chuey's on Wilshire. The food here sucks. Then I'm having a long, hot shower before I get into some normal, comfy clothes."

"Sounds great. Well, sleep well, Tyler. I'll see you in the morning for the transport home, back to our time."

"You got it, Alysha. Sleep well too."

I shut the door and turned to the bed.

"See? I wasn't lying."

"But I, I don't ...." he trailed off.

I stepped closer to him, taking his hands in mine. "Please help me. Escort me to Whitechapel and Spitalfields tonight. You can follow us to the transport site tomorrow and watch us go, if you like. It will be a once-in-a-lifetime experience for you."

"Spitalfields is an exceedingly precarious place to be at night. All manner of criminal sorts roam the city."

"That's the entire point. To be as terrified as Mary Jane Kelly will be tomorrow. That's the only way I can portray her believably. You'll keep me safe, won't you?"

He waited a full minute before he spoke again, and I thought he was going to refuse me.

Then his gaze locked onto mine. "Then terrified you shall be. I'll take you," he said.

There was something in his eyes that made me take a step back. The calm way he responded was off somehow, and it caused a cold shiver to run down my spine. I could almost see his underlying anger boiling just below the surface.

But I ignored it. Because I was Alysha Beck. I lived a charmed life. I was naïve enough to believe nothing evil could ever touch me. Why would I ever think otherwise? I had the world at my feet. I convinced myself I was wrong, that I was only letting the Ripper stories get inside my head. I shook off any misgivings I had and put my trust in the handsome stranger in my hotel room.

I now know the moments we are the most secure, the most assured, are also when we are the most vulnerable.

THIRTEEN
ALYSHA

1888, London, England

I dressed hurriedly, not paying much mind to the ensemble I threw together. After seeing what the women in Whitechapel wore, whatever I pieced together had to be an improvement.

"What time is it?" I asked.

My handsome stranger pulled out his pocket watch and glanced at it.

"It's gone eleven now. Half past."

"Will you be able to find us a carriage at this time of night?"

"My buggy awaits outside. Although the driver will not venture into Spitalfields at night. We must walk some of it."

"That's fine. As long as he can get us close and back here by the time everyone leaves for the portal, I don't care."

He nodded in acknowledgment. He was not a man of many words. That was clear. I had no time to worry about that though. We needed to get out of here and to the east end of the city. I didn't have long before I would need to be back here. I snatched my evening bag off the dresser, then thought better of it. I wouldn't need that.

"I'm ready when you are," I said.

He took my arm and led me to the door. I peeked out into the hall to make sure none of my fellow travelers were there. I did not need any of them to catch me sneaking out. Tyler seemed to have me on radar all of a sudden. As far as they knew, I was having an early night, and I wanted it to stay that way.

We made our way outside into the biting cold. Thankfully, my companion had a covered buggy as the rain broke the minute we left the hotel. I slid closer to him, laying my head on his shoulder. He stiffened, but didn't move away. I couldn't figure him out. We slept together. We did things I was certain he had never done before and wouldn't soon forget. But he was uncomfortable when I sat next to him in a carriage. Whatever. That was his problem. I closed my eyes and relaxed, willing the driver to get us to the other side of the city quickly.

I must have dozed off, because he shook me as the buggy came to a stop outside Spitalfields. He lifted a black bag from the floor of the buggy and offered his hand to help me out.

"What is that?" I asked.

"My travel bag."

"You planning to travel somewhere?"

"I don't dare leave it in the buggy. As I said before, the residents here are not to be trusted."

The gas lamps were the only thing lighting the night, and they were dim. The moon and stars hid behind the fog that shrouded the city. I took his arm as we walked the block to Commercial Street. It looked remarkably different at night. Shouts and conversation came from all around us as we rounded the corner where the Ten Bells pub loomed large. That's where we were going first. My escort protested, saying the pub was a vile den of sin. I laughed and told him it sounded like my kind of place. He wasn't amused and was quickly becoming very boring. I had been able to hold on to my forced enthusiasm for the last few hours, but I had my limits. Nevertheless, I pushed on because I was determined to at least see the inside of the Ten Bells. Because if there was even a slight chance Mary Jane Kelly was there, I had to try.

Prostitutes lined the pavement outside the door. They looked our way, but none of them stepped forward to solicit my companion. I suppose without me there, he would have been fair game. I inhaled deeply as we stepped into the noisy pub. There were men and women alike in all stages of drunkenness. Some women sat on the laps of men, hoping to have them buy them a cider or ale. A few women lay passed out, sprawled across tables, their heads resting on their arms. We found empty chairs and waited for the barmaid to come over. It was seedy and smelly. My brilliant idea to come here was quickly losing its appeal.

Finally, the server appeared and looked us up and down.

"Bang up to the knocker, ain't ye?" she said, looking at me.

"Two gins, if you please," said my escort. He kept his hat on and his face angled away from her.

"Where's yer dosh? Most haven't a sixpence to scratch with 'ere," she said.

His eyes flashed as he lifted a few coins from his jacket and pushed them across the table to her. I didn't understand most of what she said, but I figured out she wanted to see his money in advance. Judging by the rest of the clientele, I couldn't say I blamed her.

"Do you know Mary Jane Kelly?" I asked.

"A diamond of the first water, she is. Half sprung somewhere or earnin' her brass. Not 'ere."

"Thank you," I said, assuming she meant Mary Jane wasn't there. The unfamiliar phrases, the accent, it all made it challenging to follow anything she said. At least my stranger was more refined than the people in the pub.

We finished our drinks, and I was glad to be out of the loud, overheated building. I welcomed the crisp air on my skin after the heat of the crowds.

While my mystery man stepped under the streetlamp to search for a cigarette, I leaned against the building when one of the prostitutes approached me.

"Miss, be wary of that one," she said, her voice low as she motioned toward my companion. "He ain't as plump in the pocket as ye might think. A true rake, that one."

"A rake? I don't know what that means," I said.

"Don't be gulled. Careful with him," she said, before stepping back into the shadows of the building.

I shook my head and walked over to him.

"What is a rake? She called you a rake," I asked, looking back at the woman.

He turned to face me, frowning. "Nothing." But he glared in her direction.

"Can we go to Mary Jane Kelly's house now, where they will discover her tomorrow? I don't have long. What time is it?"

He drew out his pocket watch and held it up to the gas lamp.

"Gone two o'clock now."

"Crap. Let's hurry. I have to be back before any of them get up. That brochure I brought said we access 13 Miller's Court from a passageway between 26 and 27, Dorset Street."

"There's a quicker route," he said as he placed his hand on my back and guided me away from the pub.

We wandered down the dim street leading further into the heart of Spitalfields. The further we got from the Ten Bells, the quieter it got. I began to think this wasn't such a great idea after all. Rats scurried across the street in front of us, and a stray dog growled as we passed. After ten minutes, I was ready to forget the entire plan and go back to the hotel.

I became more uneasy with each step. That little voice in my head told me I should be leery. The same voice I disregarded back at the hotel now refused to shut up. It screamed at me until I could no longer ignore it. Just as I opened my mouth to speak, my companion gestured toward a shadowy alleyway. I stopped short, peering into the inky darkness.

"Right this way, merely a moment longer," he said, tugging on my arm.

I wanted to say no. I *knew* I should say no. But I didn't. Every instinct I had shouted at me not to do it. Not to follow him into that alley. I glanced backward nervously. The street was completely deserted. I decided it was more frightening to stay out there alone, so the alley was my only choice. I hesitated briefly before allowing him to lead me deeper into the passageway. Windowless two-story brick buildings lined each side of the alley. We had only walked about fifty feet when he stopped. I tried to see his face clearly, but it was too dark. All I could make out was his outline.

He shoved me against the wall, pinning me with his forearm. I struggled to get loose, all the while trying to comprehend what he was doing. He must realize he was hurting me, and I didn't understand what was happening. When I was certain the pressure would cause me to pass out, he let go. I gasped for air, unable to speak yet.

"If you move, I will kill you," he said calmly.

What did he say? My thoughts were hazy as I sucked in precious air.

He reached into his bag and drew something out. As my eyes adjusted to the dark, the knife in his hand became as distinct to me as if I were holding it myself. But my mind still grappled with what I saw.

Then the panic set in and took hold. I attempted to run, but it was no use. He grabbed me and slammed me into the wall. My head cracked as it bounced against the brick, and I slid down to a sitting position. My vision had adjusted enough by then that when he crouched down to eye level with me, I saw the ravenous look in his eyes. He was an animal who had cornered his prey.

"Why are you doing this?" I whimpered.

"You are no better than a common whore. Just like all the others. And like them, your destiny now lies with me."

"I don't understand. You were going to help me. Let me go, please," I begged. "I leave in a few hours, and you will never see me again. I will be over a hundred years in the future. I won't tell anyone what you did. You're protected, don't you understand? I can't turn you in to the police. I won't be here!"

"Stop talking, or I will make certain this lasts much longer than it ordinarily would," he said, removing a leather apron from his bag and slipping it over his clothing.

My heart pounded furiously in my chest.

This can't be how it ends for me. It just can't.

I felt like a stranger looking on as it happened to someone else.

"Who are you? Why would you do this to me?" I shrieked as fresh tears welled up.

No matter what I thought he was about to say, nothing could have prepared me for what came out of his mouth.

"Who am I? You can call me ... Jack," he said, as a smile slowly spread across his handsome face.

Instantly, the realization dawned on me, escalating my heartbeat. He might as well have sucker punched me in the gut, it so paralyzed me with fear.

I couldn't breathe.

I couldn't move.

I snapped out of my shock and made one last effort to force myself to fight the terror that engulfed me. I screamed louder than I ever had before, while I battled against his grip. But he was much stronger than me, and I was powerless to break free.

"Scream all you wish. We won't be interrupted. No one is coming to save you, Alysha. You are mine to do with as I please," he said, his eyes glowing with excitement.

I knew he was right. No one was coming to help me. That was the exact moment I gave up. I realized there would be no escape. There was only acceptance in those last minutes.

All I could do was watch as he lifted the knife to my neck and sliced into me. I no longer fought him because I wished it to be over. But my body reacted nevertheless by lurching forward, my hands instinctively reaching for my neck. The warm blood seeped through my fingers, and after a moment I let my hands drop. I felt the life ebb out of me with each passing second, helpless to do anything about it. Then the knife twisted into my stomach. I tried to scream again, but I was unable to make any sound after he cut my throat. He drew the blade up with a vengeance I was thankfully too numb to fully feel.

He had kept his promise to me. I asked to experience the terror Mary Jane Kelly felt at the hands of Jack the Ripper. I just didn't realize to do that I would replace her when the Ripper found me instead. What a vicious twist of fate.

I thought I had him eating out of my hand, but instead, I was his prey all along. And he played me perfectly. I followed him blindly, with no idea who he really was, as he led me right into the fire.

Those were my final thoughts as I succumbed to the blackness and allowed the nothingness to swallow me.

I closed my eyes and welcomed death.

FOURTEEN
JACK

1888, London, England

I lay in the unfamiliar bed and sensed the woman beside me studying my face. I wished to be elsewhere. Almost anywhere else would do. The preceding two hours had been pleasurable. There was no mistaking that. She was a beautiful woman. But with the gratifying part of the evening now over, I longed to slip out undetected.

I had tasks to attend to before the sun rose. I had already chosen my next target. I knew her routine, but one could never be too prudent in these types of endeavors. I knew where she lived. I even knew the nicknames the other trollops at the Ten Bells had given her. Fair Emma. Dark Mary. Black Mary. Soon to be immortalized. She wasn't as beautiful as the woman lying next to me, but she would do rather nicely.

The woman quite rudely yanked me back from my daydream when she asked me my name. I chuckled to myself inwardly. There would be no name exchange on my part. Certain she would faint away dead should she learn my true identity, I kept that to myself. Although she differed greatly from most women I was acquainted with. She was far more brazen and assertive. Those traits were slightly entertaining earlier in the evening, but now those same attitudes bordered on vulgar. It only caused my head to pound as she blathered on and on.

I only half listened to Alysha—that was her name—when she said something that caused my heart to race. On the inside, I panicked. But my expression would never reveal that. I worked hard to keep my face neutral and my voice steady.

"What did you say about Mary Jane Kelly?" I asked, sitting up.

"You know, Jack the Ripper's last victim."

"The most recent murders attributed to him were Catherine Eddowes and Elizabeth Stride. All the papers reported it," I said, my composure slipping somewhat more with each word.

"I've done my research, believe me. Mary Ann Nichols found August 31, Annie Chapman, found September 8, Elizabeth Stride and Catherine Eddowes both found September 30, and Mary Jane Kelly found November 9."

"But today's date is 8 November. How could you possibly know Mary Jane Kelly is to be the Ripper's last victim tomorrow?"

I watched a glimmer of fear cross her face. It was so slight someone else may have missed it, but it was there. And I saw it. I was already planning my move should I need to silence her. I did not revel in killing merely for the sake of it. My pleasure came from taking my time and savoring it. But some things were necessary. If this woman somehow knew who I was or what I had planned, she would need to be quieted. I would simply have no choice in the matter.

I listened to her folly about coming here from the future, much as I would read a lively story in the papers. Clearly, she was slightly unhinged, or worse, completely mad. I would no doubt do her a considerable service by killing her and putting her out of her wretched existence. She droned on with no relief. And the familiar fury built inside me. She dared to ask me to escort her to Whitechapel. That was my private place. Where I went to do my deeds. I refused to share that with anyone, least of all this lying whore.

"Do you take me for a simpleton?" I asked, rising from the bed and gathering my clothes. Red-hot anger consumed me.

She became almost frantic then, telling me she had proof. She grabbed a dress and lifted the hem, where there was something secured in it. She held the items out to me. I took them from her, intending to put them aside and get on with what I needed to do. The coin and paper she handed me so enthralled me, I temporarily forgot about that dilemma. I held the articles for a full five minutes. It was difficult to believe my eyes. They couldn't be legitimate, but I had seen nothing like them before. The paper was sleek and colorful. The photographs were of Whitechapel, I recognized it. But the people wore a strange manner of dress. Everything appeared wrong with the photo except the buildings. They remained the same. I didn't understand what to make of it.

I knew I should kill her quietly and leave before anyone saw me in her company. However, upon further reflection, I realized that would be a needless risk.

I spent a few more minutes studying the objects. I could only conclude they were genuine. But what did that prove? That this woman came from the future as she claimed? That was preposterous. Such thoughts were absurd. But try as I might, I came up with no other explanation. And that angered me further. If this was a hoax, I did not appreciate being made a fool of. If she told the truth, then I wasn't certain what to think.

The turmoil in my mind clouded my thoughts, and all I managed to say was, "But, how?"

She offered no detailed information other than it was a normal practice in the future to travel back in time to either study history or simply for entertainment.

So flummoxed was I, when the knock on the door came, I tensed instantly. The situation was spinning out of control, and I felt my grasp slipping. Thankfully, she opened the door only enough to see the visitor, but not before promising me this would give me further proof of her existence in the future.

The man played along well, and suddenly it became obvious to me. She told me she was an actress. Of course, that had to be it. They were an ensemble of American actors traveling across England. How dare she try to trick me like this? But my mind kept going back to how she knew Mary Jane Kelly was my intended next victim. Had someone trailed me as I followed Mary Jane, planning her murder? I failed to work that out unless she was a spiritualist. I had little time to think about it as in the next moment she asked me again to take her to Whitechapel.

She stepped closer, grasping my hands. "Please help me. Escort me to Whitechapel and Spitalfields tonight. You can follow us to the transport site tomorrow and watch us go, if you like. It will be a once-in-a-lifetime experience for you."

Her ruse continued as she begged me to take her. I played along for the moment.

"Spitalfields is an exceedingly precarious place to be at night. All manner of criminal sorts roam the city."

"That's the entire point. To be as terrified as Mary Jane Kelly will be tomorrow. That's the only way I can portray her believably. You'll keep me safe, won't you?"

Keep her safe, indeed. I didn't answer her immediately. Anger boiled to the surface once again. She was an accomplished actress, and I almost believed her. Almost.

I leveled my gaze at hers. "Then terrified you shall be. I'll take you," I said.

My answer pleased her, but her hesitation showed for a brief moment. Almost as if she looked into my conscience and saw something that terrified her. Perhaps she *was* a spiritualist after all. But likely not. Because, had she seen a glimpse into my soul, she would never have gone with me to Whitechapel.

We dressed in silence. Her absence of modesty shocked me. Did the woman have no scruples? She acted like the whores in Whitechapel, with no worry about who saw them in any stage of undress. It simply made me dislike her more. But I controlled my emotions, as I so regularly did. I focused on what was to come. Fate had handed me another victim, and she couldn't have been more perfect if someone had delivered her to my doorstep. I still planned to seek out Mary Jane Kelly and keep to my original plan, but this opportunity was not to be missed.

She wrapped her arm through mine as we made our way to the hotel lobby. Her touch burned against my skin, so revolted by her I was. I stepped off the lift and looked around cautiously. Because of the late hour, only the service staff remained in the lobby. It was easy for me to avoid contact with them, so I didn't concern myself that someone might remember seeing us together. Once in my buggy, she moved to lie against me. I stiffened at her body next to mine, but I recovered rapidly and allowed her to rest her head against my shoulder. It was a modest price to pay in exchange for her life.

When we arrived in Whitechapel, she insisted we go to the Ten Bells. I tried to dissuade her, but she was relentless. It was all I could do to control my fury. I did not want anyone to see us together and identify me as her escort. When they discovered her body tomorrow, the police would want to know what she was doing there and who her recent companions were. I had kept out of sight in Whitechapel for the most part until now, only going there when I chose my victims. Mary Jane Kelly caught my eye on my last trip, and I felt a compulsion to make her part of my faction. I wouldn't allow this woman to jeopardize that.

While inside the pub I kept my hat on and never looked directly at the barmaid. I hoped that would be enough. I remained convinced that even if I was identified as her companion, no one would suspect me capable of the Ripper crimes. I covered my steps far too thoroughly. I had a stellar reputation and alibis for each murder. It would just be much easier not to have to defend myself against a police interrogation.

Much to my relief, after one drink we left the pub. As I stood outside, I lit a cigarette. A recent indulgence of mine I quite enjoyed. Alysha wandered along the pavement in front of the building, doing who knew what. I paid her no mind. After a moment, she approached me to ask the definition of a rake. Everyone knew what the term rake meant. A man of considerable sexual appetite and few morals. She pointed to one of the prostitutes at the far end of the building, the one who called me the disparaging name. I recognized her as one I had carnal knowledge of. I glared at her, and she turned away quickly. I suspected she knew I would not forget her remark.

I offered my companion my arm as we strode along the dim streets. It pained me to feign affection toward her, but I knew I must for her to trust me. As we walked deeper into the slums of Whitechapel, familiar urges flared. When I was no longer able to control my cravings, I found the perfect place. A long, blackened alleyway away from the main street. I wanted my privacy, although I wasn't worried about anyone interrupting me. My previous murders had seen to that. No one would offer help if they heard a scream, for fear of encountering the Ripper themselves. Who knew what such a maniac would do? The notion made me smile. I had the entire city at my command, held in a vise of terror.

I pointed down the alley, telling her it was a shortcut to 13 Miller's Court. She hesitated long enough that I thought I would have to force her into the alley. But she agreed after glancing around the deserted street, taking my arm and allowing me to lead her forward.

Once we were well into the alley, I took her by surprise. I pushed her against the building and used my arm against her windpipe to subdue her. I studied the confusion on her face, wishing to preserve it, along with my arousal, in my memory forever. As she faded, I removed my hold. I knew she would try to run. They all do. I also knew from experience I had time to retrieve my knife from my bag as she struggled to fill her aching lungs.

When she moved to escape, I threw her against the brick. As expected, the hit stunned her into submission, and she slid down the building in a heap.

"Why are you doing this to me?" she sobbed.

It is a question they all ask. The answer is so simple, yet so complicated at the same time. Because I must. Yet I answered with the simplest of explanations.

"You are no better than a common whore. Just like all the others. And like them, your destiny now lies with me."

Naturally, why I do what I do entailed so much more than that. But I owed her no explanation, nor did she deserve one. My reasons were my own.

Her continued pleading distracted me. "Stop talking or I will make certain this lasts much longer than it ordinarily would," I said as I slipped the leather apron on.

Then came the question none of them could help but ask.

"Who are you?"

"Who am I? You can call me ... Jack."

I so enjoyed her moment of realization. She should be honored that I, Jack the Ripper, chose her. Unsurprisingly, once the initial shock wore off, she screamed and fought. I expected no less. I embraced it. It fueled my arousal more than she realized.

Then something happened I didn't expect. She resigned herself to her fate and went slack. The fight left her. I swear I saw it palpably exit her body it was so absolute and immediate.

NO. I wouldn't tolerate that.

I raised the knife to her neck. Still, she didn't flinch. That infuriated me further. How dare she deny me this pleasure? I drew the blade across her pale, perfect neck with ease. If she insisted on denying me, I would draw this out and make her suffer unduly. She lurched forward, her hands grabbing for her neck. At last, the reaction I had hoped for—panic. I needed her to fight and be terrified. Next, I plunged the weapon into her abdomen while she was still very much alive. She tried to speak or scream—I couldn't tell which—but she still didn't move. Her eyes locked with mine and I thought I saw the corners of her mouth lift slightly.

Was she mocking me?

I pulled the knife upward, tearing through flesh and muscle as the blind rage overtook me. In my frenzy I didn't hear the couple behind me until they were upon us. I twisted quickly, the bloody knife in my hand.

"Ripper! It's the Ripper!" The old woman screamed.

FIFTEEN
MADISON

1888, London, England

Everything was fine that evening, right up until the knock at my door. Tyler called out my name, his voice an octave higher than normal and slightly frantic. Even for *him*.

But Tyler tended to be a little over-dramatic, so I wasn't panicked yet. Not until I opened the door. I took one look at him and Tori and I knew right away something was terribly wrong.

"What's the matter?" I asked, my voice sounding jittery.

"Alysha is missing," said Tyler, wringing his hands.

"What do you mean, *missing*?" I asked as panic squeezed my chest. I felt my heart sink into the pit of my stomach.

"As in, we can't locate her. She's not in her room. No one has seen her, and we've searched the entire hotel," said Tori.

Considering Alysha had taken until our last day there to shape up, I don't know why I was so surprised when it all fell apart. I really should have seen that coming.

Derek jogged up behind them. "Did you find her?" he asked, catching his breath.

They shook their heads.

"Shit!" Derek hissed. "When we find her, I'm going to fire her ass. She's gone too far this time."

"Okay, calm down, everyone. She can't have vaporized into thin air. People don't just disappear for no reason. You said she was in her room earlier, right Tyler? That's what you told me after dinner," I said.

"She was. I checked on her before I went to my room."

"That was only a few hours ago. She can't be very far. She has no transportation and no money, for goodness' sakes. Plus, she doesn't know anyone here but us," I reasoned.

"This is Alysha we're talking about," mumbled Derek. "She knows how to turn on the charm when she needs to."

"Uh-oh," said Tyler.

The three of us turned to him at the same time.

"What do you know, Tyler?" asked Tori.

"It's probably nothing, but I saw her talking to a man. A gorgeous man, actually. They were a stunning couple."

"Tyler!" I said, my patience running out.

"Sorry. That's why I went to check on her. To make sure she got to her room okay and hadn't taken off with him or done something stupid, you know?"

"She was alone in her room, right?" I asked. My voice had taken on a desperate tone by that time, and I held my breath waiting for Tyler to answer.

"Sure. Well, I assumed so. I mean, I didn't go inside. She wasn't dressed, and it seemed rude to barge my way in. She answered the door in a sheet. She said she was tired and going to bed early."

"Oh, God," moaned Derek. "Alysha wrapped in a sheet any time before midnight after meeting a man only points to one thing."

"She wouldn't. Would she?" gasped Tori.

"Ha! You should have seen her on location when we filmed *Tarnished Souls*. I think she dated half the men in town and most of the production crew, if I were a betting man," said Derek.

Okay, none of that was good, and I was getting a very bad feeling in my gut.

Derek ran a hand through his hair and exhaled loudly. "Shit. I know where she is."

It was my turn to moan. "Please don't say what I think you're going to."

"What am I missing?" asked Tyler as his head swiveled between me and Derek.

"She was hell bent on seeing Whitechapel and Spitalfields at night. She evidently found someone to take her," said Derek.

I threw my hands up in exasperation. This entire trip had been a real hoot, but this was my worst nightmare come true. The emotion washed through me, and I let it run its course before I spoke again.

"Well, let's not just stand around. We have to go find her," I said.

"I'll go look for her and bring her back here to the hotel. I'll take Mark with me. You can all go back to bed," said Derek. "She'll hide until the last minute, anyway. Then she'll show up and wonder why we're pissed."

That information was neither helpful nor reassuring, and my frustration with Alysha grew by the minute.

"Not a chance. I'm going with you, Derek. This is my company. It's my responsibility."

I turned to Tyler. "Tyler, you and Tori make sure the others are ready for transport. We'll go find Alysha, come back here and grab our luggage, then meet you at the callout portal by five a.m. Don't wait for us, no matter what. We'll see you there."

Tyler glanced at Tori and hesitated for a moment before answering me. "You got it, Boss," he said.

"Tyler, how did you figure out she was gone anyway?" I asked.

"Mark went to her room, and when she didn't answer, he was worried and came to get me."

I knew there was something going on between Mark and Alysha. I could see why Derek was concerned. She didn't seem to be particularly discreet.

"What did this man look like, Tyler?" I asked.

"Let's see. About five-ten, maybe five-eleven. He had dark hair and a mustache, very nicely dressed. And as I mentioned before, *extremely* good-looking. He stood out in the crowd. Just like Alysha."

"You don't think something has happened to her, do you?" asked Tori.

"She's fine," said Derek, before I could answer. "Alysha does what she wants, when she chooses, and damn the consequences. She's a loose cannon and because of it, it costs the studio an arm and a leg to insure her. But this is the last straw. I'm replacing her in this film when we get home."

I didn't respond, allowing Derek his rant. He mumbled all the way to his room to get his coat.

I did the same while I dressed, muttering under my breath about everything I wanted to say to Alysha when we found her. How dare she endanger everyone else here? She had some nerve. Someone needed to call her out on her behavior. And I was just the person to do it. By the time Derek knocked on my door to leave, I was fuming.

"Let's go find a way to get across the city in the middle of the night, Derek."

He curled his lip and strode to the bank of elevators. Once we got to the front desk, I let Derek speak to the attendant. I hoped the hotel employee hadn't heard from the concierge that we were travelers from Hungary who spoke no English. We didn't have time to have Tyler come down and pretend to translate for us. And I was not in the right frame of mind to be nice enough to persuade some poor soul out of bed to haul us across town at this time of night. The more time that passed, the more incensed I became over Alysha. This was narcissistic, spoiled behavior, and I planned to tell her so.

It took Derek and the front desk almost forty-five minutes to find someone willing to take us to Whitechapel. Time I feared we couldn't spare. We had to find Alysha and get to the portal by five fifteen. It wouldn't stay open past the fifteen-minute grace period after our scheduled transport time. And that made me tense. I couldn't help but feel the time running down as we sat and did nothing.

"It's going to cost us dearly," said Derek as he joined me again.

"I took all the remaining money from Tyler," I said, handing it to him. "We plan to be out of here early enough that we don't need it anyway."

We waited on the settee in the lobby, both of us restless, until the front-desk man finally waved to us that our buggy was outside. I hurried inside the carriage straight away to get out of the chill. It wasn't much warmer inside, but at least it got me out of the drizzle that seemed to never end. Derek was paying the driver and presumably giving him direction on where we were going. I'm sure the driver was as thrilled as we were to go to Ripper territory in the middle of the night.

Derek climbed into the back with me, trying to brush the water off his coat. "He won't take us farther than Commercial Street, so we'll have to walk the side streets. The entire East End is in a panic because of the Ripper murders."

"That's just terrific. We get to hike the streets everyone else is too scared to roam at night, searching for your MIA actress." I was pissed, and I didn't care if he knew it. All this did was remind me how in over our heads we were.

"I'm not thrilled about it either, trust me, Madison. I want to strangle her myself right now."

I sighed and leaned back in my seat. We didn't talk for the rest of our ride to Whitechapel. What was there to say? We were both too aggravated for small talk. Every single controversy on this trip centered around Alysha, and I think Derek was as sick of it as I was.

I used the time in the buggy to think about how much extra money I was going to bill the studio for her antics. Down time, endangering myself, my employees, and the other travelers. Possibly messing with the timeline. I'd come up with a figure, and it was going to be a good one. I was determined not to let her get away with this conduct.

Our carriage stopped, snapping me out of my reverie. Derek glanced over at me and looked uneasy. Which did nothing to soothe my own doubt. I nodded at him, and he jumped to the ground and held his hand out to help me down. I think the driver left before both my feet were on the ground. We remained in the middle of the street, not entirely sure where to begin. It was deadly still, but for the rats scurrying from one building to the next. A dog barked in the distance, and somewhere a baby cried. The clip-clop of horses' hooves from somewhere nearby echoed through the empty street as I shivered and pulled my coat tighter to stave off the cold.

When Derek finally spoke, it pierced the silence, causing me to jump. His words seemed intensely loud, even though they were hardly above a whisper.

"I guess we should start walking and see if we spot her. What's your normal protocol for a situation like this?"

"There is no protocol, Derek. My clients don't typically wander off in the middle of the night. Or ever, for that matter. I suppose your plan is the best course of action. I'm not sure what else we can do. Alert the police, maybe?" I suggested.

"I think it's too soon for that, Madison. She's here somewhere. There aren't many places she could be. Let's see if the Ten Bells is still open. That's as good a place to start as any, I suppose. If I know Alysha at all, she'd make a pit stop there, since Mary Jane Kelly frequented the pub."

"Why does she want to be here at night, Derek? What's the allure, anyway? Because right now I'd rather be anywhere else, to be very frank," I said as we walked to the pub.

"She plays Mary Jane Kelly in the film. I know she wanted a real sense for how she lived. And died. These actor-creative-types are a breed all their own. I've worked with many of them who insist on method-actor immersion like this. There have been many film stars who take it to the extreme. Were you aware Jack Nicholson lived among the actual patients in the same psychiatric ward where they shot *One Flew Over the Cuckoo's Nest*? Or that Billy Bob Thornton put crushed glass in his shoes for *Sling Blade*, forcing him to limp in preparation for his role as Karl? And Nic Cage had a few teeth pulled without anesthesia and spent five weeks with his face in bandages for *Birdy*. De Niro even got his cabbie license and worked twelve-hours shifts in New York City for *Taxi Driver*."

"That's insane. No wonder they get paid so much."

"Alysha wants to be a world-class actress so badly she will do just about anything to achieve that," he said. "Sadly, I don't think she will ever get there. Her ego gets in her way. She'd be a brilliant actress if she would smarten up and quit worrying about where her next boyfriend is coming from and how she can get her picture in the news. And if she'd stop pulling moronic stunts like this and listen to her director once in a while."

I nodded, even though he wasn't looking at me. As we walked along the dark cobblestone street in the bitter cold, in the midst of Ripper territory, all I could think about was how the odds were undeniably against us. And that Alysha Beck was free to work on her personal demons on her own time, as far as I was concerned.

SIXTEEN
MADISON

1888, London, England

The Ten Bells pub was pitch dark.

"Looks like they're closed for the night," said Derek.

I tested the door anyway, just to make sure. It was locked, as I knew it would be. I leaned against the building, out of suggestions. We had walked the city for the past hour and had only encountered a dog, two cats, several drunks passed out in doorways, and a couple of the largest rats I had ever seen. Derek raised his hands and let them fall in a shrug.

"I don't know where she is. She's probably with whoever the guy is, at his place. God only knows where that is," he said. "Maybe we should just go wait with the others for her to show up?"

"And what if she doesn't? I don't think we can risk that. She has no money to get a carriage back to the hotel. And even if she *did* get back there somehow, I doubt she'd find the portal location on her own. We have to find her, Derek."

He peered up the darkened road. "That's a good point. Let's get back to it then."

We continued with our forced tour of Whitechapel, neither of us happy to do so. As we ventured deeper into the city, homeless people sleeping in hidden corners became more common. I suspected more of them gathered in the pitch-black alleyways. As we passed, an occasional voice would drift to the street from the dim passageways. Each step we took caused my heart to beat faster, and my worry increased as I contemplated the possibility of not locating Alysha. If we didn't find her, I had no clue what I would do.

Stay behind and look for her myself? That was far from a brilliant plan, but I didn't know what else to do. My anger with her occupied my thoughts so completely it took me a moment to realize I heard a woman screaming.

Derek stopped and turned, grabbing my arm. "It's coming from that way," he said, pointing to our right. "Come on, it might be Alysha."

He pulled me along the road toward the screams. It wasn't until we were a few hundred feet closer that I made out the words.

"Ripper! It's the Ripper! Jack the Ripper killed her!"

My heart pumped hard from the run, but those words turned it into a wild beast trying to escape my chest.

Did they discover Mary Jane Kelly?

No, that couldn't be right. The timing was all wrong. Her landlord's assistant discovered her at home mid-morning. We were still hours away from then. That realization made me pick up the pace. Derek must have had the same acumen because he sprinted ahead of me. I tried to staunch the terror building inside me, but on some level, my gut already told me who it was. I prayed I was wrong.

Please, God. Don't let this be Alysha.

When we reached the alley, a man held a sobbing woman in one hand and a torch with the other, highlighting a corpse.

The dread overwhelmed me as I rounded the corner into the alley. She was a grotesque shape, like some morbid art display, and it took me a minute to fully grasp the scene in front of us. As my gaze traveled to her face, I glanced over at Derek. His expression confirmed what I didn't want to accept, and the air left my lungs much like I imagined it would when falling into a chasm. I slapped a hand over my mouth to prevent a scream or sickness. I wasn't sure which.

It was Alysha. There was no uncertainty. The anger left me in an instant, replaced with a mixture of fear and regret.

Derek leaned over to be sick, the spasm racking his body.

Seeing Alysha this way shook me to my core. The image would never leave me, no matter how much time passed. The picture was planted in my mind for eternity. The vacant eyes, the mutilated torso. The blood. God, so much blood. It ran in currents down the alley, mingling with the rainwater.

As the initial shock and numbness wore off, I became instantly claustrophobic in the narrow alley. I longed to turn and run until I collapsed. Instead, I stumbled backward until I hit the building behind me, my breath coming in ragged gasps. I was trying to keep from falling apart but doing a miserable job at it. I felt the bile rise in my throat and was sick before I had a chance to thwart it.

Derek was in shock. He stood stock still, staring at the grisly remains of the film star he introduced to the world. I stepped closer to him, more for my own comfort than his.

"How?" was all he said.

"I don't know," I whispered as fresh tears welled up.

"We have to go before the police get here," he said, making eye contact with me.

"But shouldn't we tell them who she is? We can't just leave her here, Derek," I whispered.

He tugged at my arm, moving us further out of earshot from the other couple. "What are we supposed to do, drag what's left of her mangled body around London? We can't take her back to 2032 like this. And if we get stuck here for the investigation, we'll miss the transport home ourselves. I don't like the situation any better than you do, Madison. But what can we do?"

He made an excellent point. What alternative did we have, really? Telling the police who she was would do no good. She didn't exist in this timeline. She only arrived three days ago. But it nevertheless felt hugely disrespectful to walk away and leave her behind in that damp alley, in the middle of a slum, with strangers. Granted, she wasn't my friend. I hardly knew her. I couldn't even say I liked her. But she deserved better than that, and the guilt washed over me like a wave. I said a quick prayer for her soul and followed Derek out of the alley. I glanced back once to see her watered-diluted blood trickle into the street and disappear between the cobblestones.

There would be no funeral for Alysha Beck. Murdered in a dark, dank, filthy alley in the most horrendous manner imaginable.

Internationally successful actress. Paparazzi favorite. America's sweetheart.

I realized I knew nothing else about her. Did she have a family? She was someone's daughter, maybe even someone's sister. All she was reduced to now was an unidentifiable corpse who would receive an anonymous burial. My nausea returned at the thought of it.

This was so bad. Things like this weren't supposed to happen. People weren't supposed to die on one of my vacations. It was my fault, and there was nothing I could do to fix it. The world would never forgive me for this. I would never forgive *myself*.

As if reading my thoughts, Derek spoke. "This isn't due to any negligence on your part. None of us have any liability in this. It was solely her decision to go to Whitechapel after you forbade it. We were all aware of the dangers, even during daylight hours. But coming here with a stranger at night, well, that's just downright idiotic."

I was more than a little shocked at his callousness. He was right, but it came across as harsh and insensitive so soon after finding Alysha. I didn't want to have that discussion just then, so I kept quiet. Instead, I sought to come to grips with what had happened and what we should do now. The sun was breaking over the horizon, which left little time to get to the portal.

"What time is it, Derek?"

Derek patted his suit pocket for his pocket watch. "It's almost four thirty."

"We have to hurry. The Langham is just over three miles from here. Then almost another mile to the park. We need to run if we are going to make it to the callout site by five fifteen. I can't go very fast in these boots. Why didn't you ask the carriage driver to wait?"

"I didn't even think about that. I was so focused on getting here and finding Alysha," he said. "Besides, we don't have any money left. He wouldn't have waited anyway."

Shit.

It would ordinarily take about forty-five minutes to run four miles. We had four miles to go through dark cobblestone streets and up a steep hill. Not to mention without running shoes and in cumbersome clothing.

God help us.

"We may need more than God. But if you're religious, I'm not opposed to you asking for help," he said.

I guess I had said that last thought out loud without realizing it.

"Let's go. We have no choice, Derek. With no money for a carriage, we have to run. We can do it if we don't let up. We'll have to leave our luggage. That's not good. I'll have to send someone back to get it because I can't leave anything from our time here." I looked up to meet his gaze. "Will you be all right?"

"I'm sixty, not dead," he said, frowning at me.

We ran like our very lives depended on it. And honestly, we thought they might. We didn't let up until we hit West London, where we slowed down to a fast walk. There were a few people out readying businesses to open for the day, and we didn't want to draw any unnecessary attention to ourselves. Two people sprinting at top speed through the city streets was a sure way to do that. We picked up a brisk pace again as we maneuvered our course to the park. When I saw the hill, I had a burst of energy. We were close. I had no idea what time it was, but I prayed we were going to make it. We didn't dare stop and look at Derek's watch. That would burn too much precious time when every second counted.

We crested the hillside and caught sight of the familiar clearing near the benches. The outline of the portal was unmistakable from where we were, shimmering in the distance. What was unexpected was the man facing the energy field, hesitating as if he was undecided whether to step through or not. Was it Tyler waiting for us until the last possible minute?

"Tyler!" I shouted. "We're here!"

But Tyler wasn't who turned to face us. It was a stranger. A nineteenth-century stranger.

And when he turned, it stopped me in my tracks. Derek was behind me but caught up to stand next to me. He was bent over, hands on his knees, dragging in air like a fish just pulled out of water.

Who the hell was that?

The stranger dropped his cape, then tossed something he was holding in the same direction. He smirked at me, and despite being overheated from running, chills engulfed me. He was a striking man, but something in the way he grinned at me conveyed that he was anything but the charming gentleman he appeared to be. Every fiber in my being shifted to alert as the warning bells went off in my head. He took a step toward the portal.

Don't do it. Please don't do it, I silently pleaded with him. I held my hands up, trying to warn him.

His hesitation was suddenly gone. He turned away and walked through the portal as if he had done it a hundred times.

My God. Someone from this century just transported to 2032 Los Angeles.

I gasped and ran toward the fading portal. "Run, Derek!" I screamed at him.

To his credit, Derek matched my pace as we raced the remaining few hundred yards to the portal. But we weren't fast enough. I realized we wouldn't make it in time as I watched the portal disintegrate before me, mere seconds before we reached it.

Our way home was gone.

"No!" I cried, collapsing on the grass in a heap.

Derek dropped beside me, gasping for air again.

I crawled over to the cape, looking for whatever the man tossed before he left. I lifted it up, letting the pendant dangle in the air for a moment. When I recognized what it was, I released it hastily and scooted away.

"Isn't that Alysha's necklace? Who was that guy?" asked Derek, still wheezing heavily. I only hoped he wouldn't have a heart attack and leave me on my own.

The blood-caked necklace lay coiled in the grass where I dropped it. There was only one person who could have Alysha's necklace now. The very necklace she wore last night. I just wasn't sure how he ended up at the jump portal. Did Alysha tell him the truth about where she was from? Did he follow the others because of something she told him? I had a hundred questions and no answers. But I was certain of one thing. He didn't belong in the future.

I twisted to Derek, my gaze meeting his.

"That was Jack the Ripper," I said, voicing the fear that had been playing on repeat in my head for the last few minutes. "And he's just left for 2032 Los Angeles."

"Oh, fuck," said Derek, looking at the necklace and making the same connection I had.

Oh, fuck is what was running through my mind, too. "We are so totally screwed, Derek," is what I said.

SEVENTEEN
JACK

1888, London, England

I pushed my way past the screaming woman and her companion. Her wailing echoed through the cramped alley, heightening the sound.

I didn't think they saw my face. But I couldn't be assured they hadn't either. The man carried a torch, so it was entirely conceivable they could identify me. I cursed under my breath as I vanished into the darkness, putting as much distance between us as possible.

Killing Alysha was a grave mistake. Never had there been a witness to any of my crimes. But this time someone may have seen me. The barmaid at the Ten Bells, and most assuredly the prostitute outside, would remember Alysha with me. As my mind played over the events of the evening, I realized I also couldn't be positive a member of the hotel staff didn't see me with Alysha.

What had I been thinking?

My urges blinded me, and I permitted them to overrule my common sense. I had evaded discovery for this long because of my methodical and precise planning. Now my carelessness might be my downfall. Panic swept over me as I realized what I had done. Should I flee the city? Should I go home and wait for the police to find me? Maintain my innocence, perhaps pay a local prostitute to provide an alibi for me? My mind swirled. I was extremely angry with myself. Yet I was equally angry my time with Alysha had been interrupted.

My stomach clenched at the prospect of the police at my door. If any evidence linked me to Alysha's or any of the other women's murders, that would be the end for me. I arrived home and paced the parlor, considering my options. My confidence in preserving my freedom diminished with each fleeting minute.

I considered Alysha's claim about her origin from another time. Was it possible she had been truthful? The notion both frightened and exhilarated me. She invited me to see her off for a once-in-a-lifetime experience, as she called it. The longer I considered it, the further I reasoned it would do no harm for me to observe her companions. If they left London in a buggy, I would know she lied. I doubted very much one took a horse and carriage ride to the future. But if they didn't, well, that just might prove to be the answer to my problems. I would surely be out of the reach of the London police if I were in the future.

I changed my clothing quickly as I glanced at the clock. I had little time to get to the Langham and follow Alysha's group. Out the door in ten minutes' time, I rapidly walked the several blocks to the Langham.

I settled on a bench across the street from the hotel and checked my timepiece—four thirty. She said they planned to leave at five o'clock. I sat back against the bench and tugged my top hat down further over my head to remain as anonymous as feasible. It wasn't long before six people came out of the lobby doors carrying luggage. They seemed in conflict. Four of the people waved their arms toward the street and then back at the hotel, talking loudly. I was too far away to make out the words, but clearly, they were angry. The others didn't respond in kind. A man and woman stepped forward holding their hands up in an attempt to calm them. They led the group. That was simple to determine. They herded the others away from the hotel, and as they drew nearer, I could make out a few sentences.

"We can't just leave them here. It isn't right!" said one of the women.

"We have no choice. Madison told us to get you home to 2032 and not to wait for them under any circumstances. We can't miss the callout back to LA. Whatever's happened, we'll fix it. I'll come back for them in forty-eight hours," said the man who appeared in charge.

"What are they supposed to do until then? We don't even know if they found Alysha," said another woman.

Their conversation confirmed these were her companions. I had only briefly glimpsed them the evening before. They moved up the street ahead of me before I rose to trail them. So engrossed were they in their conversation, none of them noticed me, and I kept behind trees and shrubbery as we entered the park. They sat on the benches overlooking the city while I hid behind a large bush. There were no carriage roads in the park, no way for them to obtain transport out, so why come here, of all places? It made no sense to me. I became indignant at the prospect of wasting my valuable time with such nonsense when I should have been organizing my escape.

I readied myself to leave when the younger man stood up and motioned the others to follow him. He walked toward a small hill and then I saw where they were headed. A large, shimmering arch materialized on the hill. It hadn't been there a moment ago. I would have seen it. The apparition disturbed the surrounding air, throwing off heat waves. I had seen nothing like it before and doubted my own eyes. One of the women stepped through the arch and disappeared. My heart pumped wildly as I watched them, one by one, walk through and disappear into thin air. As if they were never there at all. I blinked and rubbed my eyes. Alysha said they were actors, but perhaps some of them were magicians and they were here practicing their act. I simply could not fathom another explanation.

I waited a few minutes, yet they didn't reappear. I wandered closer and heard a low humming noise. I walked around the arch but discovered nothing to explain it.

"Hello?" I called out hesitantly. My cry was met with silence.

I ventured closer and reached my hand out toward the arch. The tips of my fingers crossed the threshold and faded from view. The humming grew stronger, and a peculiar prickling sensation engulfed me from my fingers to my shoulder. I gasped and yanked my hand back. I rubbed my hand, which still tingled.

My breathing was ragged as I stood there gawking at the strange archway. No other explanation made sense. Alysa told me the truth. She was from the future. My God, this was unimaginable.

And an extraordinary stroke of good luck.

Before me was the opportunity to propel myself years into the future. Something I was certain no other man of my time had done before me. And the timing could not have been better. The police would close in on me eventually and I would be a fugitive for the remainder of my life. Provided I could elude them at all. No part of me had any desire to live that existence.

This venture would be an uncharted risk for me. I had merely the information Alysha gave me. That she came from 2032 America. Despite my apprehension, something inside me compelled me onward.

The humming was even louder now, with an almost urgent cadence. My intuition told me it was now or never. I unbuttoned my cape, wishing the cumbersome piece of clothing off me. Then I felt the necklace. I lifted it, admiring its beauty, the dried blood reminding me how I came to possess it. I was reluctant to give it up. Holding it allowed me to relive that most exquisite moment when the light left Alysha's eyes. But I knew I must leave behind all evidence of my identity.

Movement in the distance startled me back to the present. I twisted to see a man and woman sprinting in my direction. They stopped abruptly when they realized they were not alone. I recognized the woman from Alysha's group. I shrugged out of my cape and permitted myself one final glance at the pendant before I regrettably tossed it aside. The woman's face twisted into a grimace. She held her hands out in front of her in a motion for me to halt while she caught her breath.

But I had no intention of stopping. I had made my decision. I smirked at her, knowing she could tell it was not meant as a greeting.

"Derek, run!" she screamed.

I inhaled deeply, turned, and stepped into the future with my eyes closed.

EIGHTEEN
MADISON

1888, London, England

I collapsed on the grass with one arm flung over my eyes like some swooning Victorian woman in need of smelling salts. Drama was never a good look on me. The morning dew soaking through my petticoat didn't feel awesome either, but in my current situation, wet clothing was the absolute least of my troubles. Missing the time retrieval jump was a big fat cherry on top of my already very crappy last few hours. And just to kick me when I was down, of all the people in the world to be stranded with, the universe gave me Derek Porter. I shifted my arm enough to glance at him lying in the grass staring into space. Fate obviously had an incredibly sick sense of humor, or I'd done something awful in my past and this was my karma. Either way, it was arguably the worst that could happen. I wasn't sure what shock looked like, but if I had to guess, Derek's face was pretty much on point. From the look of him, I knew I should say something to reassure him that I had things under control. But I was a little short on inspirational quotes just then.

Derek cleared his throat and sat up, leaning on his elbows. "So, you must have a transport thingy or something in your luggage back at the hotel, right? Can't you just zap open the portal? We really need to get out of here. Especially since the Ripper went back to our time."

He stood up and brushed off his pants, holding out a hand to help me up. I sat up but ignored his hand.

"Where did you get that idea, Derek? Did you pluck it from the ether? Seriously, I don't understand where that came from. It's so random," I said. "My *transport thingy*, as you so eloquently put it, only works during our scheduled trip time and only at the pre-determined jump site. Once the portal closes, so does its capabilities. And before you ask, I couldn't have used it to get Alysha home before we found her. Whoever is being transported has to be within acceptable range of the transporter *and* the predetermined callout site. Which is ten feet, by the way. Alysha was never close enough to the portal for me to be able to send her home. And neither were we by the time we finally made it here. We were still several yards away when the portal started to close. Besides I don't even have my transporter with me. It's in a hidden compartment in my luggage."

He withdrew his hand like it had been burned. "So, you don't have any way to get us home? Well, they'll open up the portal again from LA, right?"

"Yes, they will. It's just going to take them awhile."

"Define *awhile*," he said, using air quotes on the last word.

"Forty-eight hours."

"WHAT?" he shouted at me.

"It's a security feature. So no one can follow us back to the future. Or get sucked into the portal if any residual energy field remains after our transport."

"And it worked so well, didn't it? Jack-the-fucking-Ripper is in Los Angeles as we speak. And we're stuck here! Brilliant program you've got there, Madison."

"Derek, calm down and let me think!" I stood and started to pace to help myself concentrate. I was not in a calm, unfettered state of mind, yet I still had crucial decisions to make. Derek insulting me was not going to help that process.

What could I do? I needed to fix things, or we were stranded for forty-eight hours with no money, no supplies, and nowhere to stay. And there was also the small matter of Jack the Ripper roaming the streets of Los Angeles. Yeah. No pressure. I racked my brain for a viable solution but came up empty. It was, by all accounts, unfixable.

Think, Madison!

Okay. It wasn't the end of the world. We would be home in forty-eight hours. But it was those two days before then that had me in a state of panic.

"Well? What's your plan?" asked Derek, hands on his hips.

The reality of our situation? We were marooned here for the time being. There was no way for the others to open the portal and get us home until then. I paid the world's best engineers to make sure that part of the system remained unbreakable.

My much more reassuring answer? "They'll be working around the clock to override the system and get us home."

I hoped that was true. I let myself believe that, even though deep down I knew the chances were slim to non-existent they could do anything to help us before the system released the portal again.

"They'll be working around the clock. That's it? That's all you've got to say? What kind of canned bullshit answer is that?"

Derek was right. It was not a great answer. It sounded generic even to me. But I was not going to admit that to him. I lifted my chin and replied in my most convincing voice.

"It's a realistic answer, Derek. Tyler and Tori know the situation we're in. They will do all they can to get the portal open."

"Right. I'm sure they're losing sleep over our *situation*. And what if they don't know about the Ripper? They would have no reason to believe he wasn't just some schmuck who wandered into the portal by accident."

He sure was good at pointing out the obvious.

"I know, Derek! Do you think I haven't considered that? I don't know what to do, here. This has never happened before. If we can't get home for two days, we'll have to trust that they've detained him. Listen, until that time, we had both better suck it up and calm down. We need to get back to the hotel and get our luggage. We're going to need the extra clothes for warmth, because we are probably sleeping out here for the next couple of nights."

"You can't be serious, right? I'm sixty years old. I can't sleep on the ground for two nights. I have a custom-made mattress at home. Just being here for the last couple of days has me in pain. I won't be able to walk if I sleep on the ground. My back will be so jacked up. We can spend our days here watching for the portal to pop up, and sleep at the hotel," he said.

Sure. Why didn't I think of that? It was all I could do to keep from rolling my eyes at him. He made it sound like he was two steps away from a total collapse if he spent a couple of nights without a bed.

"Derek, we have to check out of the hotel this morning. We have no money to stay there."

"But you said you got all the money from Tyler before we left to find Alysha, right?"

"Yes, and I gave it all to you. And you gave it all to the carriage driver," I said, crossing my arms. "So, tell me what we should do. Because I'm open to any and all suggestions."

"Son of a bitch! Why didn't you tell me to save some?" he asked incredulously.

"How could I possibly foresee this happening? I never planned on chasing after your AWOL actress or missing the time jump!"

Derek threw his hands up and sat on the bench facing away from me. Which was fine with me. I didn't want to talk to him either. I settled on the ground again, still trying to come up with a plan.

I couldn't decide how I felt. I was furious with Alysha for sneaking off to Whitechapel, and I resented her for putting us in this position. Then there was the guilt, because I felt at least partly responsible for her death. I knew she was a loose cannon. I wished I had gone after her when she left the table at dinner, but I never dreamed she would connive her way to Whitechapel on our last night in London. Clearly, that was my mistake. I should have known what she was capable of, based on her behavior throughout the entire trip. She had proven to be selfish and inconsiderate of how her actions might affect other people. As angry and frustrated as I was, a flood of remorse still surged through me at that last thought.

Derek remained on the bench with his head in his hands. I already knew he would be zero help. It would all come down to me to keep us alive. Could I do this? A better question would be, what choice did I have?

Why hadn't I kept a closer eye on Alysha? I could have prevented all this if I had been more careful.

I sighed and stood up. Monday morning quarterbacking wouldn't do me any good. Playing the woulda-coulda-shoulda game would solve nothing. It was already done, and I had no alternative but to deal with it.

Get your act together, Madison. One of us was going to have to take charge, and I was the experienced time traveler. Oh goodie. Lucky me.

I couldn't just sit there and wait for the people at home to determine our future. A future which, by the way, looked decidedly less bright than it had yesterday. Despite my mental slap in the face, I was still fearful. But I put my best optimistic face on, even though I felt like someone wearing construction boots had kicked me in the gut. I walked over to stand in front of Derek.

"Come on. Let's go get our stuff. Maybe there's something in the hotel room we can borrow. Like a blanket or food or whatever," I said, with as much enthusiasm as I could muster.

He sneered at me, but stood up, which I took as a positive sign. We walked down the hill in silence. I predicted this would be the longest two days of my life, if we weren't on speaking terms, so I offered him an olive branch. I could be the bigger person.

"Derek, look, I'm genuinely sorry things worked out this way. But it's only two days. Maybe less if they can get the portal open before then. We can do this. If we stick together and look out for one another, we'll be okay."

"You've got to be joking, right? This is the absolute *least* favorable scenario I could ever conjure up. The studio is going to sue the pants off you for Alysha's death. And don't think I'm not going to sue you, too. My lawyers will be all over this like a bad rash. I don't care about that bullshit disclaimer you had us sign. That's provided we live through the next two days, of course. Which right now, I have serious, *major* doubts about. And you'd better pray Jacky boy doesn't get into any trouble while he's in Los Angeles, or you'll have that to contend with too."

He stomped ahead a few feet, ending our discussion. I considered responding anyway, but then thought better of it and swallowed my snarky remark. It was bad enough we were forced to prolong our time together without picking another fight. I was certain he looked forward to spending the next two days together about as much as I did.

Not to mention Derek was right, of course. The studio would probably sue me. So would Alysha's family. Obviously, Derek planned to. And I couldn't even think about Jack the Ripper. I had to hold onto the belief that my team found him and secured him. Anything else was unthinkable.

This entire mess would tie me up in litigation for years. The attorney's fees alone would be enough to shut any business down. I wasn't at all sure my company would survive this tragedy. And even if it did, how long could it endure the public scorn for Alysha's death before I would have to close the doors anyway? Something like this would ruin our reputation irrevocably. And if Jack was out there on his own, well, I was certain the public outcry to the government would shut me down in a heartbeat. Fresh tears appeared and slid down my cheeks. I wiped them away quickly. I didn't want Derek to know he had gotten to me. I wasn't sure why that mattered to me, but it did.

We walked the rest of the way to the hotel with me several steps behind him. Then we rode the lift to our rooms without ever looking at one another.

"Look for anything we can—"

"I got it, Madison. I'm not an idiot," he said, cutting me off.

Derek turned and started down the hall to his room, and I flipped him the bird as I put the key in my door. I realized it was incredibly childish, but it gave me about two seconds of satisfaction. And at that point, I clung to anything that made me feel better. I'll admit it was not one of my finest moments, but at least I was tactful enough to do it behind his back. I gave myself points for that.

I tossed the key on the dresser and collapsed on the bed, tugging the covers over my head. I guessed we still had a couple of hours before checkout time, and I intended to take advantage of it. I lay there for a bit before I took a hot bath to warm up. I was going to miss that tub over the next couple of days, and I was reluctant to get out of it.

I soaked until the water turned cool, then gathered things to stow in my suitcase. I removed all the unnecessary clothing such as petticoats and stays to make more room. I kept my two dresses only because they would provide some much-needed warmth at night. Only one blanket would fit inside, and only after I refolded it a few times. I packed two glasses and all the complimentary cheese, bread, and fruit left in the room from last night. By tomorrow I was sure I wouldn't care that it was two days old. I was tempted to eat some now, but I decided to save it to share with Derek. Not out of some misplaced loyalty to him, especially when he was being such a jerk to me, but because it was the right thing to do. I wouldn't compromise my professional or personal integrity because he couldn't be a decent human being. Until my firm went out of business, I was going to do what I thought was ethical and appropriate. Even if it killed me. I figured I stood about a fifty-fifty chance of that happening.

My mind darted to home as I secured my luggage. I worried about where Jack the Ripper was and what he might be doing. I really hoped someone spotted him after the jump. I was uncertain how long after the others he went through the portal. There was always a ten-to-fifteen-minute lag between transports, so I hoped someone in Los Angeles saw him arrive. They wouldn't know he was Jack the Ripper, but at the very least they would detain him as an unauthorized jumper until he could come back through time. The image of Alysha's bloody necklace stuck in my mind and a wave of nausea washed over me. If no one saw Jack come through the portal, that would be disastrous. I didn't allow myself to imagine it any further. But if I had, I doubt I would ever have guessed how dangerous things had gotten in Los Angeles.

NINETEEN
MADISON

1888, London, England

I answered the knock on the door to find Derek standing there with his suitcase, looking every bit as discouraged as I was. I stepped aside to allow him in.

"I assume you agree we should stay here as long as possible, right?" I asked.

"Yeah. I'm not willing to relinquish our last hour in relative comfort before we're homeless," he said.

"We can't let them come up here to boot us out. They might notice the missing blankets and other stuff," I said. I was thinking out loud, and he nodded in acknowledgement.

"When we go down there, I prefer to talk to the front desk. Maybe I can convince them into letting us stay an extra day or two with the assurance that funds are on their way."

"I don't know, Derek. I can't imagine they would agree to that under any circumstances. Not to mention the obvious fact that there *are* no funds on the way."

"They don't have to know that. What have we got to lose? Not a damn thing, that's what."

"Well, I can't argue with that," I said. "Just make sure the concierge isn't around. He thinks we only speak Hungarian."

"That lie is beginning to be a real pain in the ass," he said.

We didn't have much else to talk about. I had no clue what to say, so we sat in matching wingback chairs, retreating into our awkward reticence. I imagined hours of uncomfortable silence stretching out in front of us until my employees rescued us. It was not a pleasant thought.

"Should we go get this over with? We can probably hang out in the lobby for a bit after we check out. It will be warmer than being outdoors in the park," I said.

"Why do we have to stay in the park? I imagine it will be very isolated at night," he responded.

"I just figured it made the most sense. It will be empty at night. If we sleep in a doorway or somewhere similar in the city, we'll either be plagued by thieves, or worse yet, the police. If we were arrested and missed the portal, it would be *another* forty-eight hours before it could open again. We're safer keeping to ourselves at night. During the day, we will blend in with the other people at the park. Besides, I honestly have no idea what time of day or night the portal will open. This is all unfamiliar to me. I've never been stranded like this before."

"Well, I'm delighted you chose my vacation to undertake your little adventure," he deadpanned.

"This isn't my fault, Derek. And frankly, I'm sick of you insinuating it is. I might remind you, if you had controlled Alysha, we could have prevented all of this." So much for me being tactful.

His face dropped at the mention of Alysha's name, and I regretted bringing her up. I blamed my behavior on the fact that I was hungry, tired, and irritable. Plus, like Derek, I wasn't excited about the prospect of sleeping in a cold, damp park tonight.

"Let's just go see if I can get us an extra night," he said.

We dragged our luggage out of the room and down to the lobby while I cursed my suitcase most of the way there for not having wheels. I really missed all the little conveniences our timeline offered.

Derek wanted me to remain in the lobby, where he tasked me with looking after all our worldly belongings which were crammed into our luggage. He straightened his back and raised his chin. He looked like he was ready to storm the castle. It was ridiculous. I shook my head, more convinced than ever that our survival here would be left to me. I watched him greet the front desk clerk, his arms resting casually on the counter. Within a few minutes, his body language told me all I needed to know. His shoulders slumped and his chin fell to his chest. He took his time walking over to me, presumably not looking forward to delivering the news that we were on our own. I was already prepared to hear the predictable conclusion to our circumstances.

"I've got good news and bad news."

"There's good news?" I asked.

"Since this is our check-out day, we can have breakfast in the dining room. Which will be served momentarily. After that we can settle in the lobby for a couple of hours while we wait for our *funds* to arrive. After that, we're out."

"You had me at breakfast. Thank God something is going our way. I'm starving," I said, already rising to start for the dining room.

My appetite hadn't been strong until now, most likely because of the adrenaline and stress of last night. But this morning my stomach protested and growled noisily.

"Let's try to take some extra stuff for tomorrow. There wasn't much left in the way of food in my room," he said.

"I had some things left, but we'll need more for the next two days. I'll unbuckle my suitcase but leave it closed loosely. That way I can slip some stuff in there. Get us a table in the corner away from everyone else," I said.

I accompanied him to a spot in the farthest corner, where the nearest diners were three tables away. If no one else sat down near us, this would be ideal. We ate until we couldn't eat another bite. I stashed bread, meat, cheese, and fruit in my suitcase and buckled it up discreetly.

"Do you think it's safe to eat this tomorrow and the next day?" I asked Derek.

"Yeah, it will be fine. It's like a damn refrigerator outside it's so cold. Hopefully, your friends will get the portal opened up early on day two and we can get the hell out of here."

I drank my tea and wondered what exactly they might be doing back home to get the portal opened. I believed they would do everything imaginable. Tyler would be near hysteria with worry. Tori would be more pragmatic about our predicament, and I was counting on her efficient nature to come up with a plan.

After I ate, I felt marginally better. But I was exhausted beyond belief, as we had been up for over twenty-four hours at that point. Derek was also fatigued, so we relaxed in the lobby, where he used our luggage as a footstool. We pretended to wait for our imaginary associates to deliver our nonexistent money to pay for the hotel room we wouldn't be renting.

We both dozed off and the desk clerk awakened us when he came over and cleared his throat loudly. He glanced at his timepiece, then back at us. He had all the charm of a rattlesnake. Our time had run out, and he wanted us to leave.

Derek gave him a sour face and let his feet fall to the floor, which caused one of the suitcases to topple over. The noise caused the clerk to jump, then he spun on his heels back to the registration counter. I guessed I'd have to take this establishment off my list of approved nineteenth-century hotels. They'd never let anyone from our group back in here. Especially when they discovered we stole blankets and other property.

Provided I still had a company after this.

I was too drained to care, so I clutched my suitcase and followed Derek out the front door into the cold London morning.

The remainder of the afternoon wasn't so awful. We lingered in the park and watched people, sometimes guessing what they did for a living or what their relationship to each other was. I took a walk around just for something to do while Derek stayed with the luggage. By the time dusk came, everyone else had left the park. I watched the sun dip behind the clouds from the bench, and with that, our last moment of warmth for the day disappeared.

Derek had the idea of moving two benches together under a large tree and behind some bushes to keep us as concealed as possible. He positioned the benches together from edge to edge, so it created a double bed. We would need our body warmth at night. I piled clothing on the bench seats to cushion them and wove some through the slats of the bench backs. Derek opened the empty suitcases and arranged them at each end of the benches. He said it would afford us some modest protection. Protection against what, I didn't ask. I didn't want to think about it. I knew foxes were indigenous to the area, but I was uncertain if they had a reputation for attacking people. I refused to allow that thought to take form. I had enough to worry about. We completed our shelter by throwing a blanket over the top of the benches, topped with my parasols to create a tent, and used the other blanket and our coats to cover up with.

A room at the Langham Hotel, it was not. But it was better than nothing, which was exactly what we had without it.

We lay on the makeshift bed, even though it was too early to sleep. I was tired, but I also didn't want to wake up in the middle of the night fully awake with nothing to do but listen to Derek breathe.

Derek reached down and pulled up a bottle of whiskey which he held out to me.

"It'll warm you up," he said.

"It'll dehydrate you," I answered. "And we don't have any water."

"We're in London, Madison. I guarantee it will rain sometime in the next few hours. We have the glasses you brought. We'll have plenty of water."

"No thanks," I said.

"Don't you ever cut loose? Are you this sensible and guarded all the time?"

"I'm just trying to be practi—nevermind."

"Mmhmm. That's what I thought."

"I'm not feeling well, to be honest. I just want to go to sleep," I lied. I turned over, facing away from him.

Physically, I was in decent shape, but emotionally, I was all over the map. My one solace was that I was pretty sure there were worse train wrecks than me. Somewhere.

It took me a long time to fall asleep that night. Derek's rhythmic breathing told me he was asleep within minutes. I had never felt so utterly alone except when my parents died, and the sense of isolation threatened to drown me. I let the tears fall silently. It allowed me a moment of relief by letting my emotions out. Sadly, that was the highlight of my day.

TWENTY
DEREK

1888, London, England

Dawn of day two of my involuntary vacation extension found me in a crappy mood with a stiff neck. No thanks to the jackass deer who kept me up half the night. Anyone reading my thoughts would assume I was a real jerk. And they wouldn't be entirely wrong. No one hates Bambi, right? All I can say to that is you obviously didn't have them poking their wet noses into your bed or trampling through bushes a foot from your head all night. They didn't even have the civility to be stealthy. The little pricks.

I also reminded myself that I was camping with little-miss-proper in the freezing cold in the nineteenth century, sleeping on a park bench and drinking rainwater to survive. All with a woman half my age who apparently hated me. I challenged anyone under those circumstances to see how *their* attitude held up.

I felt bad though, about what I said to Madison yesterday. My sensitivity gene was on vacation, apparently. Or maybe my default mode was just moron. Either way, I wasn't going to sue her. I'd have to stand in line for that anyway. There would be no point to it. The court of public opinion was going to convict her the minute the world found out about Alysha's death. If she came out the other side of this with anything left to her name, she'd be lucky. Plus, she made an excellent point that this genuinely wasn't her fault. Alysha set these events in motion when she wandered off with Jack the Ripper.

Jack-the-fricking-Ripper.

Of all the men she could have met, it had to be him? I still had trouble believing she was gone. At least the numbness dulled my resentment toward Madison. I directed most of my anger at myself. How did I allow this to happen? Why didn't I pay better attention to where Alysha was? I knew what she was capable of. She was impulsive and would do exactly as she pleased. I felt partially, if not wholly, to blame for her death. But I let Madison shoulder the blame, and I did nothing to ease that burden of guilt for her. So basically, I acted like an idiot to Madison for no reason. It was hard to know how I must have come across to her, but huge asshole was at the top of the list of possibilities. The poor kid was probably already stressed constantly about the future of her company. And she had good reason to be. I made a vow to myself to be nicer to her today and try to make things right. Just in case karma was actually real.

She stirred next to me and coughed softly.

"I'm awake. You don't have to be quiet," I said.

She turned over to face me. "Sorry if I woke you up."

"Nah, you didn't. The damn deer had me up most of the night. Poking around our bed like we were a bowl of their favorite berries."

"I wondered what was out there last night. I was too afraid to find out. Are foxes roaming around here at night? I recall hearing the fox population in England was out of control."

"I'm not sure, but we're too much effort for a fox to bother with. The way you have these clothes crammed into every crevice of these benches, they'd give up quickly. The deer were just curious. Curious and noisy."

"We should probably get this stuff back into our suitcases and move the benches in case there are any early birds in the park," she said.

We climbed out of our makeshift bed. Every muscle in my body was sore, and I felt every one of my sixty years. I rolled my neck to work out the kinks, but it improved nothing.

"Let's have some breakfast and then head into the city today. What do you say?" I asked her, my eyebrows raised in question.

"Oh, I don't know Derek. What if the portal opens and we miss it?"

"Madison, you and I both know that portal isn't opening before tomorrow morning. I cannot imagine someone as meticulous as you left any chance open that someone could override it. And besides, Tyler and Tori couldn't take a chance of activating it in broad daylight when people might be here. You said yourself the system chose deserted areas during times of the day when no one would be around. And didn't you tell me in Los Angeles that the system spot checks for activity before opening the portal?"

She bit her bottom lip for a minute before her shoulders sank.

"Yeah, you're right."

"Then let's go. If nothing else, just for a change of scenery. I'd like to get a newspaper to check for any mention of Alysha."

"That's a good idea."

We packed our clothes and moved the benches to where they belonged as the sun tried, but failed, to poke through the clouds. It was a foggy, bleak day, and the air was frigid. I feared that snow was a definite possibility, and the temperature plummeting any further would bring a whole new level of unbearable to our lives.

We ate possibly the worst breakfast I had ever had. Stale bread, overripe fruit, and warm cheese. And of course, rainwater to wash it all down. What I wouldn't give for a fat-free caramel macchiato, and a bacon-and-egg sandwich. I peered at the whiskey bottle and considered taking a swig, but decided against it. Madison already had a bad impression of me. That would probably assure her I was a full-blown alcoholic. But if ever there was a time that called for a shot of whiskey for breakfast, today was at the top of that list. I struggled to remember a time I had been more miserable, physically. Or emotionally, for that matter. The only thing that sustained me was the prospect of leaving the following morning. If Madison's pals didn't come through, I didn't know what that meant for us. I told myself I would think about that tomorrow.

We gathered our suitcases and trudged down the hill into the city. It was still early, but we found a newsboy on a corner hawking papers. Madison distracted him while I stuffed a newspaper into my coat. I wasn't proud of that. I'm sure his family needed the money. But what else could we do? We didn't have a cent to our name. Or pence, to be accurate. I placed the only thing of value I had at that moment—my timepiece—onto the stack of newspapers and hoped the universe recognized I tried to do the right thing for the kid.

We sat on a bench in front of a modest café, which turned out to be a mistake. My stomach growled furiously as the scent of fresh bread and tea wafted out the doors.

"Oh, for God's sake. Let's find another bench. This is torture," I said.

"Hang on a second," Madison said, rising.

I watched her walk through the doors of the café, wondering what she was up to. She emerged a few minutes later, balancing two cups and a loaf of bread. I could have kissed her.

"We can have as much tea and bread as we want," she said, handing me the steaming cup.

"How?" I asked.

"My earrings. They were real gems."

"That was a great idea. Thank you, Madison," I said, cupping my hands around the hot cup. The heat radiating from the tea felt so wonderful I could have wept. But I kept myself in check.

We sipped our drinks and ate the warm bread. When I finished, I spread the paper open to the front page of *The Star*. She leaned closer to me, and we read the headlines.

The Ripper Strikes Again!

"Listen to this," I said as I read aloud.

"*There is a maniac haunting Whitechapel. His expression is sinister and seems to be full of terror. His eyes are small and glittering. His lips parted in a grin which seems to be excessively repellent.*"

"Wow. That's over the top. A nineteenth-century version of a tabloid," she said.

"If it bleeds, it leads," I said as I scanned the rest of the article. "They have no idea who Alysha is. But several witnesses place her with a handsome gentleman earlier that evening."

"The man we saw walk through the portal was definitely good-looking. I can't believe I didn't think to ask that couple at the scene if they'd seen someone. I guess the shock didn't help. I wasn't thinking clearly," I said.

"I don't know," she replied. "They might have seen something."

Madison sipped her tea, deep in thought.

"Maybe that's why he went through the portal," she continued. "If Alysha told him anything about where she was actually from and there was a witness to his crime, maybe that drove him to follow the others. I have been wondering why he would go through the portal. I mean, this would be a huge thing for him, right? If he was determined to disappear, then it makes sense."

"When we get to Los Angeles we can ask him," I said.

Madison was right. The man at the portal yesterday would undeniably be described as handsome. Based solely on his looks, I would cast him in a movie in a millisecond. It all made sense. I could understand why women were drawn to him and even trusted him. Why Alysha had trusted him. He sure didn't look like the crazed serial killer I always imagined Jack the Ripper to be. The dichotomy sent a shiver down my spine. That story angle would make a brilliant film, but I shook my head to get that out of my mind. Alysha was dead, and there was no possible way I could continue with this movie about the Ripper now.

I realized Madison didn't answer me, and that made me uneasy. I hoped to hell her friends had Jack secured and waiting to transport back to this century. If not, we were in serious trouble.

TWENTY-ONE
MADISON

1888, London, England

By the time we made it back to the park, it was late afternoon, and the area was deserted. The insufferable weather kept crowds out of the park, I imagined. We had spent the day wandering around the city, going into as many free museums or shops as available to get out of the cold.

Now we were outdoors again, and I shivered almost uncontrollably. We had to wait until dark to move the benches and pile on our blankets. We didn't dare take a chance of someone seeing us, because the last thing we needed was the police asking questions. I leaned against the bench and tried to imagine myself on a sunny beach. It didn't work, and my thoughts wandered.

The sudden finality of Alysha's death had been on my mind all day, as I'm sure it was with Derek. And to add to my list of items to make me miserable, I woke up this morning feeling lousy. As if my lie to Derek the previous night about being unwell had prompted my body to join the party and make an honest woman of me.

I was so excited when I learned my company landed a tour with a movie studio. Now, as I sat shivering on a park bench in London, I wished I had never laid eyes on any of them. It was such a random event. Escort a couple of actors and a few of the movie crew on a research trip. A routine tour. Somehow that made what happened that much worse. Oh, and the guilt. That was the worst part of all this. The truth was, I was jealous of Alysha at first. So beautiful and confident and perfect. But that was before I got to know her, and her horrible personality and bad attitude became obvious.

There it was again. The crushing guilt. I was angry at Alysha, and I hadn't liked her. But I felt terrible that she was dead when there might have been something I could have done to prevent it. I suspected this would have me in therapy for years.

Derek snapped me back to the present when he moved the other bench to our sleeping spot. I hadn't noticed it was almost dark; I was so lost in my thoughts. I set up the bed in the same manner I had the night before, adding many layers around the bottom and sides of the benches. I wanted to keep as much body heat in our tent as possible.

I climbed into the bed, still shivering, Derek close behind me. We got settled, pulling the blankets and extra coats over us, but it did little to ease my chills.

"Come here," he said, holding his arms open.

I could hardly make him out in the fading light.

"You're shivering, Madison. You need to get warm."

I hesitated, unsure.

"I'm old enough to be your father, for goodness' sake. You're younger than my son," he said.

I hadn't seen that coming. I had trouble picturing Derek as anyone's father. I remembered reading online he was single, and the article hadn't mentioned any children.

I scooted closer to him and let our body heat warm me up. He reached down for the bottle of whiskey, taking a drink and offering it to me. I started to say no, but thought twice and grabbed the bottle. *Why the hell not?* I thought, taking a huge swig. The minute it hit my throat I felt the burn. I managed to swallow it, but instantly coughed and gagged. Derek patted my back and laughed as he took the bottle back.

"Take it easy. Maybe try smaller sips to begin with. I get the feeling you're not exactly a heavy drinker."

"I only ever drink wine. And then just the sweet stuff," I said.

My mind flashed back to the gin I had on our first night here while I soaked in the tub. That was the first hard alcohol I'd had in months.

"Really? I'm shocked to learn that," he said laughing.

Genuine laughter escaped from me for the first time in what felt like forever, while I relaxed and allowed the whiskey to course through my veins and warm me. We continued to drink over the next couple of hours, me taking much smaller sips. I surprised myself by having an enjoyable chat with a man I seemingly had absolutely nothing in common with. There was something about Derek that made me comfortable, and I was at ease for the first time in days. If we weren't complete strangers sharing a bottle of whiskey in a deserted park, it might have been a charming domestic scene of two friends having a moment. In reality we were two slightly inebriated time travelers doing whatever we could to stay alive and warm until our rescuers showed up.

"I'm a horrible person, Derek," I blurted out before I could stop myself. The whiskey was loosening my inhibitions.

"No, you're not. What happened with Alysha was her fault."

"No, not that. Well, that too, obviously. But I was talking about Fred, who is probably going to starve to death because I didn't come home on time. All because I refuse to give my neighbor the passcode to my apartment. She's a harmless old lady. What's wrong with me? Why can't I trust anyone?"

"Fred? Your boyfriend needs a neighbor to feed him to stay alive?"

"Fred is my cat. And he already hates me. Even Tori says so. Maybe she remembered to feed him."

Derek laughed so hard tears ran down his cheeks.

"I'm sorry. I don't mean to laugh at you, Madison. But your cat hates you? How is that even possible? The creature who depends on you for his very survival can't stand you?"

"Right? I suck. All I do is work and then come home and eat and sleep. That's my entire existence. The story of my life is enough to send anyone into a coma," I said, my own tears welling up.

"Hey, come on. You're not a bad person, you're just a business owner who takes her career seriously. You have a very interesting life story. You are the only person on earth who knows how to time travel. With a cat who hates you," he said, erupting into laughter again.

I hit Derek's shoulder with the whiskey bottle before taking another swig. He was right. The alcohol warmed me, and I had stopped shivering.

"Madison, I'm honestly sorry for the way I spoke to you yesterday. I feel awful about it. One of my many faults is to speak before I think. Just so you know, I have no intention of suing you. I don't want you to worry about that."

"Well, thanks for that. Although we both know this is the end of Taylor Travel, after this."

"Not necessarily. I've been thinking about it. Why does anyone have to know what happened?"

"Huh? We have to go to the police when we get home Derek, and report Alysha's death. And tell them about Jack the Ripper, too, if my employees don't bring him back here when they come to get us."

"Oh, of course. We'll have to tell them she is dead. I get that. But is it necessary for them to know how she got that way? If Tyler and Tori have Jack secure and transport him back tomorrow morning, then we are the only two people who know what really happened. You shouldn't lose your business over this. Alysha made her decision, and it turned out to be a fatal one for her. That wasn't your fault."

"What happens if they don't have him?" I asked, although I knew the answer.

"Well, then I guess we're screwed, and we come up with a Plan B somehow," he said.

I took a long pull from the bottle. I was glad he seemed to be willing to help if it came down to that. I didn't feel so alone because of it.

"You know, I didn't really like you when we first met, Derek. You may have picked up on that."

"Yeah. I worked that out, Madison. And now?"

"I've since changed my opinion."

"Good to hear," he said, patting my hand.

"You're a good person, Derek. And I hear you make great movies."

"Yeah. Big damn deal, huh? I'm a household name. I make millions. I'm in demand. What more could I want?"

Where to start? A family? Some privacy? A life?

I was obviously in no position to offer anyone else life hacks, so I reined in my sarcasm and kept my mouth shut. Then I brilliantly decided a change of subject might be in order.

"Was there ever a Mrs. Porter?"

"Yes, a long time ago."

"Interesting. Did she run for the hills after discovering your cranky side?" I asked, chuckling.

He smiled softly and then looked away. After a moment, he responded.

"She died. She had cancer, and they found it too late to do anything. So I watched her fade a little more each day until she was gone."

What in the hell was wrong with me? Saying the wrong thing was becoming my signature move.

"Oh, Derek," I gasped. "I'm so sorry. I had no idea."

"It's fine, you didn't know," he said, shaking his head. "Like I said. It was a long time ago."

"No one since then? You're rather a good catch for the right woman."

"Well, I try to be as unappealing as possible. And as you so kindly pointed out earlier, that seems to be working well. And by the way, *the right woman*? That's certainly a diplomatic way of saying I'm old," he laughed. "But to answer your question, no. There's been no one since my wife. She is the ruler by which I will forever measure all other women. I'll never love anyone the way I did her."

"And your son?"

"He was only fifteen when she passed. It was a tough time for both of us. He took it pretty hard. Our relationship deteriorated over time, and we haven't really spoken in five years now. My failed relationship with Mark is my biggest regret in life. And now I might not ever get the chance to fix it."

"It's never too late to fix it, Derek. Please don't worry. I'll get us home. I promise."

"I sure hope you're right, Madison. But as far as Mark goes, I've tried. He won't talk to me or see me." Derek was quiet for a beat before he put the whiskey away and pulled the covers tighter around us. "Hey, we'd better get some sleep before the deer come out and wake us up. We need to be fresh in the morning for our trip home."

"Okay. Goodnight," I said, snuggling further under the blankets. It was clear he wanted to end the conversation, so I left him alone with his memories.

At some point, I fell asleep. But when I woke for the *nth* time, I finally gave up. It wasn't the deer or any other creature that kept me up. My fear and worry wouldn't leave me alone. I didn't want to keep thinking about Alysha's lifeless, mutilated body, but I couldn't stop myself. Closing my eyes only made it more vivid, so I stayed awake, hoping for some relief. I sat up, trying not to wake Derek, and watched the sun rise over the horizon as the night quietly slipped into day. Then the fog rolled in, obscuring any view at all.

It was deadly quiet as I strained to hear anything above the sound of my own heart beating in my chest. I focused on the portal opening today to take us home. I prayed Jack the Ripper would be with Tyler and Tori when they arrived to get us, coming back to where he belonged. I refused to consider the alternative because those consequences would be devastating. And there would be little I, or anyone else, could do to prevent them.

Derek woke shortly after me. We packed our clothing in our suitcases and folded the blankets on the benches after moving them to their rightful place in the park. We thought someone might like to have the blankets after we left. We sat in silence, Derek's leg bouncing up and down rapidly in a nervous dance.

By then the fog was so thick we could only see about ten feet in front of us. I wasn't sure where the portal would open, so we stayed put to let our rescuers find us. It would do no good to roam the park and miss them, and it would be easy to do in the fog.

After an hour, my knee was shaking too. Neither of us voiced it, but I knew Derek was thinking the same thing I was. What if they never came back? My mind conjured up a few worst-case scenarios, such as Jack the Ripper murdering the entire group we traveled with when they landed in Los Angeles. Absurd maybe, but it didn't stop me from imagining it.

We had both passed on breakfast. Our cheese was inedible, the bread stale and the fruit rotten. I told myself I would have an enormous cheese omelet when I got home, as my stomach grumbled. I drank the last of my rainwater before turning to Derek.

"They'll be here."

"Okay," was all he said, without looking at me.

I was about to suggest we search for them when I heard voices in the distance. I leaned forward, straining to hear better.

"Do you hear that?" I asked.

"It has to be them. Who else would be out here in this weather and at this hour?"

"Tyler?" I called out.

The voices stopped abruptly. I called out again.

"Tyler? Tori?"

"Maddie? Where are you?" I recognized Tori's voice.

We stood, ready to find them, when I saw Tyler and Tori both materialize through the fog. They ran toward us, smiling.

Tori reached me first, throwing her arms around my neck and squeezing me to tightly I had to ask her to let go so I could breathe.

"OMG! There you are. I was so lost in this damn fog. I couldn't tell which way was out," said Tyler, taking his turn to embrace me.

"Maddie, I'm so sorry. We tried to open the portal sooner. IT never left the office, working straight through the last two days. They couldn't get it to open, and the engineer subcontractors wouldn't help us without authorization from you. Which was so stupid because we told them you were stuck here and that was the entire point," said Tori.

"It's okay, Tori. I'll fix that rule with them when we get home," I squeaked out, trapped by Tyler's bear hug.

Tyler finally released me and gave Derek a wave. "Ready to blow this taco stand? Where's Alysha?" he asked, peering behind us.

"We should get back to the portal," said Tori, glancing around for Alysha too.

"Alysha isn't here. She didn't make it," I said, lowering my head.

"Where is she? We don't have a lot of time to find *Ms. Thang*," said Tyler.

"No, you don't understand," said Derek. "She's dead. She's not coming home with us."

Tyler took a step backward, his hand over his mouth. Tori frowned and glanced between me and Derek, confused.

"What about Jack the Ripper?" I asked, holding my breath for their answer.

"Who? What happened to Alysha?" asked Tori.

"The Ripper happened to Alysha. And he followed you back through the portal. We saw him. We missed the callout by seconds," I said.

"Jack the Ripper? I don't understand any of this. Alysha is dead and Jack the Ripper came through the portal?" said Tyler, his breath coming in gasps.

"Yes," I said.

"We didn't see anyone," Tori responded. "You're saying that he came through the portal two days ago?"

"We got to the landing site at the office and ushered everyone into health and safety for their wellness checks right away. They were all pretty upset, as you can imagine," said Tyler.

"So no one has any idea where he is then?" I asked, dreading what they would say, but already knowing the answer.

They shook their heads in unison.

I looked at Derek and saw my own fear reflected in his expression.

"We are in deep shit, people," said Derek.

"That might be the understatement of the century. We need to get back to LA. Now. Every minute counts," I said.

I had to fix this. I didn't know how I was going to do that, but I had to. The four of us made our way to the portal where we stepped through time, returning to 2032 Los Angeles to try to fix the unraveling nightmare we were caught up in.

TWENTY-TWO
JACK

2032, Los Angeles, California

In what felt like merely a moment after stepping through the peculiar arch, I was in an unfamiliar building. Bright sunlight streamed through the large windows. I spun around, searching the room to establish I was alone. The room was unoccupied, and that eased my fear somewhat. Although I did not know how long that would remain so.

I walked to a window and peered out. My jaw hung slack as I studied the scene below me. The view was incredible. I was above the street, looking down, but I was higher than the double-story in my home in London and even higher than the Langham Hotel. It was as if I were on a grand hill peering down.

A young man strolled by, his hair brightly colored and standing on end. Was he a member of some local tribe? I had seen nothing like it before. I was so distracted by him it took me a moment to notice the other curious things I saw. Horseless carriages made of metal moved up and down the street at alarming speed. Humongous signs with colored pictures lined the next avenue over. A horseless carriage raced by with red and blue lights flashing from the top. The offensive noise it made forced me to cover my ears in protest. I had never seen so many grand buildings before. All shapes and sizes, some reaching impossibly high into the sky.

I stumbled backward from the window to catch my breath. There were no chairs in the vacant room, so I leaned against the wall to gather my thoughts. I had no clue where I was or indeed what year I was in.

There was no doubt Alysha told me the truth—I had been taken to the future. But where and when? I remember her mentioning California in the year 2032, but I had no means by which to substantiate that. I realized I could not stay in the room forever, but I was hesitant to leave. Beyond the room lay the unknown. Doubt seeped into my veins as I questioned my decision to come here. Perhaps I should have stayed in London, but I wasn't even clear on how I got here, much less how to get back to 1888 England.

I gathered my courage and opened the door. I peered down a long hallway that ended in what appeared to be another hall at each end. I stepped past the doorway and chose to head left for no particular reason. I walked slowly, passing two closed doors. When I reached the end, I turned left again. Halfway down, a man rounded the corner ahead. My heart pumped wildly at the prospect of discovery.

He smiled at me and stopped.

"You look lost," he said. He eyed me up and down and let out a low whistle. "Dude, wardrobe really outdid themselves with you. So authentic, man." He held his hand up just above his head and grinned. I stared at his palm, not understanding the gesture.

"Yeah, okay. No high five is cool too," he said, lowering his arm. "I get it, you're uptight about your trip. No need to be. Madison is great. She takes care of all our guests. If you're looking for the head, it's just down the hall to your right," he said, pointing. "Have a safe trip, my man."

He continued past me in the opposite direction, unmoved by my presence here. His lack of curiosity shocked me. He did not ask my name or what business I had there. Apparently, he thought me to be someone called Dude, and he assumed I belonged. I understood none of this. I simply knew I did not wish to meet any more people before my good luck ran dry.

I was not sure about where I was going or what I hoped to find. I just did not want to stay here and risk encountering anyone else. I turned at the next hallway and almost collided with a woman pushing a cart of clothing.

"Hi. Um, this area is for employees only. Do you need to find wardrobe? Why did they let you go to the bathroom unattended? Oh, never mind. I swear those people get lazier every day. I'm headed that way, so I'll walk you back there. It's easy to get lost in these old buildings with a million hallways," she said.

I nodded at her. I could think of nothing else to do at that moment.

"Well, come on," she said, gesturing down the hall toward the way I had just come from.

She pushed the cart ahead and glanced back to make sure I followed her. I had no intention of going to wardrobe with her, wherever that was. She made it sound as if she expected people to be there, and that meant nothing good for me. She continued to talk about the people in wardrobe and I allowed her to move farther ahead. She didn't look back at me and I seized my first opportunity to flee. I turned right, only to discover the hall ended after only ten feet. It dead ended into a door marked *To Basement*. Brilliant. A dark hideaway was precisely what I needed while I determined my next move.

I twisted the knob and pressed the door open. It led to stairs and I began my descent. I counted eight flights of stairs before I finally reached another door labeled *Basement*. The door did not have a knob, but rather a long metal bar attached across the width of it. I wasn't certain how to open it. I touched the bar gingerly, but it did not budge. I looked up at the door on the landing of the last flight of stairs marked *Floor 1*. I might have no other choice but to see where that led. But I realized I must be cautious roaming through the building. Each person I met presented another chance of being recognized as an intruder. Anger overtook me at my plight, and I slammed my palm against the bar on the door. To my surprise, it opened with ease to a dim set of stairs. I smiled and stepped through the doorway but remained at the top of the stairs until my vision adjusted to the darkness. It was a massive space, full of metal racks on which cartons of all sizes were neatly stacked. A small window straight ahead let in just enough light for me to maneuver around the racks. I was thirsty and hungry, but more than that, I needed rest. I retreated to a shadowy corner of the basement, covered myself with a stiff canvas cloth I found nearby, and allowed myself to sleep.

I don't know how long I slept, but voices awoke me with a start.

"I don't know, Sienna," came a man's voice. "All I can tell you is Alysha Beck and Derek Porter went on that trip. That is for *sure* because I did the disclosures for everyone on that tour. And there were no health statements signed for either of them when the tour ended. Which tells me they didn't come home. And why was our team meeting postponed yesterday? Madison *never* misses those meetings. And the cancellation email didn't even come from Madison. Tori sent it out. Weird. I'm just saying, it's a massive coincidence, if you ask me," he said.

"Yeah, you're right. It's weird. But you don't seriously think the tour team would leave Alysha Beck and Derek Porter in the past, do you? I mean, people like that would be missed, for sure. Especially in Hollywood. And Madison would *never* do anything illegal," the woman's voice responded.

"I'm not sure what to think. Maybe something happened to them when they were there? Who knows? I'm not trying to start rumors or anything, but I'm just saying. Something isn't right. Anyway, help me grab some water bottles and snacks for the lunchroom. Load up my cart and I'll haul it up these frigging stairs. This is *not* in my job description," said the man.

"Who are you kidding? You aren't happy unless you have something to gossip about. You're worse than an old lady," said the woman.

"Whatevs. There's something going on. I'll find out what, eventually," he said.

I heard heavy boxes being loaded onto their cart and then dragged up the stairs. When the door slammed shut, I inhaled deeply. The man mentioned bringing water upstairs, and my mouth was so dry I instantly sprung from my hiding spot to search the racks nearest to me.

I used my bare hands to rip open the boxes, finding nothing more than paper and small wrapped items I was unfamiliar with. I moved to the next rack. There I located a large container wrapped in a smooth, clear material stronger than fabric. The label said *Drinking Water,* and it held several strange looking cups inside. I shook the package. The strange cups appeared to hold water, and I struggled to free them from the transparent casing. I eventually tore a small corner enough to remove the wrapping. The cups spilled onto the floor once they were loose, rolling away, some under the racks. I scurried to grab them, thinking the water would spill. But they remained unscathed. It took me a few minutes of trying before I worked out the lids were twisted off, rather than pulled. I drank three cups of the water and settled into my corner to sleep.

When I woke again, darkness flooded the basement, but through the window I saw a strange streetlamp illuminating the road outside. It was much brighter than a gas lamp and exuded a brilliant enough light to allow me to see my way to the stairs. I crept up the steps as stealthily as possible and nudged the bar on the door. It made a loud clanging noise as the door opened. I held my breath for a minute to be certain the noise alerted no one. The stairway was darker now. Only a small, clouded light cast a dim stream onto the stairs. I listened for any sound from above, but heard nothing. I started my climb and decided to begin with the first door I came to. I opened it as quietly as I could. I looked out to the hallway and saw only the same dim lights as the stairwell to light my path. I stepped into the hall and turned to my right. I resolved to explore as much as possible. The building felt abandoned, but perhaps the residents were only sleeping. So I took extra care to be quiet.

I stood in front of a door with my ear against it listening for any sound from inside. After a few minutes of silence, I walked into an area large enough for a table and chairs, a large white container with a handle, and an array of unfamiliar machinery lining the shelves. My gaze settled on a basket of apples on the table. I loaded as many as would fit into my jacket and pockets. I found some small cakes under a glass dish, and I gathered them too. My hunger overrode my curiosity, so I returned to my basement to feast.

Tomorrow was a new day, and I would explore then. Tonight, I would eat and sleep to regain my strength.

127

TWENTY-THREE
MADISON

2032, Los Angeles, California

I exhaled with relief as I opened my eyes in the transport room. I was so thrilled to be home. Had I been alone I might have dropped to the floor to give it a hug. Thankfully, Tyler was there before me, sparing me from embarrassing myself with such a stupid move. We waited impatiently for Derek and Tori to transport home. I wouldn't relax until Derek was back in Los Angeles.

Fifteen minutes later, he stepped through the portal, all smiles. He held his arms open wide, and I stepped into his embrace. Tyler looked on, his face frozen halfway between puzzled and appalled. I guess it was a surprise for him to see me not only getting along with Derek, but obviously happy about it. It was true our friendship had grown in leaps and bounds over the past several days. To be fair, we didn't even *have* a friendship before then. But we experienced a tragedy that bound us together. And we still had the Jack the Ripper problem to solve. He was the only other person aware of what really happened to Alysha. I had to tell Tyler and Tori, of course, although they weren't provided any details of her murder. And I knew they were trustworthy.

Derek stepped back and held me at arm's length. "What's our plan?"

"I think we could both do with sleep, some decent food, and a hot shower. Perhaps not in that order," I said.

"Amen to that. So why don't we meet at my place later this morning? What time is it, anyway?"

"It's seven o'clock," said Tyler.

Before I could answer Derek, Tori came through the portal.

"Everybody's back safely, thank goodness," she said.

I turned to Derek. "I have to check on my cat. I can do without sleep, but I definitely need a shower and something decent to eat."

"I have Fred," said Tori. "He's been a sweetheart. He has a crush on my cat Suzi."

I rolled my eyes. "Of course. He would be perfect at your house. See?" I said, facing Derek. "He hates me."

"He just needed some company, Madison. He has a girlfriend now, so he's on his best behavior. The honeymoon stage, ya know?" said Tori, laughing.

"Madison, why don't you go home and clean up and then come over? I'll have my chef prepare us something fabulous for brunch," said Derek.

"You have a chef?" I asked.

"As in, at your disposal?" asked Tyler.

"Yes. Why do I suddenly feel guilty about that?" said Derek.

I shrugged. "Okay, when?"

"How about eleven o'clock? We can come up with a strategy while we eat."

"Sounds perfect. Send me your address and I'll see you later."

• • •

Tyler drove me home, and I'd never been so glad to see my apartment. I smiled when I stepped off the elevator onto the fifth floor. I glanced in both directions, not wanting to run into anyone looking like I did. The door across the hall opened a crack, and I called out. "Hi, Mrs. Fitzgerald."

The door slammed shut without a word from her. I suppose I deserved that. I purchased my apartment five years ago, and I'd never bothered to get properly acquainted with Mrs. Fitzgerald. But I planned to correct that. I should be at least a little friendly with my neighbors.

I had changed into sweatpants and a tee shirt I kept at the office, and while the clean clothes helped, I was still certain I oozed grime from every pore. I took a long, hot shower and let the water run over me long after I was done. I wanted to get any trace of 1888 off me. Unsurprisingly, the events of the last few days struck me head-on in that moment. A sob tore through me. Then another, until I was leaning forward, my hands braced against the tile, crying uncontrollably. I thought a proper cry would ease my guilt and worry, but I was wrong. I felt just as awful when I got out.

I dressed in jeans and a light-blue cashmere sweater. November in southern California meant the weather was cool, but it seldom dropped below the low seventies until after December. I slipped on my favorite boots and blue stone earrings. I made the effort to put product in my hair and blow dry it into the beachy waves I paid a fortune to maintain every couple of months. I even used black eyeliner and mascara, which made my blue eyes stand out. A little lip gloss and I was ready to go.

No one would guess by looking at me what I was about to do. I was going to reveal to the police that Alysha Beck was dead because of me. My business was probably going to be shut down, and oh yeah, Jack the Ripper was now part of the general population because of my time machine. At least I was having a decent hair day. I would try to enjoy that while I still could. Because once my company went under, those expensive blonde highlights would be out of the question and a thing of the past.

I knocked on Mrs. Fitzgerald's door on my way out, but got no answer. I tried not to let that offend me, because I knew she was in there ignoring me. I didn't want to drive to Hollywood where Derek lived and fight the traffic, so I opened an app for a ride service and waited in the lobby.

Thirty minutes later, we pulled up to Derek's house. More of a mansion, really. It was sharp angles, sloped roof lines and huge windows, set at the top of a long driveway. I walked up to the massive glass doors, but before I could knock, Harper pulled them open.

"Hi, Madison. Come on in. Derek is in his office. I'll tell him you're here."

I stood in the foyer for a second, in awe. Classic movie posters adorned the walls on both sides, and a massive crystal chandelier hung from the ceiling where the double spiral staircase led upstairs.

"Make yourself comfortable in the living room," she said, gesturing to her left as she walked off.

I walked around the corner into a room with cream colored furniture and stunning modern artwork on every wall. Derek's place was straight out of a magazine. The Oscar on the fireplace mantel drew my eye, and I couldn't resist running a finger down the statue.

"I picked that up for *Tarnished Souls*," came a familiar voice.

I spun around to face Derek. "Hey there. Just admiring everything. You have a beautiful home."

"Thank you. I had absolutely no hand in any of it. Left to me, there would be a pool table and a beer keg in the middle of the living room. God created designers for men like me who have no taste."

"Well, whoever designed it sure knew what they were doing. They did an amazing job."

He smiled and motioned for me to follow him. "I hope you're hungry. Bradley went overboard and prepared a ton of food. I made the mistake of mentioning that I wasn't sure what you preferred, since our shared breakfast experience has only consisted of tea, stale bread, and rainwater."

We reached the open plan dining room, and the sight stopped me in my tracks. A buffet of breakfast foods filled the table. Eggs cooked in every way imaginable, waffles, pancakes, bacon, sausage, ham, and fresh fruit. Muffins and pastries lined the sideboard, with carafes of juice and a coffee urn. It was like I'd walked into an all-you-can-eat-buffet at a Las Vegas casino.

"Your chef made all this? How many people did he think were coming for brunch?" I asked.

"I know, right? He tends to go big rather than be caught short. The rest of the staff will finish it, trust me. Make yourself at home," he said, pulling out a chair for me.

The rest of the staff? I had one cleaning woman who came in once every two weeks, and that felt overindulgent.

The extravagance didn't stop me from enjoying the food, though. I dug in as if I hadn't eaten in weeks, and the meal was heavenly. After breakfast, we passed the time making small talk as we sipped coffee and discussed what we would say to the police.

"We should report everything in chronological order, ending with Jack the Ripper coming through the portal," I said.

"Have you considered what to do if they don't believe us or don't want to do anything?"

"No. They'll have to do something, Derek. We're reporting a death. They can't just ignore that."

"I hope you're right. I only worry because the situation is unusual, at best."

"True. But however bizarre the circumstances are, there *was* still a crime committed."

"I was thinking, Madison. Why can't we just go back and create a do-over? Go back to 1888, to the day before Alysha took off, and then we'll prevent her from going to Whitechapel with Jack."

"It doesn't work that way, Derek. We don't exist in that timeline. We were only visiting. If we went back, Alysha wouldn't be there for us to save."

"Okay. I thought it was worth a try."

"It was. I'm just sorry it won't work. Believe me, if it could, I would be the first one back there to make this right."

"I know that. Well, let's get this over with, shall we?" he said, rising and placing his napkin on his plate.

Derek had his own driver on payroll, which shouldn't have surprised me, but it still did. So the ride into downtown was stress free. I was beginning to think I could get used to his lifestyle. We exited the 101 freeway onto West 1st Street, where the driver dropped us at the Los Angeles Police Department's central headquarters. We waited at the entrance for the automatic glass doors to open and glanced at each other before we stepped through. It was surprisingly quiet inside. A woman with two children talked to an officer who sat behind a wall of bullet proof glass with a plaque that read *Information* tacked to the partition. Four other people sat in the reception area. We settled into hard plastic chairs and waited for our turn.

As the last person before us turned to leave, we walked forward to the counter before anyone else cut in line ahead of us.

"How can I help you?" said the uniformed officer, with about as much enthusiasm as you would expect from someone in a coma.

"We're here to report a murder," I said.

I figured that would generate some life in him, but he looked at me like I had recited my breakfast menu to him. I thought he hadn't understood me.

"Name of the deceased?" he said, rotating his chair toward his laptop.

"Alysha Beck."

He sighed and I swear he rolled his eyes a little. He continued to type as he asked questions.

"Where did this homicide take place?"

"In Whitechapel. In London. Three days ago. Well, actually it was in 1888. It's somewhat complicated." I said.

"As in England? Across the Atlantic Ocean? And did you say 1888?" he said, raising his eyebrows.

"Technically, yes. But there are extenuating factors involved."

He stopped typing and swiveled his chair to face us. "So let me understand if I have this straight. You're reporting a homicide that took place in another country and in another century."

The officer didn't believe a word I was saying. It was all over his face. He stared at us through the glass like he was trying to explain the theory of relativity to a gopher, and no matter how hard he tried, he couldn't break through to us.

"That's pretty much the sum of it, yes," I said defensively.

"That would be out of the jurisdiction of the Los Angeles Police, ma'am." He peered around us. "Next in line," he called out, waving an elderly man forward.

"No, wait. You don't understand. We were on a time travel vacation to nineteenth- century London with my company. The Taylor Travel Group. Maybe you've heard of it? The man who murdered Alysha followed my employees back here to Los Angeles, to our timeline. We know who murdered her. And he's here in Los Angeles."

The old man took a step closer to us. "Excuse me, it's my turn. Someone stole my lawnmower from my front yard. I want them found and arrested."

"Do you mind? We aren't finished here yet," said Derek, turning to confront the man.

"Well, he said you were," he said, pointing to the officer.

"He was mistaken. We aren't done," Derek hissed at him.

The old man glared in our direction and shuffled back to his plastic chair in the corner.

The officer groaned and swung his chair toward the computer again. "They don't pay me enough to deal with this BS," he mumbled. "Suspect's name?" His fingers were poised over the keyboard, ready to type.

"His legal name?" I asked.

"That's generally how this works, ma'am." His expression hovered somewhere between boredom and irritation.

"I don't know his real name."

"His current address?"

"He doesn't live here. He could be anywhere in the city," I said.

He pursed his lips. I could tell his patience was wearing thin.

"How about a description then?"

"Well, let's see. He's about five-ten or five-eleven, or maybe even as tall as six feet. It was hard to tell from where we were. Oh, and very good-looking," I said.

"And he has a mustache," said Derek.

"A tall, good-looking guy with facial hair. How extraordinary. I'm sure we'll apprehend him in no time. You just described half of LA and most of Hollywood. You two have been very helpful. We'll be sure to keep our eyes open for him," he said. His poker face did nothing to improve my opinion of him.

"We are telling you the truth. I think Jack the Ripper is in Los Angeles," I said.

His eyes glazed over, and I knew we were getting nowhere with him. And in the meantime, there was a madman running loose in Tinseltown. At that moment, a group of officers walked through the door into the lobby, laughing and talking loudly. I raised my voice to be heard over them, but once they got to the inner doors, it was quiet again. Which meant I was shouting at the desk officer for no apparent reason. He frowned at me, but I stayed the course.

"We need to see a detective. Or a supervisor. Someone!" I begged.

"Ma'am, please, keep your voice down."

Derek stepped closer to the partition, resting his elbows on the counter.

"Listen, I'm Derek Porter. I am going to insist we talk to a supervisor. We do not have the luxury of dicking around with you in a pissing contest right now, okay?"

"Derek Porter, huh? I'm guessing you think that should mean something to me?"

He was clearly unimpressed. I realized he must think we were crazy, so I took a deep breath and dialed it down.

"Please, can we just talk to a detective? There is a murderer in this city. A brutal hunter who won't stop killing once he starts," I said, as calmly as I could.

"You know what? You're going to be someone else's problem in about two minutes," said the officer, motioning to someone behind him.

The old man materialized behind us again without me noticing how he got there. He sure was stealthy for a geriatric. He was also starting to really annoy me.

"How much longer is this going to take? I like to be home to watch my game shows by two o'clock," he said.

I gave him my best incredulous look, hoping it would scare him off. He crossed his arms over his chest and lifted his chin in defiance. Great. A stand-off with a senior citizen. Just what I needed.

Another officer approached the desk, which ended my stare-down with the pensioner.

"Collins, can you put them in interview two, please?" asked officer friendly.

The relief coursed through me. Finally, we were getting somewhere. I needed to convince the police to listen to us, whatever that took.

The officer glanced sideways at us and shook his head. He motioned the elderly man to the counter while Collins buzzed us into the inner sanctuary of the LAPD.

TWENTY-FOUR
MADISON

2032, Los Angeles, California

We followed Officer Collins to a door marked *Interview Room 2*. I tried not to feel like a lamb being led to slaughter. He flipped a switch next to the door frame and a red light lit up over the top of the door. That must signify it was occupied, and my stomach flipped at the thought of an actual police interview.

Collins opened the door and stepped aside, motioning us into the room. Four metal chairs and a trash can in the corner flanked the cheap imitation wood table.

"Wait in here, and as soon as a detective is available, they'll come see you." He walked away without waiting for a reply.

I chose a chair facing the door, and Derek sat next to me. He lifted his chin to the small camera installed in the ceiling's corner.

"Big brother's watching. Cue the ominous music," he said.

"Always the director, huh?"

"Can't help it. It's what I do."

Muffled voices from outside drew our attention.

"Showtime," whispered Derek, straightening in his chair.

The door swung open and a man about my age entered. He was looking down, smoothing his tie against his dress shirt. When he looked up, he paused as the door quietly clicked shut behind him.

"You've got to be joking. What are you doing here?" he demanded, eyeing Derek with a scowl.

"This isn't a social call. I had no idea you worked at this substation," answered Derek.

My gaze bounced between them as I tried to figure out what was happening.

"You wouldn't, would you?" the detective said as he gripped the back of the chair in front of him, leaning closer to Derek.

"How could I? You refuse to speak to me," said Derek, sounding more than a little angry.

I started to interject, but they ignored me and kept right on going. The detective raised his hand to cut Derek off.

"Let's not do this here. What do you want, Dad?"

Oh, my God! Dad? This is Derek's son?

Derek turned to face me. "Madison, would you mind giving us a minute alone?"

I started to stand, but the detective held his palm up to me. I immediately sank back into my chair, trying, but failing, to fix my gaze anywhere but on them. It was like a car wreck I couldn't look away from.

"Miss, you can remain where you are. I'll leave and send in another detective."

I nodded at him. What I kept to myself was that it would take a team of wild horses and a forklift to pull me out of the room right now. I had to see how this played out.

"Fine, Son, we'll just continue to pretend we're not family. We are here in a strictly professional capacity. To report a murder. Your mother and I raised you better than this. Suck it up and do your job."

"Don't you dare bring Mom into this. Don't even say her name to me."

"I loved your mother. I was devoted to her until the day she passed. Something you wouldn't understand, obviously, because your loyalty is nonexistent. You've distanced yourself from the only family you have," said Derek, standing up, as if to challenge him.

This was becoming uncomfortable enough that I now wished I was anywhere else but in the same room with these two right then. I was shocked at how swiftly their hostility intensified.

"You're going to have to speak with us, Mark. You're a homicide detective and we have a homicide to report." Derek turned to me, then continued. "Madison Taylor, this is my son, Mark Porter." Derek took his seat again.

I peered up at Mark and tried to smile, but I'm sure it was more of a grimace at that point. "Hi," I said.

"Madison, I apologize you had to hear all this. It's nice to meet you. Are you *the* Madison Taylor? Who owns The Taylor Travel Group?"

"I am," I mumbled, suddenly struck speechless. I could only get out a couple of words at a time. I just wasn't sure what to say to either of them.

Before he could respond, the door opened, and another detective entered.

"Hello everyone," he said. "Sorry I'm late for the party." He wore a huge grin as he took the seat across from me, oblivious to the tense undercurrent in the room. Not a great sign for a detective.

Mark pulled out the chair next to him and sat down. "This is my partner, Detective Miguel Salas. This is Derek Porter and Madison Taylor."

"Hey, you two have the same surname," he said, pointing between Derek and Mark. "And you have the same name as that time-traveling lady," said Miguel.

"Derek is my father, and Madison *is* that time-traveling lady, Miguel."

His jaw fell open. "No kidding? Nice to meet you both." He rose to shake Derek's hand and then reached over to do the same with me. "Wow, I didn't even realize Mark's dad was in LA. What else are you keeping from me, partner?" he said, laughing.

Mark and Derek glared at each other across the table. Miguel glanced at them and then at me. I shrugged and shook my head at him to indicate I had no clue what was going on.

"All right, then. So what brings you two to the LAPD today? I understand you witnessed a homicide?" said Miguel.

"Yes, sort of. We didn't actually witness it. We came upon it right after it happened," I said. "The circumstances are a bit unusual, though."

"Okay, how so?" asked Miguel.

Derek ended his visual deadlock with Mark and shifted his gaze toward Miguel. "The movie studio releasing my next film hired Madison's company to take me, Alysha Beck, Jake Martin, and a few of the production crew to 1888 London. We were there on a research trip. The studio signed Jake and Alysha to star in a film centered around the Whitechapel murders. A love story set amongst the Jack the Ripper killings."

"Go on," said Mark.

Derek and I took turns filling them in on the trip, right up to the moment we saw Jack enter the portal.

"But you can't be sure it was Jack the Ripper who went through your time tunnel," said Mark.

"Transport portal," I corrected. "And who else could it be? He had Alysha's necklace. It still had her blood on it." I shuddered saying those last words.

"I realize it certainly seems that way, but we deal with hard facts. And Mark is right. The fact is, we really don't know who it was," said Miguel.

"But what about Alysha's murder?" asked Derek.

"That's a tricky one. I believe you when you say she was murdered. But these are uncharted waters. The homicide occurred in another country over one hundred years ago, technically," said Miguel. "Other than reporting her as deceased, there isn't anything else to do in the way of investigating."

"Look, it was him. It was Jack the Ripper. You didn't see the way he smirked at us. There was nothing but evil in those eyes. And the papers reported Alysha was with a handsome man the night before. He was definitely handsome." I looked from Mark to Miguel, trying to establish if they believed me.

"Well, unlike the way Hollywood portrays detectives," Mark glanced at Derek when he said it, "we don't keep our own hours, or dispatch our own investigations. We can't just run off on our own to save the day. There are procedures we have to follow. We have a sergeant we answer to."

"He's right," said Miguel. "We have to account for our investigating time with reports. Sarg has to be updated on developments. Besides, there have been no Ripper type murders in our unit in the last few days. We're all aware of what other detectives are working on. Unless one of the other substations has something, there is no proof that whoever came over has committed a crime, much less a homicide. I'll search through the agency-wide register for the past three days to see if something stands out, but other than that, I'm not sure there's much we can do."

The disappointment settled in my stomach like a brick, and I suddenly regretted eating such a big breakfast. Derek's expression told me he was just as discouraged as I was.

"If we find anything in the system, I'll call you," Mark said to Derek.

"Do you even have my phone number?"

"I'm a detective. I can find your number."

"Just take it down, will you? It's one of those ultra-private numbers I had to pay a fortune for. Why make it harder on yourself?"

Mark flipped open his iPad and scowled at Derek as he waited for him to recite his number. He looked over at me next and I rattled off my number to him. Miguel stood to shake our hands again, but Mark moved near the door, ignoring his father. I walked out of there feeling hopeless. We would never find Jack on our own. It worried and petrified me beyond belief, because I was certain my psyche couldn't handle the guilt of another person's death. We didn't speak until we were out of the building, when we stopped to perch on a low retaining wall around a fountain.

"Are we going to talk about what happened in there with your son?"

"No. Not now, anyway. Maybe never."

"Okay. Just thought I'd ask. The rest of the meeting wasn't very successful either, huh?"

"We did what we could, Madison. They do have a point that without a crime here that points to Jack, their hands are tied. They can't do anything about him following us back."

"I'm not even sure they believe it *is* Jack," I said.

"I don't think they do either. My biggest takeaway from that meeting is that they'll do a cursory search for a Jack-like murder, and if they find nothing, they'll file our report under *Hollywood nutjobs*. But I don't know what else to do. We are by no means equipped to hunt down Jack the Ripper in a city of 5.5 million people without one clue where he is."

"I know. I just feel like we're wasting precious time doing nothing. When they finally realize we're right, it will be too late. Jack will have already killed some innocent person, Derek."

"Let's see what they turn up when they check with the other stations. It's all we can manage for now." He took his phone out and sent a text to the driver to alert him we were ready to go. "Do you care if we swing by the studio? It's on our way home and I need to tell them about Alysha. I should have done that this morning, but I chose to come here first."

"No, I don't mind."

Like I have something better to do? Go home to an empty apartment? Sit at the office and act like everything is normal?

None of my options were very tempting. The studio trip perhaps the least of all, but I figured I might as well get it over with. Once the studio found out about Alysha, there would be no stopping the impending legal avalanche that would come my way. My company would be out of business in a matter of weeks, if not days.

Who would want to book a time travel vacation after hearing I let Jack the Ripper murder Alysha Beck?

No one. That's who.

TWENTY-FIVE
MADISON

2032, Los Angeles, California

I stared out the window of the limousine as it sped along the 101 freeway into the center of Hollywood.

"I know what you're thinking," said Derek.

"I doubt that," I said, laughing nervously. Although there was nothing amusing about the situation.

"I'll make it understood they aren't to blame you or your company for any of this."

"Well, I appreciate the sentiment behind that, Derek, but there is no way I'm getting out of this unscathed. We both know it. Even if the studio takes it easy on me, the public will lose their minds over this. Taylor Travel won't be able to recover. Besides, the studio has to have a fall guy. Their lawyers will keep them as far away from any liability as they can. They booked the tour, so I'm sure they'll want to deflect from that fact. Alysha's fans may criticize them for sending her on the trip in the first place. No, they'll have to prevent people from going there. They'll have no choice but to denounce me and my company."

"There are always choices," he said but averted his gaze when I looked at him. He must have realized I was right. This wasn't his fault, and I knew he felt bad. But I felt worse. Still, there was no delaying telling Majestic Pictures about Alysha's murder.

We pulled up to the guard post, and Derek buzzed his window down. Security waved us through the gates, and we began my drive into purgatory, where we stopped in front of a series of 1940s bungalows. It was hard to tell if they were original to the property or if they built them to match the look of it. Either way, they were charming and gave the entire place an old Hollywood feel.

"I'll be back as quickly as I can. This shouldn't take over twenty or thirty minutes. I've gone over this story in my mind so many times now I have it memorized."

"Are you going to tell them about Jack coming through time?"

"I see no reason to. Their only business should be Alysha's death. Plus, I'm sure you want to spread that rumor and start a city-wide panic about as much as I do."

I nodded and watched him enter one of the cottages. I thumbed through my phone and answered emails to keep myself busy, but I couldn't help glancing up at the door every few minutes. After forty-five minutes, I was a wreck. I convinced myself they were plotting my swift demise with some obscure branch of the government who was prepared to padlock my company doors as quickly as possible. When Derek walked out an hour after he entered, I was seconds away from a full-blown panic attack.

He got into the car and lowered the tinted glass to the chauffeur's section. "We need to go to lot twelve. To the news podium, please."

I peered at him apprehensively.

"They've announced a press conference for fifteen minutes from now," he said.

"So soon?"

"They don't want to prolong the inevitable."

"What about Alysha's family? They have to tell them first."

"Her sister was all she had. They've already notified her."

His words sank like a stone in my stomach. I fought back the tears, but it took great effort to do it. I focused on breathing so I wouldn't break down.

"Try not to worry. It'll be okay," he said.

He must be joking. Nothing was okay, and I couldn't imagine how it ever would be again.

That's when four men in expensive suits exited, and I watched them walk to an SUV parked nearby, heads huddled together in private conversation. I looked away as we drove past them. Somehow, I knew they would be the group to address the press. The executives and attorneys who would ruin my life and shatter the business I worked so hard to build. I opened my window a crack for some fresh air, suddenly nauseous. It was a short drive to lot twelve, and that did nothing to ease my tension. I had hoped for a little more time to prepare myself. My anxiety spiked when we pulled up to the press area to hordes of reporters surrounding the stage. They must have already been at the studio to have arrived so quickly. I twisted in my seat to see more arriving every minute. My pulse quickened and my palms were clammy. I wasn't at all sure my legs would support me. Derek reached over and squeezed my hand. I smiled at him, even though I had little to smile about at that moment.

"Come on, let's go see what they have to say."

Do we have to?

My mouth was dry, and I couldn't bring myself to respond aloud. I followed him into the crowd and waited for the words that would end my career. When I saw the news vans for every local channel in Los Angeles there, I was sure I would be sick.

The four men I saw earlier stepped up to podium, one of them tapping the microphone to get the crowd's attention.

"Good afternoon, ladies and gentlemen. Thank you for coming on such brief notice. For those of you who may not know me, my name is Len Palmer. I am the CEO of Majestic Motion Pictures. It is with deep regret that my associates and I announce the unexpected, tragic passing of a truly extraordinary actress, Alysha Beck."

A collective gasp escaped the journalists as cameras clicked and murmurs spread through the crowd like a wildfire. Reporters shouted questions at him hoping for answers, but the CEO raised his hand to quiet them.

"I'll take questions in a moment. For now, please allow me to finish. Ms. Beck was an exceptionally talented actress, one of our most popular box-office draws, and beloved by fans around the globe. Her death deeply saddens all of us, and we ask that you respect the privacy of those close to her during this difficult period. As you may know, Ms. Beck recently left on a time travel vacation with The Taylor Travel Group. Along with her costar,

Jake Martin, they planned to take part in a method-actor immersion trip for their much-anticipated upcoming film, *Heart's Desire*."

Here it comes. I held my breath and squeezed my eyes shut tightly as I braced myself for the speech I was certain I would never forget.

Len Palmer cleared his throat and continued. "Ms. Beck died when the horse she was riding became spooked for unknown reasons and threw her, causing her fatal injuries. This occurred while on an unsanctioned activity in 1888 London, England."

What? Did he just say she was thrown from a horse? What the . . .

My eyes shot open, and I gawked at the stage in disbelief. The crowd erupted again, but the CEO ignored them and continued.

"Employees of The Taylor Travel Group warned Ms. Beck not to separate from their guides or the organized activities while in London. Unfortunately, despite their repeated warnings of the potential danger, she did just that, unbeknown to her travel companions or The Taylor Travel Group employees. That disregard sadly resulted in her fatal accident. We'll open the floor to questions now."

I turned to Derek, stunned. He grasped my hand and tugged me toward the limousine. I twisted to look back as he pulled me nearer to the car. He nudged me into the backseat, slid in beside me, slammed the door shut, and pounded on the partition to let the driver know we were ready to leave.

I shifted to face him, my breath coming in gasps as I struggled to understand. "What the hell just happened back there?"

"Alysha's contract had a confidentiality clause, which included a death disclosure provision. Any information obtained or shared during the preparation for the film is proprietary and confidential. The studio maintains absolute discretionary control over all publicity associated with the project. That includes all publicity relating to her role. Jake signed one too. It's pretty standard for major celebrities."

"So they can just spin her death any way they choose to?"

"In a word, yes. And I told them if they were smart, they would align themselves with you rather than throw you under the bus, because eventually that would turn against them. You were right in pointing out that they *did* book the trip and insist we all go, after all."

"That's crazy. How can they concoct a fantasy about how Alysha died?"

"That's Hollywood, kid. It happens more often than you'd think. Remember Guy Atwood? Single vehicle accident on Mulholland Drive at three in the morning last year?"

"Of course. It was all over the internet and television. Everyone knows who Guy Atwood is."

"It was also complete bullshit. His agent found him at the Beverly Hills Hotel dead from a heroin overdose, his favorite call girl with him."

My mind had trouble registering what he told me. I wondered how many of these cover-ups had been fed to the unsuspecting public. I considered a comment about Guy Atwood, but quickly realized there was nothing to say. There was so much wrong with what he was telling me I wouldn't even know where to start.

"So that's their story, and her fans will never know the truth?"

"That's right. As far as the world is concerned, she died an unfortunate death as the rebel she preferred to portray herself as. The press will romanticize it for months. Jake will give interviews and cry for the lost love of his life, even though they couldn't stand to be in the same room together. The studio couldn't buy publicity like this for any amount of money. Don't take that wrong, Madison. I don't think it's right either. But she signed that agreement and it's legally binding. Whether or not we like it. Plus, the good news is you won't be blamed, and your company will remain untouched. It would be unfair for you to lose everything because of Alysha's poor decision."

"I can't help but think I should have done more, though. If I had questioned her when she left the dinner table or checked on her before going to bed, maybe she wouldn't be dead now."

"Don't do that to yourself, Madison. Alysha was a grown woman. We could not have prevented her from doing what she did any more than we could have stopped a hurricane. None of us had any inkling what she was up to. And Tyler checked on her before bed. Once Alysha got an idea in her head, she was doing it, no matter what you, I, or anyone else said. The only way to stop her would have been to tie her to her bed with someone guarding her. And then she would just have sued you for false imprisonment."

"But what if—" he cut me off before I could complete the sentence.

"I think I know you well enough now that I need to remind you that you, Tyler, and Tori, all signed confidentiality agreements with the studio. If your conscience gets the better of you, remember one fact. You cannot disclose anything that took place on that trip. Including the details of Alysha's death."

"Would they really come after me for that, though?"

"They'd enforce it in a heartbeat. It would definitely be actionable, and they would have you in litigation for years. And they can afford to. They have very deep pockets."

Half of me was steeped in relief they didn't implicate my company in Alysha's death. The other half was ashamed to be associated with the lie. I told myself I had done nothing unethical. I was honest with the police, and Derek told the studio the truth. The thought of the studio suing Taylor Travel petrified me. The cost of defending that would force me out of business. Plus, I signed their agreement. Still, the entire situation felt shady, and I wasn't proud of myself for going along. I pretended to be okay with it. But I wasn't.

I thought about what Derek said the entire ride home, and deep down, I understood he was right. The regret and shame were still there, but would subside, little by little. After Derek dropped me off, I went up to my empty apartment, wanting nothing more than to sleep for the next twelve hours. I felt I had earned the rest of the afternoon to myself while I came to grips with all that had happened in the last few days.

I gravitated to the couch like a homing pigeon, landing in a heap with the last ounce of energy I could muster. The television played in the background, where all the channels ran Alysha's death as their top story of the day. It must have seeped into my subconscious because I dreamt of Jack. In my dream he was in my apartment, and I woke with a start sometime after dark. I grabbed a bottle of water and went to bed, where I stayed until morning.

I was awake early, ready to deal with our remaining problem. All we had to do was locate Jack the Ripper among the millions of people in the city before his urges took over and he went on a killing spree to rival the Night

Stalker. And to get him back where he belonged—to 1888 London. Okay, so that might not be easy, but I had to try. I knew Los Angeles was not ready for Jack. Not the City of Angels. None of us were. But I vowed to do my best to stop him before it got to that point. I grabbed my cell phone and tapped it to life.

"Call Derek Porter," I said as I sprung out of bed, gathering clothes before heading to the shower.

When he picked up, I didn't wait for a greeting. "Derek, hey. It's Madison. Hope I didn't wake you. Let's go see if your son has found anything yet. If not, we need to start our own investigation. We cannot let the sun set on another day without trying to find Jack."

TWENTY-SIX
JACK

2032, Los Angeles, California

I had been in the unfamiliar city for two nights. Confined to the dim basement of an enormous building during daylight hours. On my second night, I realized the people here during the day did not reside here. This was a workplace for them. They left at sundown or shortly after, the last person leaving by six o'clock. That allowed me the opportunity to roam the building as I pleased. I watched them go, one by one from my cellar window, where I tracked their movements with a clock I took from upstairs.

I discovered more food in the cellar, stowed away in boxes, which had sustained me this long. The food was unlike anything I had eaten before, and quite frankly, not particularly flavorful. Most were wrapped in colorful, glossy paper, and the majority of them were biscuits. Hardly sufficient to gratify my hunger. That night, I planned to explore the room again where I found the fruit my first night here. With any luck, they had replenished the supply, for I worried the food I had would not last much longer.

I likewise learned a bobby patrolled the building, and his movements were rather predictable. He roamed the entire space once every two hours, always along the same route. I followed him each night, and his habit never varied. I had counted eight staircases up. He never used the lifts, which worked to my advantage. It would be much more challenging to track him if he did. On the eighth floor, something peculiar always occurred. I did not understand what it was, or how it worked. Red transparent lines suspended in midair crisscrossed the hallway to a room marked *Information Technology Operations*. The meaning of the words was a mystery to me. The bobby used his nightstick to touch one of the red lines and the most horrendous piercing noise would fill the entire building. The first time I heard it, I nearly gave away my presence, so shocked was I. However, the shrieking was so loud, it shrouded my noisy retreat down the stairwell. I was prepared the next time it happened. Each time the bobby did this, he went to a panel on the wall after a few moments where he pressed a numbers pad that stopped the alarm. I did not dare approach it for fear of setting it in motion. When he started to the eighth floor each night on one of his many rounds, I had a few moments where he would not hear me, should I require conducting a task that would ordinarily be too loud. I trusted that knowledge would be useful at some point.

I stood by the window that night as two women left for the evening. They walked with their heads close together, laughing softly. I strained against the glass to watch them as long as possible. A familiar sensation started at the base of my spine, traveling upward until it reached my skull. I realized in that moment how much I longed to be out of the basement that had become my jail cell. My cabin fever had grown to an intolerable point. I wasn't certain how to get home, but I could not stay here much longer. I needed to construct a plan.

When the clock reached eight o'clock, I left my hideaway and made my way upstairs. My stomach grumbled loudly, thinking about something to eat other than the sweets in the basement. I opened the door and was elated to find more fruit on the counter. Gathering the fruit, I piled it on the table. The same enormous white container I saw on my last trip here sat in the room's corner. I eyed it warily as it radiated a low humming sound. The box beckoned me, although I was unsure if I should dare open it. I stepped closer and inspected each side. Nothing but a white solid box with a handle. It was cold to the touch and as solid as a rock. My fingers gripped the handle and I tugged it open quickly before I lost my nerve. I jumped backward and released it almost instantly as a bright light from inside startled me. The door stood ajar, and I could feel the cold coming from within. I moved cautiously to get a closer look inside. Unfamiliar items lined the shelves. Not unlike the colorfully wrapped sweets in the basement. I opened a bowl that was remarkably flexible, with a fitted lid. I pried the lid off and the most delectable aroma wafted from it.

Chicken!

I devoured the entire meal within a minute. Then I searched the rest of the box. There were packaged meats, cheeses, butter, and sweet creams. I gorged myself, then placed everything else in the basket with the apples. Next, I rummaged through drawers and cupboards and found eating utensils and dishes. I added a set to my basket.

When I tugged open the last drawer, I stopped short. Knives of every size filled the space. My heartbeat increased at the sight of them. It was at that moment I knew I could not control my yearning. My cravings were too powerful. And I did not wish to suppress them. That was who I was. The very fiber of my being. So be it, then. If I must endure in this new world, I shall be true to myself. I am, after all, Jack the Ripper. I chose a large knife with a serrated edge and secured it in my waistcoat.

I hurried back to my secret hideout, where I stashed my food. I needed to find a way out of here. I lingered on the first-floor staircase until I heard the bobby start his rounds. He would be gone on rounds long enough for me to leave without being detected, and I would slip back in later, before the sun rose. I strode to the glass doors that led to the street and pushed against them. They didn't open, just rattled slightly, but remained closed. Why were they locked? I reeled around to make sure I was still alone. I tested the doors again, shoving harder this time.

Nothing.

My rage was instantaneous. I scoured the room for other means of escape but found nothing. When the eighth-floor alarm sounded, I shouted as loud as I could, releasing the anger that exploded inside me.

I knew of no other way out, so I retreated to my hideout. Safely back in my cellar, I paced for an hour until my frustration dwindled to a manageable level. I collapsed in the corner, panting from exertion. The realization that I was a virtual prisoner enraged me anew.

How dare they!

They would not hold me here any longer. I was obsessed with getting outside, no matter the cost. I took the knife from my waistcoat and closed my eyes, imagining all the ways I would use it. The memory of the two women I watched earlier flooded my mind, and I smiled. I simply needed to think. Surely there had to be a way to escape, and I would locate it, given enough time.

I slept that night with a full stomach. When I woke to find daylight streaming through the lone window, the answer was obvious.

The window!

I could not believe I had not thought of the solution last night, but my anger blinded me so. I sprang up and rushed to the window. I ran my fingers around the edge. It wasn't as dark on that side of the basement, and I could see the window had no lock. They clearly meant it to be stationary. It was wide enough to squeeze through, nevertheless. And that was all that mattered. If I had to break the window to escape, then I would. I knew I must leave that night.

The idea of leaving exhilarated me. I nibbled at a breakfast of fresh fruit, meats, and cheese while I planned my escape. My mood was the finest it had been since my arrival at this strange place. I spent the day in a state of anxiousness, waiting for the sun to set and the people to leave so I could make my way out the window. It was late afternoon, and I sat thinking of my impending freedom when the basement door opened, letting in a stream of light with it. I was so accustomed to being there alone it took me a moment to understand someone was entering the basement. The unmistakable sound of footsteps descending the stairs snapped me to attention. I bolted up and sheltered behind a large box next to a bare shelf.

"He's here somewhere, Derek," said a woman's voice.

"I want to believe that Madison, I really do. But a couple of missing lunches don't prove anything. And whoever it was your employees saw on the day the others got back could be any one of your clients. Either lost or just curious and trying to get a look at the operation," said a man.

The sound of boxes moving and scraping across shelves filled the vast space. I shrunk further into my dark corner.

"Well, we have to begin somewhere. And it was more than a few missing lunches. The entire refrigerator was cleaned out overnight. I sincerely doubt that George the security guard is stealing food. He must be seventy years old.

He came with the building, and I don't have the heart to get rid of him. And we know for sure Jack came here when he transported in. So we start here, right?"

"You're right. I only hope Mark and Miguel see it that way. We really need their help with this."

"Derek, look!"

My pulse quickened as I feared they had discovered my lair. They would realize I had been staying here. The basement would no longer be my secret.

"Well, this makes things more interesting," said the man.

I peered out from my hiding place to see who they were. To my surprise, there stood the same man and woman who had come upon me in the park on the morning I left London. The two who dashed toward me as I stepped through time to the future.

"We have to call Mark. We shouldn't disturb anything. He will want to see this exactly as it is. What if there is DNA or something?" she said.

"You're right, Madison. I don't have any reception down here. Let's go back upstairs and call him. Have security lock down the building and activate the alarms. No one comes or goes until he gets here. Then you can clear out all the employees and we can conduct a floor-by-floor search for him."

"That sounds good. Let's go," she said, leading the way up the stairs.

The door slammed shut, and I stumbled out from behind the box. My time had run out. They would bring others back to search for me. The woman—Madison—unsettled me. I felt it in my bones. She realized what I was capable of. I saw the way she looked at me that morning in London. And now she referred to me as Jack, so I was certain she knew I was Jack the Ripper. An uneasy feeling washed over me like icy fingers clutching my soul. She would be the one to be wary of.

I patted my waistcoat to confirm the knife was there, packed some food into my jacket and crossed the basement to the window. I placed a pail against the wall to stand on and used my elbow to shatter the glass. The sun was setting, so I would have the cover of darkness on my side. I swept the glass shards from the frame and poked my head out. I welcomed the fresh evening air against my face and inhaled deeply. I peered up and down the street and saw no one nearby. Time was of the essence, so I pushed my way through the small opening, landing in a heap on the walkway below. I quickly regained my footing, rose, and brushed the dust from my coat. I glanced left, then right. There were fewer lights to my left, which suited me fine. Unlike most people, I was comfortable in the darkness. I walked away from my prison without ever looking back. Like a bat from its cave.

TWENTY-SEVEN
MADISON

2032, Los Angeles, California

I arrived at Derek's to find him as keyed up as I was. We agreed to launch the hunt for Jack at Taylor Travel. It was the only place we knew he had been for certain, and I hoped he had somehow left a trail to help us figure out where he was now. It was a long shot and we both knew it. But it was our only starting point.

Derek called Mark and learned Miguel's county-wide database search revealed nothing to make him believe Jack had committed a crime or was even in the city. Yet. I knew he would strike soon, and my nagging sense of urgency to find him wouldn't leave me.

Derek insisted we have his driver chauffeur us around again, arguing he would pay him either way, so we may as well take advantage of it. Personally, being taxied around all the time was starting to get old. It seemed completely indulgent to have someone drive me all over Los Angeles when I was able to drive myself. Derek lived this lifestyle every day, but for me, it was completely foreign. Not that I was in need of money. My company did remarkably well. However, I refused to become a complete Hollywood cliché by flashing that fact all over town. That wasn't my style, but I didn't voice that opinion to Derek. I didn't want to offend him. So I got in the limo and tried not to think about it.

When I tried to question Derek about his call to Mark on the way to the office, he didn't say much. I was glad they were talking, even if it *was* about Jack the Ripper. Baby steps. That's what I told him. He only scoffed at me before turning to stare out the car window.

When we reached the office, I planned to call Tori and Tyler in to devise a strategy on how to question my employees about whether they had seen anything out of place. I had to be careful not to alarm anyone, and I certainly wasn't going to tell them I suspected Jack the Ripper was loose in our building. But I also couldn't take the risk of putting any of them in danger. I decided to send everyone home with paid days off and cancel tours for the next week with full refunds. I had to resolve this before resuming normal business.

I told Derek my plan, and before I could call Tori and Tyler, they both burst into my office.

"Thank God you're here," said Tyler.

Tori stopped beside him and shook her head. "Maddie, everybody is freaking out. There's a line outside the HR office."

"What? Why?" I asked. The panic rose inside me as I sought to push it down and appear impassive. Although I didn't imagine I looked even remotely calm.

"The lunch situation, Madison. People are not happy right now and are demanding an investigation," said Tyler. "And seriously, I don't blame them."

"What are you talking about?" I asked. My relief was so intense when I realized it had nothing to do with Jack, that I sank into my desk chair in a heap.

"I sent you a text. Didn't you read it?" said Tori. "Someone stole all the food from the refrigerator. Everything! Someone ransacked the entire kitchen last night."

"People bring food for the whole week and store it in there. And you know, everyone has something these days," said Tyler, waving his arms and rolling his eyes. "Gluten intolerance, no sugar, no fat, whatever. The point is, they go to a lot of trouble to prepare stuff and now it's all gone. They're gossiping about how much money they are out and how the security guard must have done it. The rumors are getting out of control."

"Jeez, people take their lunches seriously here," Derek mumbled to himself.

"I hardly think George is stealing lunches, Tyler."

"I'm just telling you what's being said, Boss."

"Well, reimburse them. Have them submit an expense report. Whatever it takes. I have bigger things to worry about. Tori, I need you to put out a company-wide email asking the staff if they have seen anyone unfamiliar in the building since the day you got back from London."

"But we didn't see anyone follow us back. Do you still think it was Jack the Ripper? I figured that theory was off the table, with no proof and with no one turning up."

"I don't know for sure, but I don't want to take any chances. I thought the police would have made more progress by this time, but apparently Jack is laying low. I also need another email to follow that. Essential positions should be issued a work from home order for time and a half pay. Everyone else has the week off with pay. Tyler, please cancel all upcoming tours for the next seven days and refund the clients in full. Schedule another tour for them on our first available date at a fifty percent discount and offer them a bring-a-friend-for-free deal to keep them happy."

They looked at one another like I had lost my mind, then back at me.

"What do we do about the lunch dilemma?" asked Tyler.

"All I can do is reimburse them. I have no clue why anyone would—"

My hand flew to my mouth as the realization struck me. I spun to face Derek, my eyes widening.

"Oh my God. It's him. He's stowed somewhere in the building," I said.

"That's a gigantic leap, Madison. Missing food proves nothing," said Derek.

"I think you're wrong. I think it means he's still here and doing what he has to, to stay alive," I said. "This is the perfect place for him to stay out of sight until he gets his bearings."

"Well, if you're right, we should call the police!" said Tyler.

"Let's not panic. Let's search the building ourselves. You and I take half, and Tyler and Tori take the other half," said Derek, nodding his chin toward them.

I paced behind my desk, struggling to work out a better plan, but coming up empty.

"You don't have to do this, either of you," I said to Tyler and Tori.

"I'm fine with it. I personally don't think JTR himself came after us. I mean, I know you said you saw someone come through and I believe that. But that doesn't mean it's Jack the Ripper. It's probably some poor sod who is scared half to death because he can't figure out how he got here or where he is. We'll find him and send him home with one hell of a story to tell," said Tyler.

"I agree with Tyler. I doubt it's really Jack the Ripper," said Tori. "We'll take floors five through eight. You two take one through four."

"Okay. Just be discreet. Don't set off a panic," I cautioned.

"Then can I suggest you hold off on sending anyone home for the week and canceling tours? At least until we do a search?" asked Tyler. "I know I'm usually the drama queen of the group, but I really think you're overreacting, Madison."

I was sure I was right. Jack was here. But if I *was* wrong, then I would frighten my employees over nothing. My thoughts bounced back and forth, making me more unsure than ever. It was difficult to trust my instincts after what I allowed to happen in London. Because full disclosure, my inner voice had already proved itself to be untrustworthy. I continued to question myself but ultimately let them persuade me to delay doing anything further until after the search. The doubt still niggled at my brain, but I stupidly ignored it.

We split up into pairs and started the search. We stopped in occupied offices to ask employees if they had noticed anyone they didn't recognize. We searched the storerooms and bathrooms. There weren't many vacant offices. Taylor Travel had teams of IT support and operations, tour guides, sales personnel, customer service coordinators, travel consultants, historians, researchers, and, of course, wardrobe staff. The lower-level floors held the human resources, accounting, and marketing departments. After three hours of searching and interviewing staff, I was starting to believe I had been mistaken. That Jack had already made his way into the city. I was in the lobby with Derek when Jim Davis from accounting rushed in.

"Madison, I'm glad you're still here. I just remembered something. A few days ago, I saw a guy wandering around the transport floor. He was in costume, so I figured he left wardrobe to use the bathroom and got lost going back. It was unusual because I've never seen a client in full dress outside the transport or wardrobe areas before. I pointed him in the right direction, and he took off. I forgot all about it until now."

My eyes darted to Derek. "Jim, do you remember what day it was? And what he looked like or what he was wearing? This is very important."

"I know exactly when it was. I had to bring a receipt up to a guest who said they never received it and who refused to leave for his trip without seeing proof I'd sent him another one. The tour guide had me run it up to him so the client wouldn't delay the trip. I guess he was being totally unreasonable about it. That was on November 9th. I looked it up before I came to find you."

"What period of clothing was he wearing?" I asked, already knowing what he was going to say. Guests went straight from wardrobe to the transport rooms. If they needed a bathroom break, or when we had the occasional client who panicked before a trip and needed the chance to calm down, there were bathrooms and quiet rooms available in wardrobe.

"Um, well, I'm not an expert or anything, but it could have been the Victorian era. He had on a jacket and waistcoat with a top hat. Spats on his shoes. That kind of stuff."

"Thank you, Jim. You've been very helpful."

Jim nodded and left for his office, and I pulled Derek aside. "See? He was here."

"I don't doubt that. But that was three days ago. We knew he had a two day head start, but I can't imagine he's stayed here this whole time."

"Call it intuition, or whatever you want, but I don't think he ever left here. We still have the basement to search. It's full of supplies and stuff for the vending machines and old boxes from the previous owners. I've never cleaned it out, so it's a dumping ground for anything I don't know what else to do with. It would be easy to hide down there undetected for a few days."

"Sounds like a thrill a minute. Lead the way, Nancy Drew," he said, but I was already walking to the stairs.

I stepped into the dark basement and felt along the wall for the light switch. The dim light made little difference in the large room. Boxes lined the shelves, and we stacked larger ones against the walls, with a narrow path that allowed us to walk around the shelving to get to supplies. It smelled damp, and dust motes floated in the air all around us. We didn't come down here regularly, and it showed. We moved boxes around the shelves, but it was unlikely anyone could hide there.

We walked around the space looking for anything to suggest Jack was hiding there. The lighting was dim, and it was hard to see into the shadowy corners. I also wasn't prepared to search every creepy square inch of the place. Even if I didn't find Jack, I was sure there were spiders or vermin down there I didn't want to encounter.

I was about to turn around, convinced we had reached another dead end, when something caught my eye. A small pile in a dark corner appeared out of place among all the boxes. I walked closer to find a crumpled paint tarp littered with food wrappers.

"Derek, look!"

"Well, this makes things more interesting," Derek said, moving to stand beside me.

We glanced around the immediate area but saw no one. Was he still living here, or had he already gone? It was possible he had left somehow, but in his nineteenth-century clothing, someone would have noticed him exit the building. Wouldn't they?

We didn't touch anything for fear of disturbing it for Mark and Miguel. I hoped they could pull DNA or other evidence from the items to tie it to Jack later. Because I knew in my gut that he was going to strike sooner rather than later. And when he did, we would need everything we could get our hands on to help find him and tie him to his crimes.

We went upstairs to call the detectives, and I was hopeful for the first time in days that perhaps we could stop Jack before he did something terrible. But that's the thing about hope—it's complicated. It can help you get through the darkest of times. Or trample whatever faith you have left when it fails to deliver.

TWENTY-EIGHT
MADISON

2032, Los Angeles, California

Mark and Miguel arrived in thirty minutes and followed us down the basement stairs.

It's right over there," I said, pointing to the far end of the room. I stood rooted where I was. Knowing Jack had been there gave me the creeps, and I had no desire to be anywhere near his hideout again.

The two detectives inspected the area wearing latex gloves and carried large plastic evidence bags. Miguel used tweezers to pick up a large scrap of paper, or maybe it was a wrapper, and slide it into a bag. I didn't recall seeing that before. Then again, I was only there for seconds before we went upstairs to call the detectives. It was possible I missed a few details.

I followed Derek to the stairs, where we sat on the bottom step and drank coffee while we waited for Mark and Miguel to complete their inspection.

"What if we can't find him?" I asked.

"I don't know, Madison. I think they'll take us more seriously now, though," he said, gesturing toward his son and Miguel.

"They'll have to," I said, although I wasn't convinced yet.

The two men walked the basement, probing behind containers and shelving. I didn't know what they were searching for, but they were the detectives, so I figured they knew what they were doing. When they reached the far side of the room, they disappeared behind a few large boxes. Almost immediately after, they called us over.

Derek and I exchanged a nervous glance before joining them. They stood at the window, and I saw instantly why they wanted us there. A cool breeze flowed through the shattered window, making me shudder. Broken glass littered the floor and the top of a pail which was used as a stepping stool to reach the window.

"It looks like someone broke this recently. The surrounding dust is disturbed and rubbed away, and it hasn't been damaged long enough to allow new dust to settle."

"So it was probably him," said Derek.

Mark glanced back at his dad. "It was likely whoever has been camping out in here, yes. However, I'm not yet ready to say it was Jack the Ripper come forward in time to wreak havoc on LA."

"I've got a good latent print," said Miguel as he waved a device over the windowsill.

"Great. Then we'll find out who it is in no time," said Mark.

Miguel input data into his handheld and looked up. "We should have an answer in a few seconds."

The device beeped, and I held my breath. The government fingerprinted everyone in the United States. Teenagers submitted their prints in school and the law mandated that adults born after the legislation passed were required to submit fingerprints within ninety days. The government even fingerprinted homeless people. And anyone the police encountered was checked in the system for compliance. If your prints weren't in the system, they were input immediately. That started five years ago, so by now, everyone's fingerprints were in the database. Unless you were a prepper hiding from the government enforcers or somehow living on the fringe of society.

Miguel frowned and tapped the keys again.

It beeped again almost right away. "That's strange. No record of that print in the system."

He handed Mark the gadget, who typed something in and scanned the screen. "Well, I'll be damned. I've never had that happen before."

"He wouldn't have his prints on file here, Detective Porter. He's from 1888. Now do you believe us?" I asked.

Derek crossed his arms over his chest and lifted his chin. "She's right, Mark. This just proves he is who we said he was. Jack the Ripper."

"This may lend itself to the position that he came through time from the nineteenth century as you said. But I'm with my partner on this. There is nothing to suggest this was Jack the Ripper," said Miguel.

Mark turned to Miguel, and a look passed between them I couldn't read.

"Madison, we found a note to you on top of the blanket. Did you read it when you were here before?" asked Mark.

"A note? There was no note. I would have seen that. There was nothing on the blanket except some used food wrappers," I said.

Mark looked at Derek next. "Did you see it?"

"Definitely not. There was nothing there. Like Madison said, just a bunch of food wrappers around the area."

"You said it was addressed to me. Can I see it?" I asked.

Mark lifted a plastic evidence bag from his case, handing me the note. I walked under the bulb hanging from the ceiling in the middle of the room, and Derek followed. I tilted the plastic bag under the light to see the writing clearly.

My dearest Madison,

Whilst I cannot understand how I have come to be in this time and place, I now realize your Alysha was truthful when she alleged to be from the future. Such a shame she had to die. But alas, we all must. Fate determines when and how we perish, and I am afraid her destiny was to meet me. I must confess, I so enjoyed our time together. However, I fear she might not feel the same about me. I am also compelled to share that I have devoted the past several evenings to thoughts of the many pleasures a night with you might bring me. I felt a connection to you that morning in London when our eyes met. You did not fool me, dear Madison. I saw the way you looked into my very soul. Yet I now sadly must accept that we are not to be. For circumstance once again decides my future. I shall satisfy my longing with others who await their fate, simply because I must. I shall be most keen to meet them. Perhaps another day we will have the opportunity to speak in person. Until then, I remain yours truly,

Jack the Ripper

I swallowed my dread with a sip of my drink as the uneasiness churned in my stomach with the coffee. If I wasn't sure before, I was now. Jack the Ripper was in Los Angeles and free from the confines of my office building.

I turned to Mark and Miguel. "You've read this letter, and you still think this isn't Jack the Ripper? He provided you a signed confession to Alysha's murder."

Mark shuffled on his feet and shoved his hands in his pocket. "I understand what this looks like, and maybe you're right. I'm not rejecting that theory altogether, but there still hasn't been a crime that even comes close to a ripper murder. I can't arrest anyone based on a note scrawled on some scrap paper. For all we know, this is a prank. The only thing we have right now is a break-in and someone living in your basement who signed a letter as Jack the Ripper."

"So what you're saying is someone has to die before you do anything? If this is a prank it's a pretty big coincidence they picked now to write me a note pretending to be the Ripper," I said. "And apparently, he's just gained his freedom. Which means until now he hasn't had the opportunity to commit a murder. But he's out there now."

"Madison, let's let them do their job," said Derek, placing a hand on my arm.

"No, Derek," I said, shaking him off. "Something has to be done. The longer he's out there, the more chance he has of hurting some innocent person."

"What would you have us do, Ms. Taylor?" asked Miguel.

"I don't have the first clue. You're the detective."

"Look, I give you my word that we will continue to check the database for Ripper type homicides. If anything comes up, we will contact the detectives handling the case. I'm going to log all of this into my report. This is now officially an open case."

They grabbed their supplies and left, leaving me completely defeated. I brushed the glass fragments off the pail and took a seat on it.

"Hey, try not to worry. They'll do what they can. It's only a matter of time before Jack makes a move," said Derek.

The frustration flared in my chest so strong it replaced the numbness that had been there for the last several days. We had been home from 1888 for three days, and time had done little to ease my guilt over Alysha's death or bring us any closer to locating Jack. Nothing about this was getting easier. In fact, it was getting harder by the day.

"Aren't you worried?" I asked, frowning at him.

"Sure I am. I just don't know what to do to fix any of this."

My frustration wasn't directed at Derek. He just happened to be the closest, and therefore the easiest, person to take it out on. My voice softened when I answered him. "I don't know how to fix it either. I hope you're right and he does something to give himself away soon."

I only hoped that something wasn't murdering someone.

Derek offered to drive me home, but I told him I would get a car service back. It would take me some time to resolve the lunch crisis with Human Resources and authorize reimbursements to the employees. Business carried on, whether my head was in the game or not.

By the time I finished, it was six o'clock. I called for a ride and got home right before seven, hungry and tired. I realized I had only eaten a muffin earlier that morning, and all the coffee I had was making me jittery. I couldn't carry on with this level of neglect and expect my body to continue operating. I stood in front of the open freezer, scouring the meager contents. My choices were leftover freezer-burned spaghetti, waffles purchased who knew when, or a very sad looking frozen meal that promised low calories, low fat, low sodium, and no taste. Judging by the package, the low everything had more to do with portion size than nutritional content. It looked to be about three bites of food. The refrigerator offered nothing better. I found a couple of slices of turkey and half a block of cheese. I settled on a turkey and cheese sandwich on bread that had seen better days.

As I sunk onto the couch with my pitiful sandwich, I turned on the news. Alysha's death was still a leading story on all the channels, so I preoccupied myself by ordering groceries online for next day delivery. I figured the least I could do for myself was make sure I had decent food in the house.

I went to bed to finish a novel I started a month ago, but after rereading the same page three times, I conceded defeat and turned off the light, hoping sleep would come.

My ringing phone woke me a few hours later when the vibration knocked it off the nightstand. I blinked the sleep from my eyes as the cell light blinded me. I felt around the floor for the phone and brought it up to the bed with me.

Incoming Call—Derek Porter

I tapped accept and cleared my throat. "Derek? What's wrong? What time is it?"

"Sorry to wake you. It's late, after two a.m. Mark called. There's been a murder."

I sat straight up, instantly awake. "I'll be right there."

"No, I'll come to you. It's on the way. It isn't far from your office."

"Okay, see you soon."

I sprung from bed and gathered a sweater, jeans, and sneakers. I didn't bother with makeup. I washed my face, brushed my teeth, and pinned my hair up. Grabbing my purse, I tossed a bottle of water in it and rode the elevator to the lobby to wait for Derek.

TWENTY-NINE
JACK

2032, Los Angeles, California

The night was deathly still. Only the occasional distant sounds of the city made their way to me, while my shoes kept a constant tempo on the wet pavement. Twinkling lights sparkled in every direction in the distance, and I tried to imagine what they were. I passed buildings with large smokestacks and stone walls surrounding them. Factories, I surmised. I trudged on without a destination and not knowing what I would encounter. I only knew the further I got from the building I had been at for the previous three days, the more in control I was, and the freer I became.

After some time, I noticed a campfire and made that my target. Where there was a fire, I reasoned, there were people. I was shrewd enough to know I would require assistance to endure here.

I hung back, concealed in the shadows watching several people congregated around a steel drum from which the fire roared. There were makeshift shelters, although I was wary of how they would withstand the rain. Blankets and clothing were strewn about the campsite, and waist-high steel mesh carts on wheels held belongings of all kinds. I watched from my hiding place undetected. Or so I thought.

"Hey man, what are you doing out here? Are you spying on us?" came a man's voice from behind me.

I turned, startled, and his overpowering stench hit me full force. I coughed and struggled to keep from gagging.

"I beg your pardon, sir?" I choked out.

"You beg my pardon? I'll just bet you do," he chuckled. "You cold? Hungry? You're staking out our camp and hiding in the dark, I gotta believe you're both."

"I . . . yes. I am."

"You homeless?"

I stared at him, not sure how much to give away about myself.

"You know, unhoused. Without a home. Nothing to be embarrassed or ashamed of, my man. We all hit a rough patch now and then. Why don't you come over and warm up by the fire?"

The prospect of a bit of warmth was too tantalizing to resist, and I followed him out of the shadows.

"Nice threads, by the way. The hat's a statement piece, for sure," he said, looking me up and down.

I nodded in acknowledgement. "Name's Chuck," he said. His greasy, shaggy hair brushed his shoulders, where bits of leaves clung to it. His beard was just as neglected and peppered with gray. I touched my own mustache and beard stubble, wondering what I must look like now. Chuck's attire was no better, with holes in his gloves, his shirt and pants tattered and filthy.

"You can call me Jack."

"Well, pleased to meet you, Jack. Hey, everybody, this here's Jack," he announced as we entered the encampment.

The others watched us approach, though none of them greeted me. It was clear I would need to ingratiate myself into their good standing, should I intend to remain here for any period of time.

"Pretty fancy clothes for a homeless guy," said a woman sitting in front of one of the cardboard shelters.

"Don't be like that, Francine. We're supposed to support each other here. The man just needs a little help, that's all," said Chuck.

Francine snorted and turned away after glowering at us. The others made room for me by the fire, and I sighed with contentment as the warmth enveloped me. A woman heating stew in a pan over the flame dished out servings. When she reached me, she handed me a bowl and smiled.

"Nice to meet you, Jack. I'm Cassandra."

"The pleasure is all mine, madame."

"From across the pond, are you? Interesting. I love the accent," she said, smiling as she moved on to the next person.

After we ate, Chuck passed a bottle of whiskey around the group. The potent alcohol warmed me, and after a few sips I relaxed more. Chuck told stories of his years in the army, and his tales of bullets that flew from the sky destroying entire cities both unnerved and thrilled me. I realized I had seen so little of this place yet. I peered up at the stars and watched as flashing red and white lights danced across the sky. Was it possible man could fly through the heavens that high? I dared to dream about the possibilities.

I studied Cassandra sitting across from me. The firelight softened her features, and she wore her dark, wavy hair loose, where it reached the middle of her back. Her face resembled that of a noble woman, and I couldn't help wondering how she ended up in a homeless encampment. The people here rivaled the destitute in Whitechapel. Filthy and living in squalor, hardly better than an animal. But Cassandra seemed unique. She caught my eye and didn't break contact. So brazen, the women of this era were. I recognized the lust in her eyes, and I returned the look.

Chuck nudged me and leaned closer. "That's off limits, my man. Cassie is a little lost right now. I look out for her. I know I may come off as a good-time Charlie, but make no mistake. I was Army Special Forces, and all that training is still in me. Don't make me regret inviting you here. Stay away from Cassie, Jack."

I didn't bother to acknowledge him or even glance in his direction. Why should I? He was clearly beneath me. I balled my fists and tamped down my irritation. I would not be told who I could or could not keep company with. Especially by someone who was no more than a common vagrant.

Later that evening, I would recall that same feeling when Cassandra came to me. I refused to heed Chuck's warning.

Everyone slept, but I was wide awake as I sat by the campfire in a rickety chair. I stared at the sky, searching for more flying machines, but the clouds hung thick and low, restricting the view to my nearby surroundings. The air was different here than from London. Heavy, and it smelled of machinery and smoke. I missed London, and I longed to go home. What once seemed like an excellent idea to flee England and a potential police investigation was swiftly becoming the worst mistake I had ever made. Though I was at a loss as to how to rectify it, and my future loomed bleakly on the horizon. I was drifting to sleep when movement caught my attention. Cassandra crawled out of her shelter and stretched. She ran her hands through her long hair and glanced my way. We locked eyes for a moment before she walked toward me. She took the chair next to me and passed me a bottle of wine she pulled from inside her coat.

"So, what's your story, Jack? Why are you wandering Los Angeles alone at night dressed like that?"

I took a drink from the bottle and handed it back to her. "I find myself without housing at the moment. Also, with pockets to let. You could say I have had a turn of unfortunate luck recently."

"With pockets to let. First time I've heard being broke described that way. I like it," she said, laughing. "But that's everyone's tale in this city. What makes you any different? A handsome guy in clean clothes isn't something we see around here very often."

"My misfortune is rather recent. A fortnight ago I had the world on a string, it seemed."

"And now?"

"Now I am afraid I cannot imagine a grimmer future for myself."

"Chuck says you can stay here. We don't have much, but we get by. I wouldn't object if you stayed."

I studied her face closely. Despite her ragged clothes and undeniable need for a bath, she was a beautiful woman. Her high cheekbones and full lips gave her an exotic appearance. I still marveled at how she happened to be here, but I didn't ask her. I had no interest in hearing her tale of woe. I had my immediate future to consider, and that had to be my sole focus. But when she stood and grabbed my hand, my resolve was forgotten as old weaknesses bubbled to the surface.

I stood without speaking and let her lead me away from the camp. We strolled through long grass, damp from the earlier rainfall. She stopped at a tattered settee in the field and pulled me down to her. Liquor bottles littered the area as far as I could see, and the rubbish suggested this was a frequently used spot. Her intentions were unmistakable, and I was equally enchanted and revolted. She was behaving like a common harlot. I thought she was special, but I understood in that moment she was anything but. She knew I had no money, so she was not prostituting herself. Prostitutes did not bed a man for free. That somehow made her more repulsive.

The entire scene was so distasteful that I reached into my coat for my knife before I realized I was gripping it. Her scream died on her lips within seconds. I plunged the blade into her abdomen with such force it required a great deal of effort to free it. I was fixated on my hatred, and it was all I could focus on. I already knew I would butcher her, mutilate her until it satisfied the hunger in me, and I looked forward to it. It seemed the perfect set of circumstances. It was well into the late hours, and we were alone in a desolate field. And no one knew I was with her.

I took my time with Cassandra, and I must admit it was some of my finest work. I normally strangled my victims, but I hadn't done that with Alysha, and I didn't do it with Cassandra either, for reasons I did not understand. Perhaps I was evolving.

I had intended to take my time with Mary Jane Kelly, but of course, my plans had to be adjusted. She was meant to be my most spectacular kill to date. I felt unsatisfied, and quite frankly, cheated, that I was unable to spend time with her. Not to mention my evening with Alysha was interrupted. So I used the opportunity with Cassandra to quell my desires. And beautiful Cassandra did not disappoint me. I squatted in the damp grass and mopped the perspiration from my brow while I admired my handiwork. Just lovely.

A loud thrashing sound disrupted my thoughts, and I sprung to my feet. The piece of plastic I found nearby to use as an apron fell off me as I spun around. Chuck stood a few feet from me, carrying a silver tube that radiated light from the end. He pointed it at the couch and Cassandra. He stood gawking at her mangled body in shock before letting the bar slip from his grip when he rushed toward her.

"No! Cassie," he cried. He wanted to embrace her, but her body cavity was open and there was so much blood, he recoiled.

By the time he twisted around to confront me, I was long gone. I walked away from the field fully prepared to kill Chuck if the demand arose. I truly did not want to, as I considered him a mate now. However, if I had to defend myself, there was no question that I would. But he didn't pursue me. His cries for Cassandra pierced the tranquil night until I was too far away to hear him any longer. All his talk of protecting her aside, when the time arrived, his agony over losing her overtook his ability to react. It was indeed for the best, as now Chuck would live another day.

I walked until my feet could no longer carry me. Then I slept in an abandoned building until the sun peeked over the horizon. My stomach grumbled with hunger as I commenced my journey to search for a new camp. I was convinced that was the answer to my predicament. The homeless seemed quite willing to welcome a stranger into their fold. And I was more than willing to be an ideal houseguest—until I wasn't.

I paused at a rain puddle to wash the stray blood specks from my coat. It wouldn't do to have that give me away. Not when starting over here. The more I pondered it, the more sense it made. I would lead the existence of a vagabond. No responsibilities, relying on the kindness of strangers. Satisfying my impulses as I pleased. I would kill whomever I wanted whenever I chose and move on afterwards. Suddenly, my prospects had a much brighter outlook. I whistled as I rambled onward, and before long, I located my next encampment. I straightened my tie and smiled as I approached my new temporary home.

Perhaps Alysha wasn't the only thespian that night in the Whitechapel alley.

THIRTY
MADISON

2032, Los Angeles, California

I made Derek send his driver home so we could take my car. I was tired of being shuffled around town like *Driving Miss Daisy*. Not to mention it would be beyond inappropriate to pull up to a murder investigation in a limousine. I was nervous, and driving would help keep my mind occupied until we got there.

"Tell me exactly what Mark told you," I said, glancing at Derek.

"Just that there was a murder that might fall into the Ripper category. He mentioned where it happened, but he had to hang up before I got any more details."

"Okay."

"Try not to worry. We really won't know anything until we get there."

"You seriously can't believe that. Of course, it's Jack. That would be too much of a coincidence."

He turned to gaze out the window, and I returned to concentrating on my driving. This late at night the traffic was light, so we made it to the east side of the city much faster than anticipated. I pulled off the freeway into a rundown industrial area. Derek glanced at his phone every few minutes while he directed me through the deserted streets. We rounded a corner where emergency vehicles lined the street, their lights flashing brightly. Police tape cordoned off an opening in a chain-link fence that led to a grassy field, and I pulled in across the street and parked behind an unmarked police car.

"What should we do? Wait here and see if we spot Mark and Miguel or try to find them?" I asked.

"Let's try to find them so they know we're here."

We stopped the first officer we found and asked to speak to Mark. He took off toward the field while we waited in the cold. It started to sprinkle, and I shivered as two uniforms rushed by us, carrying a portable awning.

Mark stepped out from around the barricaded area a few minutes later, and I could tell immediately he was not happy to see us there. His lips were pinched into a thin line, his brow furrowed. He yanked off his latex gloves and shoved them in his coat pocket.

"What are you two doing here?" he asked, his voice lowered as he grabbed Derek's elbow and steered him across the street.

I followed right behind them, not wanting to miss anything he said.

"Well, you called me, Mark. Remember? We *are* trying to locate Jack the Ripper, after all."

"Lower your voice," he hissed. "I called you as a courtesy. I never told you to show up at my crime scene and interrupt my investigation. This is completely out of line. I need you to leave. Now. I'll call you when we have something."

"Was it him? Just tell us. I need to know." I studied his face, my expression pleading for him to tell me something.

He searched the sky for answers he'd never find as he thought about how to respond. "I don't know yet. Maybe. Probably," he sighed.

Tears stung my eyes. I blinked them away to slide down my cheeks, but more came just as quickly.

Derek moved to my side and drew me close, patting my back and trying to soothe me. Mark was about to say something when shouting drew our attention. We turned in the direction Mark had come from just in time to watch paramedics carry out the dead woman on a gurney. Rivulets of rain cascaded off the body bag with each bounce of the stretcher. A scraggly looking man in badly worn clothing followed right behind them.

"Where are you taking her?" he sobbed.

When they didn't answer, he dropped to his knees. "Cassandra," he wept, burying his head in his hands.

The wheels rattled on the uneven pavement as the paramedics steered the cart to a waiting ambulance. They hoisted the gurney up and slammed the doors, where one of them pounded on the back of the vehicle to let the driver know they were done. The emergency lights went still, and they pulled away. No need for lights and sirens now. It was too late for Cassandra.

My thoughts hovered between horror at the scene in front of me and hope that we finally had enough to find Jack. Then the crushing guilt came suddenly, squeezing the air from my lungs. This woman died because of something I might have prevented.

"I've got to get back before this rain washes away any chance of us finding something. Go home. I'll be in contact later," said Mark, casting me a sympathetic look.

Mark started toward the murder site but swung around to face us after only a few steps. "Is there anything else you can tell us about this guy? Anything at all?"

If I had any information to offer, I would have done so. Surely, he knew that. We'd practically begged them to believe us from the start. But in the absence of such information, all I could do was wait. Wait and hope they caught him. Derek and I both shook our heads, and Mark resumed his walk to the fence.

Derek rested his hand on my back as we walked to the car. "Let me drive, okay? You shouldn't go home to an empty apartment, and I sure as hell don't want to be alone with my thoughts. Why don't you come to my house with me? We'll rest and wait for Mark to call us."

"I'd rather go home, Derek."

"Then I'll stay there with you. I'm not leaving you on your own, Madison."

I didn't have the energy to argue with him, although I would have preferred to be alone. I wasn't the type of person who needed to cling to someone when I was distraught. I was better off working through it myself. But it was useless to debate the subject with him, so I stayed quiet. We didn't speak on the way home, but it wasn't uncomfortable. We had spent enough time together by then that we didn't need to fill the silence with small talk.

When we got to my apartment, the sun was already up, and the city was alive and breathing. I went for a steaming shower right away. I let the scalding water run over me for a long time until I realized no amount of soap and water would ever wash away the sickening feeling that clung to my every pore. I doubted even a bleach bath would do the job at that point.

The groceries I ordered the night before were delivered while I was in the shower, so Derek made us a late breakfast. It felt good to let someone else be in charge for a while. I lay on the couch, and he covered me with a throw. It was so cozy I fell asleep until the doorbell woke me a couple of hours later.

"That must be Mark. He asked to meet us, but I wanted to let you sleep, so he said he would come here. I hope that's okay with you."

"Sure," I said, sitting up and combing my fingers through my hair. I figured Mark must think I was such an idiot. Every time he saw me I was either on the verge of a breakdown, crying my eyes out, or ticked off. I planned to try very hard to be normal during this visit with him. Or at the very minimum, give him the illusion that I was holding it together.

Derek answered the door and showed Mark into the living room, where he settled into a chair across from us on the couch.

"There's a good chance it's him. Jack the Ripper. Either that, or this was someone who researched the Ripper pretty intensely and has a connection to global law enforcement. I spoke to Scotland Yard earlier today. There are details about the Ripper killings that were never made public, and this homicide has earmarks of those characteristics. I can't discuss what they are, so don't even ask. But it's too fortuitous. And I don't put much stock in coincidence when it comes to serial killers."

"So what happens now?" asks Derek.

"We don't have much to work with. The witness from the homeless community you saw this morning is with the forensic artist now. They will put his description into the computer software and see what they come up with. Once that's completed, I need you both to look at it and tell me if it's your guy. We'll incorporate his picture among other computerized sketches of actual suspects from other cases to make it fair and unbiased. The witness said the individual's name was Jack, and he claimed to be homeless. His clothes looked old-fashioned but on the new side, and he was clean."

"That's promising," I said.

"If we can establish it's the same man who came through your time portal, that will be crucial. I think he doesn't have many options right now. He's without money in an unfamiliar place and time. The homeless community makes the most sense for him. And there are vulnerable women there he can easily prey on. It's perfect for someone like him."

"So you should be able to find him quickly then, right?" asked Derek.

"There are virtually hundreds of homeless camps in the city. We'll start our search at the nearest known camps to where he was last seen and spread out from there. This is officially an active case now."

I sighed with relief. But it saddened me that it took Jack butchering a woman to make that happen. At least they would have to take us seriously now.

Mark left, promising to call once the sketch artist finished. He would text the pictures to Derek and then we would call and let him know if any of them were Jack.

The day stretched ahead of us and waiting for the photo was agonizing. Derek protested, but I genuinely wanted to check out his movie, *Tarnished Souls*. I needed a distraction—badly. It was strange to watch Alysha and Jake on the screen now that I had met them, and bittersweet to see Alysha. Despite her qualities I wasn't crazy about, I had to admit she was a gifted actress. Her performance even moved me to tears at the end. Which was saying something, because I had cried so often recently, I couldn't understand how there were any tears left in me.

Derek was happy I enjoyed it, and I could see he was proud of his work. And he had every reason to be. I understood now why people loved the movie so much. It was a feel-good story that helped you escape reality for a while. Maybe I would make a point of seeing more movies. I hated to say it, but Tori was right. It wouldn't kill me to stream a movie or get out and see one with her occasionally. This experience had made me reexamine my priorities, so at least one good thing would come out of all this.

The text from Mark came through late that afternoon. We synched Derek's phone to my laptop and pulled the images up. We looked at one another, then back to the screen. Jack's face stared back at us with chilling detail from among the ten pictures. I enlarged the photo, and his face filled the monitor. The likeness was uncanny. The handsome face, the vacant eyes, it was all captured perfectly. It was unsettling to have a life-sized image of the monster who murdered Alysha and several other women on my laptop. I slammed the computer shut, not wanting to look at him for even another second.

Derek tapped his phone to life and made the call that would steer the manhunt in a new direction.

"Mark? It's dad. That's him. Picture number six. That's Jack the Ripper."

THIRTY-ONE
MADISON

2032, Los Angeles, California

After we positively identified the police sketch as the man we saw come through the time portal, the investigation became more focused. The homicide sergeant assigned a second team of detectives to the case, and the four officers worked what little evidence they had around the clock. They canvassed homeless communities and reached out to confidential informants for any word on the street. They were careful to keep any details about Jack out of the press. No one wanted to panic Los Angeles by suggesting Jack the Ripper was running loose in our timeline.

Mark told us that ninety percent of the time, solving a homicide came from talking to anyone and everyone associated with the crime scene and the victim. Someone might have information they didn't even realize would be useful. It was a numbers game, he said. You just kept interviewing people and pretty soon you'd get the break that would point you in the right direction. That approach seemed like a tedious process to me. One I wasn't sure we had time for. Yet there was nothing I could do about it.

The one thing I hated most about this situation, besides the glaring fact that innocent women died, was that I had so much empty time to fill. It was impossible to escape my thoughts. I couldn't help thinking it might be my punishment for allowing Alysha to wander off unnoticed in London. I was sick of feeling guilty about her, but I didn't know what to do to make it go away. At night in bed, I would try telling myself everything I could think of to make the shame disappear. It remained, no matter what I did.

I tried to go back to work but found it useless. I couldn't concentrate. So I had Tyler and Tori cover for me while Derek and I did everything possible to find Jack. If I had any hope of ever getting my life back, we couldn't sit idly by and wait for something to happen. Derek's driver took us out every day to cruise homeless camps looking for Jack, where Derek handed out cash in exchange for any information we gleaned from the residents. They were reluctant to talk to us, and I couldn't blame them. We rolled up in a limousine asking questions about someone they would consider a fellow homeless person. It felt wrong to flaunt our wealth like that. But it allowed us both to look for Jack if someone else drove.

After two days of going from one camp to the next with nothing to show for it, we became discouraged. How could he just disappear? Derek reminded me we hadn't even touched the tip of the iceberg yet. Hundreds of homeless communities dotted the city, with more cropping up every day. And in the meantime, Jack was out there plotting his next murder. It was so frustrating. I fantasized about catching him and shipping him so far back in time he would never encounter another human being.

On our third day of searching for Jack, Derek got the phone call we had both been dreading.

"It's Mark," he said, looking at his cell. "Hey, Mark." He listened for a moment, nodding his head. "Where? All right. I'll wait to hear from you."

"What did he say?" I asked.

"There's been another murder."

"Another murder?" The words caught in my throat like a piece of hard candy had lodged itself there. "Where?"

"I don't know. He wouldn't tell me. He made it clear we were not to come to another crime scene of his, and he'd call when he was done."

My chest tightened as the last glimmer of hope I had clung to slowly evaporated. How did one man, seemingly so bewildered by unfamiliar surroundings, murder a second person and slip away? I reminded myself he had eluded police in 1888 and remained one of history's biggest unsolved mysteries to date. But we had a face now. Still no name, as I didn't believe for one minute Jack was his real name. But we knew what he looked like, and that was more than anyone in the last one-hundred-forty-four years had.

We went back to Derek's and waited for the next call from Mark. I was too anxious to continue our daily search, and Derek looked exhausted.

"Are you okay, Derek? You're unusually quiet today."

"Yeah, I'm fine. Just thinking."

"About what?"

"Besides the obvious? It's selfish. I was thinking about when this is all over. I wondered if Mark will still stay in touch with me when he doesn't have a reason to."

My heart broke in two for him. He looked crushed. I didn't have kids, so it was difficult for me to imagine what it must feel like to be estranged from your own child. His face gave me a very good indication of it, though. I reached over to squeeze his hand. He returned the squeeze with a small smile.

"I'm glad we're friends, Madison. I'm sure most people wouldn't understand our friendship. On the surface, we appear to be polar opposites. A thirty-year-old entrepreneur and a sixty-something Hollywood director. But it works, doesn't it?"

"Yeah, it works," I said, returning his smile with one of my own.

Derek reminded me of my father in many ways. Maybe that was why I felt so drawn to him. Once I got past his tough exterior, I realized what a genuinely nice guy he was. I agreed with him though, people would probably not understand our platonic friendship. But honestly, at that stage I couldn't have cared less what anyone expected of me. I was focused on one task. Finding Jack.

We hung at Derek's for the afternoon. We played pool, ate lunch, and watched a movie while we killed time waiting for any news about the latest murder. I pushed it out of my mind when it crept in. I didn't want to speculate about who died this time. The stress was affecting me in ways I definitely saw. I had lost weight the past week, and the dark circles under my eyes from lack of sleep were a permanent fixture.

When the call finally came, I was ready to jump out of my skin. Mark was on his way over.

He arrived thirty minutes later with Miguel.

"Wow, this is some place, Mr. Porter," said Miguel as he stepped into Derek's living room.

"Thank you, Miguel. Please, have a seat. You too, Mark" said Derek, gesturing to them.

"So, as I said on the phone, there's been a second homicide. A near exact replica of the first one. Residents say an individual calling himself Jack drifted into camp yesterday morning. They discovered the deceased victim this morning, and Jack was gone," said Mark.

"Any idea where he went?" asked Derek.

"Not yet. But he can't be far. The coroner puts the victim's time of death somewhere between four and five a.m. this morning. He's on foot, so that limits his resources. We have uniforms out to every known homeless camp and abandoned building within a three-mile radius of there," said Miguel.

I knew I should keep my mouth shut and not question their process, but I couldn't stop myself.

"How did he get away again? This guy is in our world now. Shouldn't we be smarter than him?"

Miguel sighed and looked at Mark to answer me.

"Ms. Taylor, we are doing everything possible to apprehend him. There are lots of places to hide in Los Angeles if you don't want to be found. Hundreds of deserted buildings and alleyways are tucked away in dark corners. We are certain he will stay clear of the homeless camps now that he's committed another homicide. He won't take a chance since he's established a pattern for us to follow."

"So, are you no longer looking in homeless areas?" I asked.

"We will continue to comb those, but it's more likely he will go to ground now until his urge to kill again becomes too strong for him to control. Our profiler worked up a crime scene profile as well as an offender and victim analysis. Those reports suggest he will try to manage the impulses as long as possible, out of fear of being caught. That gives us the chance to locate him, hopefully, before he kills anyone else," said Mark.

"He's out of his element here. His former habits and routines no longer apply. Once his desire to kill strikes again, he won't be able to keep it in check for long. It will consume him because he will be under tremendous stress, and he'll look to that as an outlet for the pressure. This period right now is his weakest time. We plan to hit hard and fast to find him while he's still in this fragile state," said Miguel.

That all sounded logical to me, but I realized actually finding him would prove to be another matter. He could be practically anywhere. I had no choice but to put my trust in them and accept they knew what they were doing. That didn't mean I wouldn't continue to go out to search for Jack with Derek. I would. Maybe we would refocus on abandoned buildings too. If the profiler predicted he would go into hiding, then who was I to dispute that? It wasn't as if I had any experience dealing with serial killers.

Neither Derek nor I asked Mark or Miguel for any details about the murder. I couldn't bear hearing it. It did, however, prompt us to get back out and continue our search. As soon as the detectives left, Derek wanted to call the driver.

"Derek, I get why we need to have someone chauffeur us around. It allows us both to look for Jack. But could we consider taking a different car? The limo is so *in-your-face*. So elitist. I don't guess the people we're talking to appreciate us showing up in that when they're living in cardboard boxes and nylon tents. I don't feel great about it, and I can't imagine they do either."

"You're right. I have an older SUV we can take. It belonged to my wife, and I've never had the heart to get rid of it. It's a little beat up, but it will get us around."

"That sounds perfect. And I thought of something else. Why don't we put together some care packages for them? Food, toiletries, socks, and underwear. It doesn't have to be anything fancy. Just some items they can use. We're outsiders. They might be more receptive to us if we came bearing gifts."

"We can do that, sure. We've been giving them money, though."

"Yeah, I know. But that almost feels sort of bribery-ish to me. It would be hard for them to get access to things they need. I don't imagine stores are going to exactly welcome them in, you know what I mean?"

"You make a good point. Harper!" he shouted.

She appeared within seconds, tablet in hand.

"I need you to order some items to be delivered in the next hour, please. Come sit with Madison and me and we'll go over the list. Do you need to grab a water or anything before we start?"

"Um, no, I'm fine. Thanks, though," she said, beaming at him.

"Okay, darlin', scoot on over here and let's get cracking."

I smiled to myself. Derek treated Harper much differently now than he had when I first met him. He was really coming around, and I had to attribute that to his newfound relationship with his son. I made a mental note to speak to Mark at some point about maintaining contact with his dad. I felt strongly they both owed it to themselves to make it work. And I had no problem giving them a push on the right path.

THIRTY-TWO
DEREK

2032, Los Angeles, California

Harper had our order together in no time. Then she spoke to the driver and had him bring the SUV around for us. She actually was a pretty fantastic assistant. She never complained about the long hours, or about anything else I asked her to do. I planned to give her a raise on her next paycheck and surprise her. Maybe a bonus too.

God, Madison was turning me into a pushover.

I had seen Madison's disapproving looks when I barked out an order to Harper. I had made a point to be mellower and more pleasant when dealing with Harper because of that. Or perhaps being around Mark softened my perspective. I would be lying if I said these past several days hadn't been pretty great. I knew that sounded awful. The Jack the Ripper part of the past several days was disturbing and horrific. But Mark and I were getting along, and just being in his everyday life was a treat I hadn't had in many years. He even called me last night just to see how I was holding up through all this. A call to check on me! It was unbelievable. I tried hard to remain calm and not go overboard with my response, but I was sure my voice gave away how overcome with emotion I was by the gesture. It was more than I ever dreamed I would have again with him. I felt his mother looking down on us and smiling. Maybe Mark felt it as well. Madison had a lot to do with my improved outlook too. She had a soothing effect on me that was hard to explain. The poor kid was under as much, if not more, stress than me over this entire Jack situation. It was her company and reputation on the line. Yet she remained composed, even thinking about bringing the homeless people supplies. You never knew what went on in someone's mind, but on the outside she seemed unflappable. I might not have been her biggest fan when we first met, but that changed somewhere along the line. I considered her a true friend now. And that was a rare gift in Hollywood.

She was the type of girl I'd want for a daughter-in-law. And don't think I hadn't considered that. Both she and Mark were single. And it was about time my son settled down. Of course, I had to tread carefully in those waters. If either of them thought I was meddling like that, they would both resist. But I recognized a good match when I saw one. I cast Alysha and Jake together, didn't I? That was the proverbial golden ticket. So as far as I was concerned, that qualified me to play matchmaker with Mark and Madison.

We pulled up to the first camp of the day in my SUV with peeling paint on the hood and a dented rear bumper. I noticed the reaction immediately. The people approached us without hesitation. When we were in the limo, they hung back, staring and whispering, distrustful of us. I opened the door and hopped out, Madison right behind me. We began unloading boxes of non-perishable food and toiletries to smiles all around. Madison seamlessly turned the chatter to our purpose for being there as she asked about Jack. No one there had seen anyone like him, so we moved on.

At the third and last camp that day, we struck pay dirt. A tall man with a graying beard and a friendly smile helping us unload supplies stopped with his box midair when Madison described Jack. He reminded me a little of Denzel Washington. He definitely had the looks, and more importantly, the cool demeanor.

"I've seen a dude like that. He was here this morning," he said.

Maddie reached for her tablet and pulled up the computer sketch of Jack.

"Yup, that's him, all right. But he has a beard now. Not a proper one like mine," he said, stroking his long beard. "But he still had one starting. Something's not right with that guy. Me and Manny told him he should move on. Yep, we weren't about to let him stay here."

"Did you see which direction he left in?" I asked.

"Whatcha looking for him for. There a reward or something for him?"

"Not exactly. But if you give us information that leads to finding him, you have my word I will come back here and give you a finder's fee. In fact, if you can point us in the right direction now, I'm willing to pay you something."

"Naw, man. I may be down on my luck, but I ain't no bum. You find the dude because of something I told you, then you can come back. I won't turn down a reward I earned."

I shook his hand and he walked us over to the far corner of the camp where he pointed toward a group of old factories. "Those businesses ain't been open since last winter. Closed for good now, I think. He went that way, toward the factories. Can't say he's still there, but that's where I last saw him headed."

"Thank you. I'm Derek, and this is my friend Madison. Thank you for your help."

"Robert," he said, nodding. "Thanks for bringing us the food and whatnot. It'll help."

We got into the truck, and I buzzed my window down and called out to him.

"Robert! What did you do before? I mean, before you lived here?" I asked. Robert seemed different from most of the people we met in these camps. He didn't have that hopeless look in his eyes. Not yet anyway.

He swung around to face us and chuckled. "Same thing everyone else in this town does, Derek. I was an actor, paying the bills as a customer service rep before the company I worked for shut down." He turned and strode away.

"I knew it," I said, slapping my knee. "He's a perfect character actor, Madison. He has that every-man face. I'm coming back for Robert when this is all over. I'm going to cast him in a movie. And if he can act, I'll even give him a speaking part."

"Do you ever stop working, Derek?"

"Habit. I can't help it."

Madison smiled at me and peered between the seats to the block of factories ahead of us. I did the same. Clouds drifted over the sun, making the late afternoon turn gloomy.

"Call Mark," I said into my phone.

I glanced over at Madison as he answered the call. "Mark, we have a lead. Someone in a camp off Third Street saw him this morning. They kicked him out of the camp, and he took off toward the abandoned Ford buildings. Okay, we'll meet you there."

I disconnected and shifted toward Madison. "We've got him Maddie. I can feel it in my bones."

"Well, let's not start celebrating yet. I suppose Mark insisted we wait for him and Miguel to get here?" she asked.

"Of course."

"And are we going to?"

"Well, we should. I told him we would," I said.

The driver stopped just before the deserted factories on the pitted asphalt. The sun would sink in the west soon, and the late afternoon light cast an eerie orange glow over the place.

"This may be our only chance, Derek. If he's in there, he may already know we're here. The muffler on this thing could wake the dead," she said.

"It was your idea to take this monster, not mine."

"Let's just have a quick peek around. If we find something, we'll come right back to the car," she said.

"And what if we find Jack? Then what? How are we supposed to take down a serial killer?"

She grabbed her purse and held up what looked like a small television remote.

"This is what we use if that happens, Derek."

"And that would be what, exactly?"

"It's a transporter. I had IT get me one of the prototypes they've been working on. We are moving to this method next year instead of using the portals. If we find him, we can send him back in time. Problem solved."

"You want to go up against Jack the Ripper with a transporter? How do you even know it works if it's a prototype? And what about him standing trial for Alysha's murder? And the others back in 1838. And the two women here?" I asked her.

"Of course it works, Derek. It's been tested. And do you really think he would stand trial here? He's the first person to come through time and commit a crime. *We* know he did it. And Mark would probably prove it. But some public defender wanting to make a name for himself might get him sent to a care facility on a mental health conviction. Or worse yet, back where he came from so he could just keep murdering women. Then where would we be?"

I thought about what she said for a minute. I knew Mark would never condone transporting Jack back, but Madison made an excellent point. I didn't want to take a chance that he would end up in some cushy country club prison for mentally unstable criminals. But I also didn't want to jeopardize my newfound connection with Mark. I considered my options for a minute before answering her.

"Okay, listen. We'll just take a brief glance around. Chances are he's already moved on, anyway. Let's just try not to go too far off script here. Take the transporter thing with you, and we only use it in an absolute emergency. As in a life-or-death situation. Agreed?"

"Sure. Of course. Mark and Miguel will probably be here any minute, anyway," said Madison, although she appeared nervous.

My boots landed on the pavement loudly enough to alert someone to our presence, and Madison shot me a look. I told my driver to stay alert and honk if he saw anyone other than Mark or Miguel.

We were only a few hundred feet from the first building, but it seemed to take forever to reach it. The steady hum of traffic from the distant 101 freeway was the only sound besides our footfall. As we neared the door that stood ajar, a bird flew out of a broken second-story window and Madison jumped and squealed. It took a minute for my heartbeat to slow down from warp speed and resemble something normal again. I had no idea why I was doing this. I had no business hunting Jack the Ripper. My son was far better qualified to deal with these types of situations. Plus, he carried a gun. All we had was a prototype transporter that, frankly, I wasn't even certain worked. Hence the *prototype* label. Nevertheless, I was committed to the plan now unless I wanted to look like some pansy senior citizen. So I stepped through the door into the shadowy building, trying not to let the fear take control.

A streak of fading sunlight played across the middle of the room, highlighting a rusted metal table and several old tools. It was one large room with a couple of offices to the left, both empty, with tall glass windows. An open loft ran around the perimeter of the space above us.

"Doesn't seem to be anyone here," said Madison.

"Well, there are two more buildings. But like I said earlier, he's no doubt moved on by now."

As soon as my sentence was out of my mouth, the SUV horn beeped once. My head snapped to the door.

"I'll go check it out."

"Okay, hurry back, please," said Madison.

I dashed outside, where my driver waved and pointed to his right. I saw a man retreating, but I could already tell it probably wasn't Jack. He had long, scraggly hair under a beanie and wore a tattered green army jacket. I hurried after him anyway, just to be sure it wasn't him. When he turned at the sound of me approaching, I saw it wasn't Jack. I held my hands up and turned back the way I came. I gave my driver a wave to signal everything was okay and started toward the building I had just come from. Nothing could have prepared me for what I saw when I walked back in. Jack stood fifteen feet from Madison, grinning, and clutching a large knife.

THIRTY-THREE
MADISON

2032, Los Angeles, California

I watched Derek jog out the door and immediately regretted not going with him. I rubbed my arms to warm up, but it did me no good, so I walked to the other side of the room to peer out the window. It was still outside except for a few birds pecking at a discarded fast-food bag. A creaking noise behind me caused me to spin around, where I almost tripped over a rolling cart. I shoved it out of my way and moved closer to the front door where I tried to will Derek into hurrying back. It was creepy in the deserted building all alone.

I couldn't see where Derek was, and that made me uneasy. I perched on the edge of a rickety desk and jumped when it tilted under its broken leg. When I looked up, I almost toppled over again. Jack stood only fifteen feet from me, grinning. The sight of him turned my stomach. The knife in his hand sent a bolt of terror through me.

"Good day, Madison."

All I could do was stare at him. Even though I had seen him once before, standing face to face with him I had trouble connecting the man in front of me to the legendary Jack the Ripper. I waited for the sinister laugh, the menacing grimace. *Something.* I certainly hadn't expected a civilized greeting. And that threw me.

Once I got over my initial shock, panic washed over me for a split second before my fingers curled around the transporter in my hand. It made me feel powerful. With that feeling came courage. And that turned my fear into red-hot, seething anger. I hardly recognized my voice when I spoke.

"Don't say my name again, you miserable piece of shit. It makes me sick to my stomach to hear it even come out of your mouth."

The only person more shocked than me by my outburst was Jack, and he visibly stiffened a little. It was a small gesture, but I saw it before he recovered. It was enough to let me know he wasn't expecting that from me, and I had unnerved him. That boosted my confidence even more. That and the instrument I was clutching in a death grip.

My heart was pounding so hard it blocked out all other sounds, and I didn't hear Derek approaching. My newfound bravery didn't stop my little voice from screaming at me to run, but my feet refused to move. I thought I knew what I would say when I finally came face to face with Jack, but it was all a blank now. So I went with the more obvious and lame statement about the police coming for him.

"The police will be here any moment now. You're going to get what you deserve."

"I suppose that remains to be seen. I've learned our destiny is not carved in stone. You, of all people, should know that Madison. Take poor Alysha, for example. I'm certain her future would have played out altogether differently had you not brought her back in time to London."

"You have no right to bring Alysha into this. Her death is on you, no one else. Funny, but I just realized that at this very minute. Tell me something. Who are you? You know my name. How about you return the courtesy?" I asked.

"Madison, you know very well who I am. I am Jack the Ripper. The notorious Whitechapel murderer."

"Don't play games with me. What's your real name?" I asked again.

"Perhaps I shall whisper my name in your ear right before I kill you. I agree you deserve that consideration. You have been a formidable opponent, Madison."

He smiled, but it didn't reach his eyes. I had never known such evil before, and it chilled me to my core. Yet I pushed on, despite his smug demeanor.

"Opponent? This is all just some stupid game to you, isn't it? Well, the game is over, asshole. This is your last chance to tell the world who you are.

Don't you want everyone to know who Jack the Ripper really was? You're one of the world's greatest criminal mysteries of all time."

I was stalling for time, hoping Mark and Miguel, or at least Derek, would arrive to help me. It seemed to be working, and my mind was thinking a step ahead about how I could keep him talking.

"Madison, I had truly hoped you understood me better. I don't do this for the notoriety."

"Then why do you do it? Please, enlighten me."

He sighed and grinned at me again. "Because I must."

I let out a sharp laugh. "Really? It's that simple?"

"On the contrary. It's that complicated. I fear I could no more give up killing than I could cease to take my next breath."

"You don't think that statement is crazy from just about every angle, especially coming from you? You're more demented than I ever imagined."

"Perhaps you are right. Nevertheless, I am who I am. I have no desire to change, and I imagine that makes me the monster you think I am."

"The universe has a gaping hole in it because of you. But you know what? I can remedy that. And I intend to do just that, *Jack.*" I tightened my grasp on the transporter. "And after I do that, I will go on with my life like you never existed. Because you don't deserve any better than that. You, on the other hand, will be dust soon. It's too decent an ending for an asshole like you, but that's what I've got to work with, so it'll have to do."

He continued on, unfazed by my threats. "I believe I am going to enjoy my time with you more than any other woman I have slain. I'll tell you a secret, Madison. There are others, you know. They just haven't found them yet."

My stomach dropped at his words. Jack the Ripper stood before me confessing to murders history didn't attribute to him. He was as calm as if he was reciting the weather report to me. His depravity knew no bounds, and I decided in that instant I couldn't allow him to go on living.

"You think you're going to add me to your list? Go ahead. Give it your best shot. Give me a reason to justify what I'm about to do, other than you're a despicable person who deserves to rot in hell."

I keyed a number into my device and kept pressing zeros until the programmer wouldn't take any more.

"I genuinely admire your confidence, Madison. But I fear your time has come to an end."

"I warned you not to say my name again, you jackass," I said.

He lifted the knife and lunged for me. I didn't hesitate. I raised my arm and leveled the transporter at him. Any guilt or remorse I was afraid I would have by condemning another human being to their death left me in that moment, as if it never existed. I watched him vanish in front of me with his face twisted into a silent scream.

I stumbled backward into the desk, my hands trembling so hard, I dropped the transporter. Derek was at my side immediately. I was so focused on Jack I hadn't even heard Derek come back inside. He drew me into an embrace.

"Shhhh. It's okay. He's gone. Let 1888 London deal with him."

I pulled away, my eyes locking onto his. "I didn't transport him to 1888. Or to London."

"You didn't? Where is he then?"

"I can't be exactly sure. IT is still working out a few of the bugs with the handheld device. But the transporter estimated it at about sixty-five million years ago, somewhere in North America. With any luck, just in time for the big asteroid to get him. Well, that's assuming he doesn't wind up as a dinosaur snack before that."

Derek's jaw fell open. "Are you serious?"

I nodded. The tears welled in my eyes. "I couldn't allow him the chance to hurt another person ever again."

His face morphed into that of a proud parent whose kid had just kicked the winning goal. He pulled me into another hug and laughed. "Sixty-five million years backwards? Damn. You've got some brass ones, my little friend."

"He deserved it. He was the worst, lowest form of man. Someone who preyed on women weaker than him. Just because *he must*. He wouldn't have stopped killing, either. I think when he said those words like they meant nothing, something in me snapped. That's when I knew what I had to do."

"You're right. He would have continued right on killing women until he got caught. I'd like to think Mark and Miguel would have made a strong case against him. But it is a unique situation, so who knows what would have happened to him once they arrested him. I'm not sure the government wouldn't want to study him or some nonsense. The entire thing would have been a media circus. This was the right move. It was the only move," said Derek.

I wasn't sure if he said that to make me feel better or if he really meant it. Maybe he thought I was having some kind of moral crisis. But I wasn't wringing my hands in regret and questioning what I'd done. To be honest, I didn't need him to justify my decision. I was at peace with blasting Jack into extinction. Or maybe I was in shock. Either way, I was grateful Derek cared enough to try to put me at ease.

Approaching sirens pierced the quiet, and I inhaled a deep breath, ready to defend my actions to the detectives.

"Let me do the talking," said Derek, picking up the transporter and handing it to me.

I shoved it into the pocket of my jeans and wiped the tears from my cheeks.

A few seconds later, Mark strode through the door with Miguel right on his heels.

"I told you to wait in the car until we got here, Dad. This might be a crime scene you're trampling all over."

"It's not," said Derek.

"Oh really? When did you graduate from the academy and make detective?" asked Mark, shaking his head.

"It's not a crime scene because he's not here, Son."

"Well, maybe he isn't, but we'll check it out. And even if he's not, you may still destroy valuable evidence. Please go wait in the car, both of you," said Mark.

"No, you don't understand. He was here, but now he's gone. I mean, *really* gone. And it doesn't matter anymore, because he won't be here for you to arrest, Mark," said Derek, wrapping his arm around my shoulder.

"What are you talking about, Dad? Gone where?"

"I transported him out of here. He's no longer in 2032," I said.

"You shipped him back to 1888?" said Miguel. "Why would you do that?"

"He's not in 1888. And I had no choice. He was charging at me with a knife. I didn't want to end up like the rest of the women he's slaughtered. It was an impulse decision. It was the only way to defend myself."

"Where is he then?" asked Mark, narrowing his eyes.

"Does that really matter? I walked in as he was coming after Madison, and neither of us had a weapon. She did what she had to do. I would have done it if she hadn't," said Derek.

"You didn't answer my question. Where did you send him?" said Mark, looking at me.

"Just, you know, way back," I said, waving my arm behind me in a dismissive motion.

"Ms. Taylor, unless you want to be arrested for impeding a homicide investigation, you'll answer my question with a straightforward response."

"Sorry, Son, but that's only happening over my dead body."

"Seriously, do not tempt me, Dad."

"Stop it. Both of you. I relocated him back sixty-five million years. To the dinosaur age. Okay? Are you happy now? And you know what? I'm not sorry, either," I said, crossing my arms over my chest.

If I live to be a hundred years old, I will never forget the look on their faces. It will remain etched in my memory forever. It was a mixture of complete disbelief and confusion. I suppose I couldn't blame them. What I had just told them was a lot to digest.

After a minute, Miguel burst into laughter, clutching his side, and bent over. Mark cast him a steely look, but it didn't quell Miguel's fit of laughter.

"I'm sorry, Porter, but you've got to admit, that is priceless," said Miguel, still chuckling.

"What on earth possessed you to do such a thing, Madison?" Mark asked me.

"He didn't deserve to be around other people anymore. Anywhere I would have sent him, he would have killed again. He told me he couldn't stop himself, and he didn't want to either. I'd just trade one century of Ripper murders for another. And it would mess with the timeline."

"She has a point, Mark. Besides, she just saved us about a week's worth of reports, and the city hundreds of thousands of dollars in costs to prosecute him. Plus, they'd probably just have her send him back to London in the end anyway," said Miguel.

"I'm going to have to create a report. It was self-defense. Do you understand what I'm saying, Madison?" asked Mark.

"I do. But I honestly didn't have a choice. It *was* self-defense. He would have killed me. I wouldn't ask you to lie on your report. Admittedly, I begged him to give me a reason to do it. But it wasn't as if I just zapped him into oblivion without provocation. I saw what he did to Alysha Beck up close. I did it for her. And all the other women he's killed. He told me there were others. Women that haven't been found yet. Knowing Ripper history, I guess they never will be."

We stood in silence in the deserted warehouse, the last place human eyes would ever see Jack the Ripper again.

I couldn't help but wonder what his short life would be like, because I had little faith he would last longer than a few days where I sent him. However long he survived, I hoped it was brutal, and he experienced the same degree of terror each of his victims felt.

THIRTY-FOUR
JACK

2032, Los Angeles, California

I watched them enter the warehouse from my hiding spot behind the office door. I peeked through the crack between the door frame and the wall as they conducted a half-hearted search for me. The room was almost empty, so that provided them a misleading sense of security that I wasn't in the building. Luckily for me, they only took a cursory glimpse inside each office, but never inspected behind the doors.

Once Derek left to see what the commotion outside was about, I knew that might be my only chance to seize Madison. I didn't know how long Derek would be gone, so I planned to force her to another location, if necessary. There were many buildings there, all with dark corners for carrying out sinister deeds. And I was confident I could easily dispose of Derek if need be.

I crept into the open space while Madison was turned away from me. I wanted to unsettle her. She turned and froze, and the shock on her face told me I had succeeded in surprising her. We had a rather unsatisfactory exchange in which I learned she understood nothing about me. I thought she was shrewder than most women, but sadly, I had overestimated her. Her part of our conversation astounded me. She believed either the police would come to arrest me or she would somehow force me to surrender. How dare she speak to me like that? She had no idea what I was capable of. Her civility left little to be desired, and I couldn't wait to get her alone. She would soon learn I would not tolerate being treated in that manner.

I quickly became bored with our chat and my composure wore thin. I lunged for her, ready to subdue her before I killed her. It was then that she pointed a peculiar object at me and closed her eyes, in what I initially assumed was a brace against my charge. I now know better.

That was my last recollection of Los Angeles.

•   •   •

Somewhere in North America, sometime during the Cretaceous Period
I awoke on a bluff surrounded by large flowering plants. The air was warm and muggy. I blinked rapidly to clear my head, as I was remarkably disoriented. I had no concept of where I was or how I got there. I rolled onto my back and breathed deeply while I tried to sort my thoughts.

My throat was incredibly parched. I had never known such thirst before. I pushed up on my elbows as I looked around. Bits and pieces of my memory gradually returned as my confusion cleared. I had been in the deserted factory with Madison. Yes, that was it. She pointed a device at me, and that's all I remembered until I woke up in the unfamiliar place.

My shoulders sagged as I realized what must have happened. The dread started in my chest and spread through me like a wildfire. I shook my jacket off as the oppressive heat overwhelmed me. Where did she send me? I stood up and turned in a complete circle. All I could see were broad-leaf trees, tall grass, and flowers. Green mountains loomed in the distance, with the sea on one side. I stepped to the brink of the cliff hesitantly and peered over the side to the surf below. The waves churned furiously, slapping against boulders. Sharp rocks jutted out of the face of the crag below me, and I shuddered. I wasn't fond of heights, so I took a careful step away from the edge.

No civilization of any kind was anywhere in sight, yet I knew I must find help. I started out in search of other people and hiked for a mile before I gave up and collapsed in a meadow. The sweltering heat was getting to me. And my thirst consumed me now. It was all I could focus on. I wiped the perspiration from my brow and lay there panting. I forced myself to get up and continue on, and at last discovered a small opening in the side of a rocky hillside. It wasn't spacious enough to call a cave, but it was the best chance for refuge I had come across. I settled in for the night as the sun set. I don't know how long I slept, but I woke up shivering. How it could be so cold at night when it was so hot during the day was a mystery.

I huddled in my rock shelter as strange noises haunted me through the night. None that made me feel any safer here. I had to find other people, some type of settlement. I needed a proper shelter, food, fire, and most of all, water. My tongue stuck to the roof of my mouth as I imagined a drink of chilled water. Sleep eluded me for the rest of the night, so I sat up and prayed for sunrise.

I was certain I heard the low growl of animals and something much worse. A beast I imagined to be massive emitted a horrifying call that was like nothing I had ever heard. It sounded somewhere between a growl and an elephant trumpet, only much, much louder. But no matter how hard I strained to see anything, nothing was visible in the total darkness. I pushed back as far as I could get into the cramped shelter and waited for daylight.

At first dawn, I was determined to push on, despite my fear of whatever creatures were roaming the land. My need for water compelled me forward. It wasn't long before I came to a puddle of what was presumably rainwater. It was stagnant and dirty, but I did not care. I lowered my face to the pool of muddy water and gulped greedily. After a brief rest, I willed my feet to resume walking. I had been on the move for several hours when I couldn't believe my eyes. I stood staring at the grotto I had spent the previous night in. Somehow, I had managed to get turned around and done nothing but wander in a giant circle all day.

The hopelessness swept over me, and I sank to my knees and cried out. My head dropped to the grass, and I wept for the first time in many years. I can't say with any certainty how long I remained there. But when I heard a terrifying, unexpected sound, it brought me to my feet instantly.

I scanned my immediate surroundings. Nothing. Nothing and no one.

Then movement in the sky drew my attention. A humongous bird glided across the sky. No, not a bird. It was a creature with a wingspan so vast it blocked out the sun as it flew over me. It circled back and passed overhead again, screeching loudly. I covered my ears with my hands. I watched it swoop lower and start toward me. I paused for a brief moment before the adrenaline began to pump through my veins. My instinct told me to run, so I did. I ran like I never had before. I heard its wings beating, drawing closer with each passing second, and I raced onward without thinking about where I was going. As I neared the edge of the bluff, I knew I had no alternative. I would have to jump off the cliff into the choppy water to escape the beast. My arms and legs pumped, and I closed my eyes right before I sailed over the edge. The creature dived to seize me mid-fall, and I felt the rush of air as it missed me by a mere fraction of an inch. I splashed into the sea like a sack of rocks. The impact knocked the wind out of me, my entire body battered by the force, but I kicked my way to the surface. I whooped and cursed the monster as it screamed above me.

I escaped! I was victorious!

I treaded water in place, euphoric over my triumph against the flying creature. Then something brushed my leg. Gently as first, then with more pressure. I twisted frantically every which way in the turbulent ocean, trying desperately to locate whatever was toying with me.

"NOOO!" I shouted. "You will not win, Madison! I will not die here alone!" My fists pounded the water with every word.

I sensed a shift in the undercurrent and spun around. My mouth dropped open as my eyes moved upward in disbelief to take in the entire span of the beast's head directly in front of me. My initial instinct was to escape by any means possible. But as I stared into the massive jaws of the shark, I had a sudden and very clear perception of two points.

One, the shark was going to kill me. Whether it regarded me as food or sport didn't matter. He would kill me because it was his nature. Because he must. No one understood that more thoroughly than I.

Second, I now realized why Alysha abandoned her will to survive just before I butchered her. Her realization that resisting would merely prolong her suffering was now evident to me as well. It was of no use to fight, so I didn't attempt to swim away. Instead, I faced my attacker head-on. I was Jack the Ripper, and I would not back down or cower fearfully in the face of death.

But just as Alysha's reaction was instinctual when her hands flew to her throat after I sliced it open, so was my scream as the beast's jaws locked onto me and ripped through my flesh.

THIRTY-FIVE
MADISON

2033, Los Angeles, California

A lot had happened in the last twelve months. Sometimes I couldn't believe how much my life had transformed after only a year's time. I was a different person than I was when I left for 1888 London. I hadn't been able to accompany another tour to England yet. The memory of my last trip there was still too raw.

I thought about Alysha often, and the other women Jack murdered in Los Angeles. Not a day passed when I didn't give thanks that we caught him before he could hurt anyone else. I promised myself I would not give Jack the dignity of ever thinking about him again. But to be honest, every now and then at night, while I tried to fall asleep, he crept into my mind. I hated that he could still get to me, but I couldn't stop it. I wondered what became of him. I imagined an array of gruesome endings, none of which came even close to what he deserved. And try as I might not to, I felt a little guilty about sentencing him to a certain death. I kept telling myself I had not lowered my standards to his level by condemning him. But a small part of me still clung to the universal proverb that two wrongs don't make a right, and I had some lingering doubt. I refused to allow that doubt to consume me, though. Maybe I should have let the police and courts decide his fate instead of taking the law into my own hands. But he had already murdered too many women in 1888, and I reasoned I couldn't allow him to continue to do the same in any other timeline. I supposed I would never know if I'd truly done the right thing. But I had made the choice, and now I could only live with my decision.

When I first arrived home from 1888, I took some solace in that at least Mary Jane Kelly had been spared death at the hands of Jack the Ripper. But surprisingly, her death remained firmly ensconced in history as his last victim. Derek and I knew that wasn't possible. Jack was already in 2032 when she was killed. We could only surmise it was a copycat killer, especially because her death varied greatly from Jack's other victims. It sickened me to think that someone admired Jack the Ripper so much they would mimic his murders. And they got away with their crimes. Just as Jack had. No more Ripper killings were ever recorded after Mary Jane, so we would never know what happened to the copycat killer. It was strange to think that our small group were the only people who knew Jack wasn't responsible for her death. I also thought about the other women Jack confessed to killing, the women who would never be found and linked to his other infamous murders. I didn't know for certain how many more victims there were, but I had the feeling it would rock history if we ever knew exactly how many women Jack the Ripper had really murdered.

Derek and I remained friends and became business partners, opening two companies together. I still owned The Taylor Travel Group, and with Derek's connections, my time travel business was thriving. Movie studios all over the world now used us for method-actor immersion trips regularly. I promoted Taylor and Tori, who took over most of the day-to-day operations, while I divided my time between the travel group and the other companies I ran with Derek. I also made sure I had time for some fun in my life. And I was happier for making those changes.

The first company Derek and I opened jointly was the Porter School of Acting, where up-and-coming artists studied the ins and outs of the motion picture industry. I was more of a silent partner, as there was absolutely nothing I could contribute in the way of instructing actors, other than funds. But it never got old, saying I was a partner in an acting school. Plus, I got to meet celebrities whenever Derek arranged for them to make special appearances. For the record, I wasn't missing the irony of the situation. I said I never wanted to identify with the Hollywood flash the city built its notorious reputation on. But I finally realized there was something to be said for living in La-La Land, and I may as well take advantage of all the city had to offer.

Our other enterprise was The Alysha Beck Rescue Mission in downtown Los Angeles, and that was where I enjoyed being more hands-on. We took in as many homeless as possible where we offered drug and alcohol rehab, job training, and transitioning into careers and their own homes. It was the most gratifying work I had ever been a part of. Derek helped many of the homeless that came through our doors get their Screen Actors Guild, or SAG, cards and cast them as extras in films. The money they earned helped secure their futures, and the studio had a never-ending selection of diverse extras to choose from.

Derek also stayed true to his word about Robert, the homeless man who steered us to the warehouse where we caught Jack. Derek found him and encouraged him to get his SAG card reinstated, then cast him in a small speaking role in his latest film. The picture was a blockbuster, just like *Tarnished Souls* had been. I never doubted it would be. Derek replaced Alysha but kept the original movie script. Although he initially harbored some serious misgivings about doing that. He said it seemed disrespectful to her memory, but I convinced him to move forward with the project after I read the script. The story was too good not to share it with the world. And I didn't think for one moment Alysha would care if Derek produced the film without her. Derek let me come to the set and watch filming whenever I wanted to, and although it was strange to see another actress in the role created for Alysha, I was pleased he agreed to release the film.

Somewhere along our path, Derek turned me into a huge, geeky movie buff. We got together at least once a week when he introduced me to another classic. My vintage movie knowledge is pretty impressive now. Anyone who didn't know us would probably consider us the most mismatched friends ever. Even Mark questioned our compatibility occasionally. On the outside, we appeared to have nothing in common other than we lived in the same city. But he was my friend. It didn't matter to me how we wound up there. I missed my own dad terribly, and Derek helped fill that void for me. I wasn't sure why Derek needed me in his life, but I never challenged his motives. As he once said to me, "It just works." That was good enough reason for me.

Derek and Mark remained in close touch and were rebuilding their relationship a little at a time. It thrilled me to see them strengthening their bond. They were both headstrong, but I understood how much they needed each other, and I made sure they didn't let their progress slip. When things grew tense between them from time to time, I served as the buffer to smooth things out.

You might expect that would land me and Mark squarely in the friend zone. But you would be wrong. The truth was, the more time I spent with him, the better I liked him. And that like was developing into something deeper for me. I could tell his feelings toward me had grown too. A woman just knows. Although neither one of us had acted on those feelings—yet. No thanks to Derek, who managed to drop subtle hints about us dating into practically every conversation he had with me and Mark. He made it very apparent we had his blessing. But I was old-fashioned in that respect. I preferred Mark to make the first move, and I would wait patiently until he did. I wasn't going anywhere.

One evening, almost a year to the day after our return from 1888, during a dinner out with Derek, Mark, Miguel, and his wife, Anna, Mark broached the subject of our group planning a time travel vacation to rectify some historical injustices. More pointedly, he suggested we track down a few of history's more prolific serial killers and do the world a favor by making them disappear. He was the quintessential cop. As much as the idea tempted me, I declined the offer. Messing with the timeline went against everything I had promised my father regarding his discovery. No tweaking history or swaying it to anyone's benefit. History was meant to play out as time had written it, no matter the consequences. And after all we went through with Alysha and Jack, I wanted nothing to do with editing the past.

I did, however, want to take a vacation. We had all earned one. So after squashing the crime re-do, I brought the matter up.

"I'd like to go someplace magical. To a time when life was simpler," I said.

"Like the old west?" asked Mark, taking a bite of his steak.

"No. I've been to the 1800s so many times. You wouldn't believe how many wealthy men fantasize about playing cowboy," I said, rolling my eyes.

"I wanna play cowboy too," said Miguel.

"No way. I have no desire to visit the old west," said Anna.

"You need Paris," said Derek.

"That's perfect! Derek, you're a genius. I want to live like one of the Lost Generation. I want to wander through the streets of Paris in the 1920s like a war survivor. How fun would that be?" I said.

"Paris. Now *that's* a trip. Oh, and the dresses. The parties," said Anna, dreamily.

"Yes! The roaring 20s and the Great Gatsby. The flappers, the speakeasies. It was all so glamorous," I said.

"So, the cowboy trip is off the table then?" asked Mark, glancing between me and Derek.

"The ladies prefer Paris, Mark. I vote to give them Paris. A little culture wouldn't hurt either of you," said Derek, pointing his steak knife between Mark and Miguel.

"Oui. I can do Paris," Miguel said, grinning at Anna.

Anna clapped excitedly, beaming from ear to ear.

We spent dinner creating plans, and after much discussion, I was more excited about a trip than I had been in a surprisingly long time. I glanced around the table at my friends, thinking how fortunate I was to have them in my life. My eyes settled on Mark, and he held my gaze for a moment longer than necessary. Derek glanced between us and smiled. Yep. There was undeniably something there worth exploring, and the heat flushed my cheeks when Mark smiled at me.

"A couple of modern-day homicide detectives, a movie director and a time-travel entrepreneur in 1920s Paris sure is an odd mix," said Anna.

She made a good point. But I wasn't worried.

"True. But what could possibly go wrong?" I asked.

The table erupted into laughter, but a part of me was serious. My little voice tried to rear its ugly head, but as usual, I ignored it and told it to shut up. This trip wouldn't be work. It would be a fun, stress-free holiday.

"Seriously, I'm a professional. I have years of time travel experience, and—"

When, oh when will I learn?

My dinner companions burst into laughter again before I could say anything more, and I couldn't think of a snappy finish to my sentence. Which was a shame because I felt like I had started out making such a good point.

But I let it go and paid them no mind. Because it wasn't like I was new at this. I'd been to the past hundreds of times.

I knew exactly what I was doing.

THE END

ABOUT THE AUTHOR

Christy Cooper-Burnett is an award-winning author based in California with a degree in Administration of Justice, where she lives with her rescue beagle, Gertie. She has one grown son who inspired her to write her award-winning debut novel, *No Way Home*, part of the *Christine Stewart Time Travel Adventure Series*.

A lifelong avid reader, she began her writing journey later in life, but once she started she couldn't stop. Her work focuses on creating relatable stories and characters that transcend genres and encourage readers to imagine what they wold do if thrown into the unique, imaginative situations her protagonists end up in.

NOTE FROM THE AUTHOR

Word-of-mouth is crucial for any author to succeed. If you enjoyed *Passport to Terror*, please leave a review online—anywhere you are able. Even if it's just a sentence or two. It would make all the difference and would be very much appreciated.

Thanks!
Christy Cooper-Burnett

We hope you enjoyed reading this title from:

BLACK ROSE
writing™

www.blackrosewriting.com

Subscribe to our mailing list – *The Rosevine* – and receive **FREE** books, daily deals, and stay current with news about upcoming releases and our hottest authors.
Scan the QR code below to sign up.

Already a subscriber? Please accept a sincere thank you for being a fan of Black Rose Writing authors.

View other Black Rose Writing titles at
www.blackrosewriting.com/books and use promo code
PRINT to receive a **20% discount** when purchasing.